THREADS OF KINDNESS

THE ELEVENTH NOVEL IN THE ROSEMONT SERIES

BARBARA HINSKE

ALSO BY BARBARA HINSKE

Available at Amazon in Print, Audio, and for Kindle

The Rosemont Series

Coming to Rosemont

Weaving the Strands

Uncovering Secrets

Drawing Close

Bringing Them Home

Shelving Doubts

Restoring What Was Lost

No Matter How Far

When Dreams There Be

Waves of Grace

Threads of Kindness

Novellas

The Night Train

The Christmas Club (adapted
for The Hallmark Channel, 2019)

Paws & Pastries

Sweets & Treats

Snowflakes, Cupcakes & Kittens

Tarts & Turnovers

Workout Wishes & Valentine Kisses

Wishes of Home

Wishful Tails

Back in the Pack

Novels in the Guiding Emily Series

Guiding Emily (adapted for The Hallmark Channel, 2023)

The Unexpected Path

Over Every Hurdle

Down the Aisle

From the Heart

Growing the Circle

Novels in the "Who's There?!" Collection

Deadly Parcel

Final Circuit

CONNECT WITH BARBARA HINSKE

Sign up for her newsletter at **BarbaraHinske.com**
Goodreads.com/BarbaraHinske
Facebook.com/BHinske
Instagram/barbarahinskeauthor
Pinterest.com/BarbaraHinske
BookBub/Barbara Hinske
Twitter(X)/Barbara Hinske
TikTok.com/BarbaraHinske
Search for **Barbara Hinske on YouTube**
bhinske@gmail.com

ISBN: 9798991115179

Library of Congress Control Number: 2025914847

Casa del Northern Publishing

Phoenix, Arizona

To the exceptional group of readers who love this series. Your warmth, kindness, and support inspire and encourage me every single day.

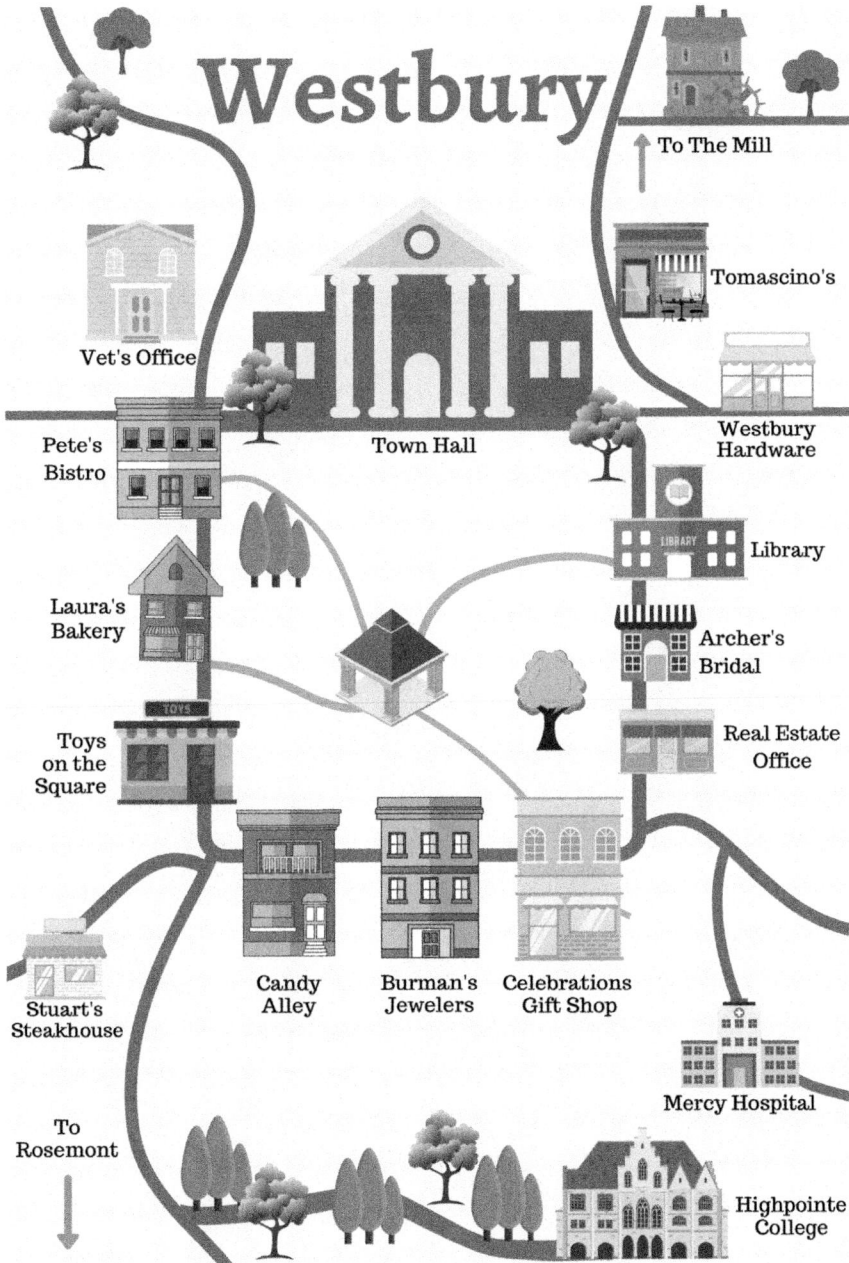

Westbury

To The Mill

Tomascino's

Vet's Office

Town Hall

Westbury
Hardware

Pete's
Bistro

Library

Laura's
Bakery

Archer's
Bridal

Toys
on the
Square

Real Estate
Office

Stuart's
Steakhouse

Candy
Alley

Burman's
Jewelers

Celebrations
Gift Shop

Mercy Hospital

To
Rosemont

Highpointe
College

CHAPTER 1

aggie Martin snuggled under the covers, her hand searching for her husband in the empty space beside her. The area where he was meant to be lying was still warm. Even on Christmas morning, it did not surprise her that John Allen, DVM, was not in bed.

She rolled onto her back and listened for sounds of him. The bedroom remained quiet. Maggie turned onto her side and opened an eye a slit. Her nightstand clock displayed 4:55 a.m.

Maggie inhaled and snuggled deeper into her pillow. She and John didn't have to be anywhere on this Christmas morning until 7:00 a.m. Susan and her husband Aaron had invited them for breakfast and to see Julia open her Santa presents. There was nothing like witnessing a small child experience the wonder of Santa Claus.

Maggie thought back to those long-ago days when Mike and Susan had been children, and she and Paul, her deceased husband, were young parents. They had been happy then—hadn't they? She had always believed that, but his later betrayals cast doubt on the truth behind her early marital memories.

Maggie squeezed her eyes shut and pressed her head further into the pillow in a futile attempt to banish the unwelcome thoughts of her late husband. She sighed and flung the covers aside. Troubled by unsettling memories, she couldn't get back to sleep.

Maggie shoved her feet into the slippers that lived at the side of her bed and shrugged into her fuzzy robe. She padded to the bank of tall, mullioned windows that over-looked the rear gardens and pulled the heavy drape aside.

Moonlight bathed the sloping back lawn that extended to a line of trees along the rear of the property. Westbury had received another two inches of snow overnight. The unblemished blanket of white looked like icing on a cake dusted with glittery sugar. The scene was magical—perfect for Christmas morning.

Breaking with years of tradition, she wasn't hosting Christmas dinner at Rosemont this year. Since Thanksgiv-ing, when it had been decided to hold this year's dinner at the Olsson House, she had been telling herself she was grateful for the break in her routine. The fall, with new alle-gations against Paul—and, by extension, herself, since he was deceased—had been intensely stressful. She should be glad that the only thing she had to do today was get dressed, go to Susan's in the morning, and join the crew at the Olsson House later in the day. She was free to do as she pleased.

As she held the curtain open, Maggie realized she was sad and depressed. She loved preparing to host a party almost as much as she loved giving the party itself. Having a jam-packed schedule was as much a part of her holiday tradition as exchanging gifts, singing carols, and gathering with friends and family. Now that the script had been flipped and she was the guest, Maggie wasn't sure she liked the feeling.

Eve, the faithful terrier mix who had adopted her on the night she moved into Rosemont, rose from her bed in the corner of the room and came to stand by her mistress. The intuitive pup rose on her hind legs and placed her paws against Maggie's thigh.

"You know I'm out of sorts, don't you, girl?" Maggie leaned to one side to stroke the soft fur of the animal she loved.

Eve wagged her tail and peppered Maggie's hand with doggy kisses.

"Don't worry about me, girl. I'm being silly. Today is going to be a wonderful day. It's going to be a different kind of Christmas from the ones I love. But things change, and I need to change with them. Before I know it, Susan will be in charge of Christmas Day, and John and I will be guests. It'll be fine."

Maggie let the curtain drop back into place and lowered her knee to the floor until she was face-to-face with her pup.

"Has your buddy, Roman, followed John to the kitchen?"

Eve thrashed her tail, nearly knocking herself off balance.

"I thought so," Maggie said. "Let's go downstairs to see what they're up to. It's time for your breakfast, too. It's time to get this Christmas Day started."

～

EVE TROTTED AHEAD as Maggie stepped onto the staircase that hugged the outer wall of Rosemont and opened to the living room. A fire crackled in the hearth and the lights of the Christmas tree that soared to the ceiling in the center of the room were on. The flickering flames threw into sharp relief their stockings, hanging from the mantel.

Maggie paused on the bottom step to survey the welcoming scene in front of her. Not a day went by that she didn't appreciate the beauty of their home. She would always be grateful for the sequence of unexpected events that had led her to Rosemont and her dream man.

The aroma of freshly brewed coffee drew her toward the kitchen. The library, dining room, and conservatory glowed with the light of their smaller Christmas trees. *All is calm, all is bright,* Maggie thought.

She padded into the kitchen to find her husband setting a carafe of coffee on a tray holding two giant-sized Christmas mugs. Beside them was a pink bakery box, its lid pulled open to reveal an assortment of croissants and Danish pastries.

"Merry Christmas, sweetheart," Maggie said, crossing to him and standing on her tiptoes to plant a kiss on his cheek.

John abandoned the tray and swept her into his arms. "Merry Christmas to you, darling." He bent, and they kissed.

When they finally pulled apart, Maggie stepped back and finally noticed what he was wearing.

"You're in scrubs," she said. "Are you going to the animal hospital?"

"Just for a bit. We're boarding a couple of surgical patients who need to be checked on. I'll look in on them this morning, and Sherry will do the same this evening. That way, I won't miss the fun at the Olsson House."

"You remember we're going to Susan's?"

"Of course. Do you honestly think I would forget being with Julia when she opens her gifts?"

"Good point. No, I don't. If there's one thing I know, it's that anything that involves her is your top priority." She pointed to the tray. "So, what's all this?"

"It's Christmas. We could treat ourselves to two breakfasts, if we like. Besides, this is just coffee and pastries."

Maggie peered inside the bakery box. "You got chocolate pistachio croissants for me, didn't you?"

"I know my best gal's favorite."

"These things have an entire day's worth of calories in them."

"As I said—it's Christmas. Who cares? We don't count calories on Christmas."

"This is awfully sweet of you, John, especially since you won't have much time to enjoy it."

"I wanted to make sure you had something nice while I went into the hospital." He pulled back and looked into her eyes. "I was worried you'd be a little bit ..." He paused, searching for the right word. "Blue today. You're normally up at the crack of dawn on Christmas, getting ready for the Rosemont dinner. I've been married to you long enough to know how much you love the hustle and bustle. I was afraid you'd miss it."

Maggie rested her hand on his chest. "You know me so well. I was pretty melancholy when I got out of bed this morning. But coming downstairs to see the beautiful trees lit, and to smell the aroma of coffee coming from the kitchen, where my dreamboat of a husband was waiting for me, well ... the blues just vanished."

"I'm thrilled to hear that, my dear." John took a quick glance at his watch. "Let's take this into the living room. I've got time for a quick cup of coffee and my favorite cherry Danish before I have to leave for the hospital."

He picked up the tray, and she followed him into the living room.

They sat together in companionable silence, enjoying their treats.

"I'd better be on my way," John said. "I promise I'll be home by six thirty at the latest. What do you plan to do in the meantime?"

"Well," Maggie cocked an eyebrow, "since calories don't

count on Christmas, I think I'll have a second cup of coffee with a cheese Danish. I'll still have plenty of time to get ready before you're home."

Bubbles emerged from the shadows and jumped into Maggie's lap. Maggie stroked the cat until throaty purring became background music in the room.

"Can I offer a suggestion?"

"Of course."

"Why don't you take a nice, long bath? I know you love to soak in the tub, and it's been ages since you've had time to do that."

"My gosh, that's a genius idea," Maggie said. "I think I'm going to like these slower Christmas mornings."

John planted a kiss on the top of her head, scooped up a second Danish to eat on his drive to work, and left Maggie to enjoy the solitude.

CHAPTER 2

*M*aggie's cell phone sprang to life with an incoming call. Maggie smiled when she heard Susan's self-recorded custom ringtone.

"Hey, Mama Llama, it's me," the phone chirped.

Maggie realized she couldn't get out of the tub, dry herself, and reach the phone before Susan's call went to voicemail. She was enjoying the rare treat of a morning bath and hated it to end.

She reclined against the bathtub pillow, running her hands through the blanket of bubbles, when Susan called again.

"Well, something must be on her mind," Maggie said to Eve, who was curled into a ball and snoozing on the plush bathroom rug. "It's time for me to get ready to head to her place anyway."

Grasping the sides of the tub, Maggie hoisted herself to her feet. She reached for the plush bath sheet draped over the small table next to the tub and wrapped it around herself. Stepping carefully onto the rug so as not to disturb Eve, she dashed into the bedroom and tapped the screen to answer the call.

"Hey, Mom," Susan said. "Merry Christmas. I didn't think I was going to get you."

"Sorry, honey," Maggie said. "I was soaking in the tub. I was going to let it go to voicemail, but when you called again right away, I knew something was up. So, what is it?"

"I hate to say this, but Julia's sick. She woke up with a 104-degree fever. Her nose began running when we got home from the children's Christmas Eve service at church. By the time we put her to bed, she had a low-grade fever. During the night, she woke with coughing fits."

"Oh no, honey, I'm so sorry to hear that. She must feel miserable."

"She's been inconsolable. We gave her children's Tylenol last night, which provided some relief, but her next dose isn't due for another hour."

Maggie heard crying in the background. She drew in a deep breath, hesitated, then continued. "Measles isn't a possibility, is it?"

"No, Mom, it's not measles. Julia is up to date on all her childhood immunizations. Her dad is a doctor, remember? He doesn't think it's measles. Aaron says it's just a virus and will clear up on its own. I'm calling you because neither of us wants you or John to be exposed to her."

Maggie was silent for a moment, contemplating how disappointed John would be to miss Christmas with Julia.

"Thank you for being so thoughtful, honey. You're right. As much as we both want to see our little girl open gifts, it's not wise."

"Julia's too miserable to open presents this morning, anyway. I don't know how we're going to handle the 'Santa brought you gifts' thing from last night, but we'll hold off for a day or two. When she's better, you can still be here when she opens them."

"That would make John's day," Maggie said.

"Then that's what we'll do. I've never seen a more devoted grandfather than your loving husband."

"I guess this means you won't be attending the Christmas potluck at the Olsson House this afternoon."

"Aaron thinks we should stay home. He feels perfectly fine, but he said we could be contagious and carriers, so we'll have to miss it, which makes me sad."

"I've been down in the dumps, too," Maggie said. "I've been saying for weeks how glad I am not to have all the work associated with the Rosemont Christmas potluck, but I woke up this morning in a terrible funk. John helped me snap out of it, but I'm having a hard time hanging on to a positive outlook, especially now that we can't come see your family."

Maggie switched the call to speakerphone and began

patting herself dry with the towel. "You said Aaron feels fine. How about you?"

"I'm not sure, truthfully," Susan replied. "I don't have a fever or runny nose or cough, but I don't feel like myself either."

"I noticed you nodding off during church last night," Maggie said.

"I know, right? It was only seven thirty, for heaven's sake. I've been swamped at work for the past two weeks, but nodding off in church before eight is unacceptable." She paused, considering what to say next. "I woke up feeling queasy, too," she admitted.

Maggie inhaled sharply. "Oh, my gosh. Fatigue and an upset stomach ... could you be ...?"

"I don't know, Mom. We've had so many false starts."

"Maybe this will be a very special Christmas present for you," Maggie said gently.

"I thought about that," Susan said. "I really don't want to see another negative pregnancy test this week. Aaron and I agreed—we'll enjoy the Christmas and New Year's holidays and test again on January second. If we have something to celebrate, we'll do it then."

"I'm sorry you've had such a difficult time with this, honey. I think that's a smart plan. Put it out of your mind for now. You'll have your hands full with a sick toddler, anyway."

Maggie heard Julia wailing in the background.

"I'd better go, Mom. I didn't want you and John to drive over here, only to have to turn around and go home."

"I'll miss seeing you, honey," Maggie said. "I think this is the first Christmas of your life that I won't have been with you."

"You're right, Mom, and I'm so sorry. But it's for the best."

"John and I will pack up a couple of plates from the Christmas buffet and drop them off for you on our way home. At least you'll get a Christmas dinner."

"That would be wonderful. We don't have much in the house to fix other than the eggs and bacon I was going to make for breakfast today. Plus, we can at least see each other through the window. That'll count as seeing each other on Christmas."

Maggie chuckled. "Indeed, it will. Take care of that little girl of ours—and yourself. Let me know if you need anything. We'd be happy to run by the pharmacy and pick up what you need."

"Will do, Mom, and thanks. Living with a doctor, our medicine chest is well stocked. Depending on how long Julia is sick, I may ask you to drop off groceries for me in the next few days."

"I'd be delighted to, honey."

"I'd better go," Susan said. "I'll see you later, Mom."

"Merry Christmas. I love you," Maggie said.

~

MAGGIE RETURNED TO THE BATHROOM. John would be home in half an hour. She glanced longingly at the tub. Getting dressed would be the practical thing to do, but it was Christmas morning. Practical things were not required.

She checked the temperature of the water. It was lukewarm. Turning the hot water tap on full blast, she loosened the drain plug, letting some water out. Maggie poured another capful of bubble bath into the tub and watched with glee as a blanket of iridescent bubbles filled it. In only minutes, the bathwater was perfect.

She deposited her towel back on the table and climbed into the tub.

Eve stirred and cracked open one eye. She thumped her tail on the rug twice and resettled her muzzle on her paws.

Maggie leaned back against the bath pillow and stretched her legs in front of her. A leisurely morning bath was the ultimate luxury. She'd have to remember to do this again.

She had just closed her eyes when her cell phone rang again. This time, her caller ID announced Judy Young.

Maggie pressed her lids tight against her eyes, then forced them open. Judy was one of her dearest friends in Westbury. She and Jeff Carson had recently married and started their life together by remodeling the stately Olsson House near the square. Now she and Jeff were hosting the annual Christmas potluck at their new home.

Maggie had offered to help, but Judy had declined, assuring her everything was under control. Maggie had replied that Judy could call for help at any time—and now Judy was calling.

For the second time in the last thirty minutes, Maggie

hoisted herself out of her bath. She clutched her towel around her as she hotfooted it into her bedroom, leaving a trail of wet footprints on the hardwood floor.

"Merry Christmas, Judy," Maggie said.

"The same to you, Maggie," Judy replied with forced cheerfulness.

"How's it going?" Maggie asked.

"It feels like we're on the Titanic over here. And we're racing around, rearranging the deck chairs."

Maggie chuckled. "Oh, come on. It can't be that bad. Besides, it's always chaotic finishing up party preparations."

"In all honesty, Maggie, you and John made hosting appear effortless. I had no idea how much preparation goes into something like this, even for a potluck. You need to set up so much stuff: serving pieces, plates, glassware, cutlery, napkins, ice, coffee, cream, sugar." Judy groaned. "The list goes on and on. Plus, you have to make sure the bathrooms are clean and there's enough soap and toilet paper."

Maggie suppressed a smile. She couldn't help but feel vindicated by Judy's frantic confession—especially after Judy had casually assured her she knew what she was doing, even though she'd never done it before. Judy had insisted that, although she hadn't hosted many parties herself, she'd supplied dozens of customers with invitations and party items. In the end, she'd wondered how difficult it could really be.

"I had no idea how much work you put in, Maggie. I'm here to tell you, I really appreciate you even more now."

A lump formed in Maggie's throat. This was no time for her to privately gloat over her friend's newfound appreciation.

"You don't need to thank me, Judy. And, believe me, we've all been where you are. So, what do you need? What can I do to help?"

"I'm not sure how to even set up a buffet—what the flow should be. Jeff and I experimented with a few different configurations. Where's the best place to put the chairs? For easy access, where's the best spot for the beverages? Do we put the coffee with the other beverages or set it up somewhere else? Will everyone bring serving utensils, or do I need to supply them? And—we forgot to buy ice. Do you have a bag you could bring?"

"We always keep a couple of extra bags of ice in our outside freezer," Maggie said. "We'll bring those. That should be plenty. I can do better than that, though. If you'd like, I'll come over in a few minutes."

"I thought you were spending the morning with Susan's family."

"That was the plan, but Julia is sick and they're quarantining. They won't be coming this afternoon, either. So—I'm happily off leash."

"I don't want to interfere with your peaceful Christmas Day," Judy said.

"You'd be doing nothing of the kind," Maggie replied. "To be completely honest, I was a little down in the dumps this morning because I wasn't getting ready for a party. You know me. I love entertaining, and I relish the hustle and bustle before a party. You'd be doing me a favor. I'm already feeling better just thinking about it."

"You promise me you're telling the truth?" Judy asked.

"Pinky swear," Maggie said. "I just got out of the tub. I can be dressed and over there in thirty minutes."

"What about John? Won't he mind?"

"I hear his footsteps on the stairs," Maggie said. "Let me ask him."

Roman raced into the room, followed closely by John.

"I'm talking to Judy," she wiggled her phone, pressed to her ear. "Susan called while you were at the hospital—Julia is sick and they don't want us to be exposed to the crud, and they're staying home today. Do you mind if I run over to Judy's this morning to help her get ready for the potluck?" Maggie's voice radiated her enthusiasm.

"On one condition," he said.

Maggie cocked her head to one side and raised an eyebrow.

"That I get to come with you and help, too. You were in such a funk this morning. I didn't want to make it worse by telling you I was feeling letdown as well."

Maggie turned back to the phone. "Did you hear that?" she asked Judy. "Would it be okay if John also came along?"

"Jeff and I would consider it our own little Christmas miracle."

"Okay—you two hang tight. We'll be there soon."

CHAPTER 3

*J*udy reached over and put her arm around Maggie's shoulder. "You're right; this was a smart idea." The two women stood, their backs to the elaborately carved front door of the Olsson House, and surveyed the scene in front of them.

A crystal vase filled with evergreen boughs, white roses, and sprigs of holly heavy with red berries soared four feet from the top of the round mahogany console table in the center of the foyer. Scattered around the base of the vase were bowls of wrapped mints, mixed nuts, and open boxes of chocolates.

"Right before a party starts, I always go to my own front door and pretend I'm a guest walking inside. I want their first view to be welcoming." Maggie placed her hand over Judy's and gave it a squeeze. "I think the treats on your entry table tell your guests they're welcome." She glanced at Judy. "The identical trees on either side of that dramatic staircase of yours are gorgeous. I think people will have their pictures taken on the first step. I love that you decorated the trees with the hand-carved wooden ornaments that brought you and Jeff together."

Judy grinned. "I brought my set home from the window at Celebrations after I closed last night. Uniting both sets here on Christmas Day seemed fitting to me."

Maggie nodded. "I couldn't agree more. I'm sure William Olsson is looking down from heaven and loving every minute of this."

"I hope so," Judy said. "Jeff says he frequently feels his uncle's presence here."

"Who knows—maybe the Olsson House has a resident ghost."

"Just like Alistair at Rosemont? Do you now believe in him?"

Maggie shrugged. "I'm becoming more convinced as time goes on."

"I'm not sure if I want to share our house with a ghost." Judy cocked her head to one side. "Is it as festive as Rosemont, do you think?"

"Absolutely! You can smell those live trees in the main parlor and the dining room from here—it's heavenly. And when you step into those rooms, the effect is magical."

"Thank you," Judy said. "I was so busy working at the shop during the Christmas retail season, I put off thinking about this party until a week ago. Once I started to plan, I realized I was way behind the eight ball on everything. I think I had a full-blown panic attack last night, worrying that I'd forgotten something major."

"Is that why you and Jeff weren't in church for the candlelight service?"

Judy nodded. "I was beside myself."

"Well … you've done it, my dear—you're ready. My advice is to grab your phone and take pictures of your setup, so you remember next time how you did things."

"Oh gosh," Judy said, "I'm not sure there's going to be a next time. I figured you'd take over the Christmas potluck next year."

"I'm happy to do that. I love to host. But you may discover you enjoy it, too. We can always share duties and alternate years." Maggie checked her watch. "It's time for John and me to scoot. We need to go back home to change and grab the dish we're going to share."

"Gosh, I've occupied you here most of the day. I hope that hasn't interfered with what you planned to make. We're going to have plenty of food—you don't have to bring anything."

"I've got a honey-glazed ham, so all I have to do is slice it and put it on a platter. I also have the smoked turkey breast that Susan was going to contribute. I picked them both up from the same retailer and was going to take it to Susan this morning. Since they're quarantining at home, I'll plate that and bring it as well."

"Sounds wonderful," Judy said, giving Maggie's waist another squeeze before releasing her. "I can't wait to get this party started."

Maggie smiled. "Your first guests should arrive in the next twenty minutes. You've already checked off everything on your to-do list. Don't review it again. Enjoy how beautiful your home looks, take a deep breath, and import a sense of calm to face the day."

"I'll give it a shot," Judy said.

"Now, where did our husbands get to? Do you have any idea?"

"If I had to place a bet, I'd say they're in the library watching a football game."

"That's a safe one." Maggie chuckled. "I'm gonna drag John out of there. The sooner we leave, the sooner we'll be back." She headed to the library. "Oh, don't forget to change into your party dress, either. I've lost count of how many times I've had to rush upstairs to change and fix my hair as the first guests arrived."

CHAPTER 4

John's car crept down the street toward the Olsson House.

"Look at all these cars," he said. "Every parking spot at the curb is occupied. Could some of these people be going to the neighboring houses, and not Judy and Jeff's?"

"Judy told me she invited her neighbors. I think everyone who got an invitation is attending—and arrived on time."

"The potluck started fifteen minutes ago, right?"

"Yep. If these cars are any indication, she'll have double the turnout we had last year."

"Well, the more the merrier," John said.

Maggie chuckled. "That's the spirit. I'm happy for them."

"Do you want me to drop you at the curb while I continue to look for a place to park?" John asked.

"No, I've got a plan. Judy's old house is up ahead on the left. No one is living there. We'll park in her driveway." Maggie pointed to the house as they drew abreast of it.

John parked and they walked back to the Olsson House, being careful not to spill any of the contents from the platters they were bringing to the potluck.

They reached the low iron fence that enclosed the yard. Maggie paused on the sidewalk, taking in the gracious three-story Victorian mansion, now transformed into a holiday jewel. Cedar boughs, tied with generous bows of burgundy velvet ribbon edged in gold, wrapped the porch railing like a festive embrace. Icicle lights traced the gabled roofline and framed the turret windows, where the soft flicker of candlelight shimmered behind the glass. Even in the pale sunshine of late afternoon, the lights glowed faintly, casting a gentle enchantment over the house.

The scent of woodsmoke mingled with the faint aroma of gingerbread, hinting at the warmth waiting inside. Judy and Jeff's painstaking restoration of the once-dilapidated beauty had polished it to a high gleam, like vintage silver brought lovingly back to life. The house sparkled from every angle. Music and laughter spilled through the open front door, wrapping around them like a welcome, and beckoned them forward.

John opened the gate and stepped aside for Maggie to precede him on the walkway. They climbed the steps to the porch and paused in the open doorway. Small groups of people crowded the foyer. Frequent bursts of laughter interrupted the low buzz of conversation. Excitement hung in the air.

"What's going on?" John asked Maggie. "It's like people are waiting for something."

"I don't know. It's Christmas afternoon—Santa has already been here and gone," she teased.

"Maggie!" She heard her name over the din.

"John!" cried another voice.

They turned toward the familiar voices calling their names. Alex Scanlon, Maggie's successor as mayor of Westbury, and his partner, Marc Benson, pushed through the crowd to reach them.

"Merry Christmas, you two," Maggie said, leaning in to kiss Alex on the cheek and accept one from him.

"We've been looking for you. I was afraid you'd miss it."

"Miss what?" Maggie asked.

"Lyla Kershaw is going to make a big announcement any minute now. Even Judy doesn't know what it is," Marc said, shaking John's hand and taking the platter of ham from him. "Alex and I will take your dishes to the buffet table and be right back."

"Thank you," Maggie said, surrendering her platter. She pointed to an empty spot along the wall to the right of the door. "We'll save a place for you if you want to join us for the announcement."

"Will do," Alex said, following Marc into the dining room where the buffet was set up.

Maggie and John planted themselves against the wall.

"Lyla Kershaw?" John asked. "Do you think this has anything to do with her son Josh?"

"And perhaps Sunday Sloan, too?" Maggie replied. "I may know something, but my lips are sealed—or they're supposed to be." She smiled at him and stood on tiptoes to whisper in his ear.

His grin spread like butter on toast. "What a wonderful Christmas Day announcement that'll make!" he exclaimed.

Alex and Marc jostled through the crowd to return to Maggie and John as Lyla climbed to the fourth step on the staircase. The petite woman in her late fifties smoothed an errant hair into place in her neat bob. She raised a glass above her head and tapped it with a knife.

Conversation stopped as everyone turned toward her. Maggie noticed that Josh and Sunday stood at the base of the stairway.

"Merry Christmas, everyone," Lyla said, lowering her glass. "I'm only going to take a moment of your time—I know better than to get between hungry people and that buffet in there." She waved her glass toward the dining room. "While we're all here, I wanted to share with you my wonderful news. My Christmas wish, a gift I've always dreamed of but never expected, is coming true this year."

Her face flushed, and she blinked repeatedly.

"I think many of you know Josh Newlon"—she pointed to her son—"and that I'm his birth mother. We reunited last year after his adoptive parents both died. I now have a lovely relationship with the son I missed every day since giving him up for adoption.

"I experienced more miracles when the rare book theft at Highpointe College reunited me with Josh's birth father. I thought Robert had died before Josh was born, but he was very much alive, and we recently married.

"And now, my embarrassment of riches continues. I'm going to have a daughter-in-law, and she's someone I knew and called a dear friend long before Josh came back into my life. Sunday Sloan has accepted Josh's proposal of marriage, and my family of one will soon blossom into a family of four.

"Christmas is a time for miracles. The changes in my life are truly that. I want to share this joyful news with all of you. Please raise a glass and let's toast the happy life in store for Josh and Sunday."

The crowd cheered and whistled as people raised their glasses and joined in the salute.

"I wish I'd gotten you all champagne," Marc said. "I'm sorry I didn't think about that." He peered at Maggie. "Are you okay?"

Maggie swiped away the moisture under her eyes and nodded. "I'm perfectly fine," she said. "Just a little emotional after hearing Lyla's toast. It's a testament to the fact that you never know when good things are going to happen."

"I'll drink to that," Marc said, raising his glass and clinking it with Alex's.

The crowd surged forward to congratulate the engaged couple.

"I think we're going to head into the dining room and get something to eat while everyone's waiting in line to speak to Josh and Sunday," Alex said. "Care to join us?"

"I'm starved," John said. "I think that's a great idea."

"Lead the way," Maggie said. "We'll see Sunday and Josh before we leave."

~

"Of course I don't mind," Maggie smiled at John. "I'm sure Jeff and the other fans are watching sports on that ginormous television in the library. I'll get a second cup of coffee and find Sunday and Lyla. I'd love to hear about the wedding plans."

"You're the best wife in the world," John said, leaning down and kissing her on the cheek.

Maggie entered the kitchen and refilled her cup at the coffee station in the butler's pantry. She took it into the dining room and made her way to the dessert selections set up on the carved mahogany sideboard.

Sam Torres, her longest-standing friend in Westbury, stood off to one side, alone, near a tall potted palm. "Tisk," he uttered, using his tongue and teeth to capture her attention.

She sidled over to him. "Merry Christmas, Sam. What in the world are you doing in here, lurking behind this tree?"

Sam chuckled. "I'm lying in wait until I'm certain Joan won't catch me. I want to grab a second slice of that Bûche de Noël, a lemon bar, and one of Gloria Vaughn's famous sour cream sugar cookies."

"I'm sure Joan wouldn't care."

"Oh, but she would. My cholesterol is high, and I've gained a few pounds—actually, twenty pounds. We're both on diets, and she's sticking to hers better than I am to mine."

"It's Christmas, Sam. I don't think she'll object."

"Even so, I'd rather my second trip to the dessert buffet go unnoticed."

"Okay—how can I help?"

Sam looked through the open door of the dining room, across the foyer, and into the parlor. His wife stood in front of the fireplace with her back to him.

"I wish she'd go sit down somewhere. I feel like the minute I load up a plate, she's going to turn around and catch me."

"I've got an idea. Why don't I load up a plate for you?"

"You'd do that for me?"

"Of course I would! It's not like I'm aiding and abetting a criminal enterprise. I was going to get myself some dessert, anyway. Sit tight—I'll be right back."

Maggie handed him her coffee cup and went to the buffet, making her selections and returning to him.

"I'll trade you this plate for my coffee cup," Maggie said, snagging the additional sour cream sugar cookie from the top of the plate. "This one's for me. It's not Christmas without one of Gloria's cookies."

Sam motioned for her to follow him farther into the

room and out of his wife's line of sight. He lifted a forkful of Bûche de Noël to his lips.

"You must be enjoying seeing this house so full of light and life. You and Jeff did a masterful job with the renovations." Maggie took a small bite of her cookie. "It's beautiful."

Sam nodded. "It took far more work than either of us expected, but we're very happy with the result. We learned a ton in the process, too. Even after forty years as a handyman, I still ran into things I didn't know. I'm sure we'd be much more efficient if we ever restored another old home again."

"Is that in the cards for you?" Maggie asked.

Sam shrugged. "We've talked about it from time to time. This place wasn't done until a week ago. We decided we'd take December off and talk about any future projects next month."

"That's exciting," Maggie said. "Would you retire from your day job and do this full-time?"

Sam finished his sugar cookie in two bites. "That's the big question. I need to talk to Joan about that, of course, but I'm not sure yet how I feel about that idea."

"I understand—it's a big decision. But I know, if you do take the plunge, you'll make a success of it." She nibbled at her cookie and glanced toward the parlor. "I was hoping to visit with Sunday and Lyla. Have you seen them?"

Sam dabbed at his lips with a napkin and pointed to the parlor. "I think they're in there, talking wedding plans."

"Then that's where I want to be." Maggie caught his eye

and smiled warmly. "Merry Christmas, Sam," she said, then walked to the parlor.

Sunday and Lyla sat on an antique sofa to the right of the fireplace. The red velvet upholstery, the crackling fire, and the fragrant, decorated evergreen nestled in the bay window created the perfect composition for an old-fashioned Christmas card. Judy and Joan stood across from them, while Anita Archer, owner of the local bridal boutique, flanked them on the other side.

Maggie entered the room as Sunday described her dream wedding.

"I'm a traditionalist at heart," Sunday said. "That makes sense, I guess, since I'm a librarian with a specialty in rare books. I appreciate old things. What can I say? I want a church wedding with a minister, a big white dress with a veil, and a tiered cake."

"That sounds lovely, dear," Judy said. "Traditional weddings have never gone out of style. Even in these days of Evites,"—she made a show of shuddering—"I still sell a lot of traditional wedding invitations."

"Good, because that's what I want," Sunday said. "When we get our details firmed up, I'll come into Celebrations and order them from you."

"I'd be happy to help you find exactly what you're looking for," Judy said.

"How many people do you plan to invite?" Anita asked.

"I think it'll be a relatively small wedding," Sunday said.

"Susan isn't here, is she?" She looked around, and her eyes rested on Maggie.

"No," Maggie said. "Julia is sick and they're quarantining."

Sunday nodded. "I think my only attendant will be Susan, if she says yes. I'd have asked you, Lyla, but you're going to be mother of the groom."

Lyla brought a hand to her heart. "That means so much— that you'd even think of me as an attendant."

"I don't have any family to invite," Sunday said, "and Josh's family is small, so I think once you add in our friends, we're looking at fifty people, if that."

"Have you selected a date?" Maggie asked.

Sunday shook her head. "Not yet. We want to secure a venue first. After the holidays, we're going to visit some of the local churches."

"Have you considered the chapel at Highpointe College?" Maggie asked. "It's absolutely beautiful. As an employee of the college, you're entitled to get married there. You can also hold the reception in the walled garden outside the chapel for a nominal fee."

"Really?" Sunday asked. "I hadn't heard that. I've never been inside, but you're right—it's stunning from the outside. We've been talking about a late spring or summer wedding, after Josh graduates. Having a reception in the garden would be pretty at either of those times."

"It's a popular venue, so be sure to book as soon as you make your decision," Maggie said. "It'll require approval from the facilities department. If you get any pushback from them over your use of the chapel or the gardens, let me know. The college should do this, at the very least, for their rare book librarian." She patted Sunday's hand. "Especially considering the risks you took to protect our collection."

"Thanks," Sunday said, closing her eyes as she remembered that night in the deserted library, alone with Nigel Blythe. He'd killed before and had been intent on taking her life. Shaking her head, she tried to forget their dramatic fight on the stairs, the one where Nigel tumbled over the railing to his death.

Conversation ceased as everyone cast their thoughts back to the decades-long crime spree. Judy broke the silence. "Have you selected other vendors?"

Sunday opened her eyes. "Some," she continued. "I'll get my cake from Laura's Bakery. She displays wedding cakes in the window of her shop and they're beautiful. Her lemon cake is tied with chocolate for my favorite flavor."

"You can't go wrong with either one," Anita said. "Pete's Bistro caters weddings. Many of my brides use him for their receptions."

"Pete's it is," Sunday said. "I came in here feeling overwhelmed at the thought of planning a wedding that we want to take place relatively soon. I think the only details I have left are the music, the flowers, and my dress."

"Have you met Marc Benson?" Judy asked. "He's here—somewhere. He's a marvelous pianist and organist. I'll introduce you before you leave."

"I'd appreciate that," Sunday said. "And I have an idea of

what I'd like for my dress." She gave Anita a rueful look. "I know I don't have time to order one, so I'll either get a used one online or buy a sample dress from one of the chain boutiques."

"Do you have pictures on your phone of what you'd like?" Lyla asked.

"What engaged woman doesn't?" Sunday pulled out her phone, tapped the screen, and scrolled. She turned the screen around and held it toward Lyla, who gasped. The other women leaned in to view her selection.

"I adore a princess-style gown," Joan said. "Your wedding may be your only chance in life to wear a dress with a skirt that big." She tapped the screen. "That dress would be gorgeous on you."

"Thanks," Sunday said. "I guess watching Disney movies my entire childhood is catching up with me. I still want to be a Disney princess."

"If you think you'll ever grow out of that, you're mistaken," Maggie teased. "We're all like that."

Anita reached out her hand. "May I?"

Sunday handed her the phone. Anita studied the dress, using her fingertips to enlarge the image on the screen.

"I'm familiar with this manufacturer," she said. "They make beautiful dresses. The yards of fabric make this a very expensive dress."

"That's what I found online," Sunday said. "I can't afford a new one, so I'm going to look for something used."

Anita handed the phone back to her. "If you find it, I'd be

happy to take a look at it and tell you if it can be altered to fit you before you purchase."

"Really? Gosh, that would be so nice. I'd appreciate that."

"And if you don't find the dress of your dreams online, I've got a small selection of gowns I've collected over the years that I sell at a steep discount. These are dresses that people ordered but never picked up. I keep them in case someone needs a wedding dress in a pinch. That happens less and less these days of ordering everything online, but I still have them. I don't have one like that, but, if you get panicky that you won't find a dress, stop by the shop and look."

"Thank you. I'll do that," Sunday said.

"Do you know where my shop is located?"

"I sure do," Sunday said. "Laura's Bakery and Archer's Bridal are both part of my regular route whenever I'm in the square. I love drooling over the dresses in your window."

Sunday opened her Notes app. "Can anyone recommend a florist? I can't wait to contact your referrals. I may have my wedding planned before New Year's."

The group around her chuckled.

"I'll fix a tray with an assortment of desserts to bring in here," Judy said.

"Terrific idea," Lyla said. "I'm going to grab another cup of coffee. Does anybody else want a refill?"

"I'll come with you," Joan said.

Maggie slid into the seat Lyla had vacated. She put her arms around Sunday's shoulders and pulled her in for a hug.

"I'm thrilled you and Josh found each other and have decided to join your lives."

"Thank you," Sunday said. "It's the miracle Lyla spoke about." She narrowed her eyes and looked at Maggie. "Were you really surprised by our announcement? Did Josh actually keep it a secret from you?"

Maggie pursed her lips into a thin line before she spoke. "He didn't tell me, but he's worked as my assistant long enough that I could tell something was different about him. I knew he had visited a jeweler about a ring. It doesn't take a genius to guess what that was about. I used all my strength to stop myself from asking him. I figured he had promised you he would keep it a secret, and I didn't want to interfere with that. Honestly, I'm not sure how much longer I could've held out before I tried to wheedle the truth out of him."

Sunday giggled. "In your position, I'm not sure I could've held off either."

"This is the best news," Maggie said. "I'm sure Susan will be delighted to stand up for you at your wedding. John and I are dropping off food for her and Aaron on our way home. I won't mention that you'd like her to be your matron of honor—but can I tell them about your engagement?"

"Of course," Sunday said. "Now that we've announced it, it's not a secret."

"Who is Josh going to ask to be his best man?"

"This may seem strange because they haven't known each other long, but he's thinking of Frank Haynes. They get along incredibly well. Josh has only been working for him part-time for a short while, but they talk multiple times every day. Josh jokes that they finish each other's sentences. What would you think if he asked Frank?"

Maggie swallowed a lump in her throat. "I think that would mean more to Frank than you could ever know. You don't always need a lot of time to develop deep feelings for someone."

"That's what I thought," Sunday said. "Josh was going to talk to him about it today, but he and Loretta and the kids aren't here. Sean and the twins are passing around a cold, just like Julia."

"That's too bad," Maggie said. "I wondered where they were."

Sunday snapped her fingers. "You've given me an idea— Josh and I will take food to the Haynes family on our way home. If Frank can step outside for a moment, we can share our happy news and Josh can ask him."

"Great idea," Maggie said. "I think you're on track to plan this wedding in record time."

CHAPTER 5

Alistair

Maggie and John weren't the only ones feeling down in the dumps this Christmas Day. I don't want to overstate it, but I was drenched in melancholy.

During my many decades as Rosemont's butler, I'd seen my share of parties. We had thrown some real doozies. When Silas Martin died and the house was boarded up, my communication with the outside world came to an abrupt end. I had been inhabiting the attic for years, and, while I sometimes relished the solitude, it was a lonely existence.

I was initially annoyed when Maggie disrupted my slumber that snowy evening years ago. But trailing behind her through the empty house, watching her wander from room to room, pulling dust sheets off the furniture and admiring the home's treasures, warmed my heart. By the time she curled up in the big chair by the French doors in the library and fell asleep, I was smitten.

Then came the whimpering of that pathetic terrier mix, shivering in the icy wind outside the library. I knew what I had to do. I created a disturbance to wake Maggie. She rescued the little dog and took her into her heart, as I'd hoped she would. In that moment, I knew she was the perfect person to move into Rosemont and bring light and life back into the home I loved so dearly. A home I had devoted my life and afterlife to.

And I was right. Under Maggie and John's auspices, Rosemont played gracious host to Easter brunches, carnivals, Thanksgiving celebrations, the annual Christmas potluck, weddings, and engagements. I looked forward to each of these happy incursions into our otherwise quiet lives. So, when I noticed Maggie wasn't polishing silver trays and John wasn't hauling extra chairs in from the garage, I began to worry. It wasn't like Maggie to procrastinate. Something was off.

They had gotten up early, as usual, but, instead of kicking into high gear, they enjoyed a leisurely cup of coffee by the fire. After that long bath of Maggie's and John taking off and returning, they both went out again in old clothes, only to come home in mid-afternoon to change into dressier attire. They placed a few slices of ham and turkey on platters and left again.

I spent the day floating from room to room. The cats were true to form. Blossom and Buttercup cuddled on the rug in front of the now-cold living room hearth. Bubbles pestered Roman in an attempt to start a game of chase, but Roman was wise to her antics. He curled into a tight ball on his kitchen bed, tucked his nose under his tail, and ignored her until she grew bored and wandered off to nap in a sunny patch under a window in the conservatory.

While Eve stayed at Maggie's heels when she was home, the dog sank into the memory foam of her kitchen bed and spent the day snoozing whenever her human was away.

The afternoon sun crossed from the back of the house to the front. The leafless trees along the driveway cast long shadows. I was considering retreating to my attic and turning in early when the garage door opened.

I roused myself and floated downstairs to the kitchen. My hope was that Susan, Aaron, and little Julia would be with Maggie and John. That tiny girl gladdened my heart. I wasn't positive, yet, but I suspected she was one of those rare humans who could sense my presence. Maggie and John entered the kitchen alone. My spirits plummeted.

John dropped his keys on the counter and pulled Maggie into his arms.

"Christmas turned out nice, didn't it?" she said, resting her head against his chest.

"It did," John agreed. "I think Judy and Jeff enjoyed hosting Christmas as much as we do. Everyone certainly had a great time."

"The news about Sunday and Josh is wonderful," Maggie said. "Lyla is over the moon."

"Robert was in the den with us. Living in England until recently, he's not into U.S. sports. So, while we watched the games, he talked about Josh and Sunday and the happy life he and Lyla are building. I agree with you—it's wonderful."

Maggie pulled back and looked at him. "Are you hungry?"

"I stuffed myself at the potluck. I don't need anything else tonight."

"Me too," Maggie said. "I think I'll go upstairs and get ready for bed. But there's one thing I need to do before that."

John studied her face.

"I've got one little gift for you," Maggie said. "I'd like you to open it before I head up."

"I thought we agreed not to exchange gifts this year," John said. "We were going to take a week off and go somewhere this winter instead."

"We're still doing that," Maggie said. "But I found something you had to have. I couldn't resist. It's fine if you don't have a gift for me. That was our agreement."

"Well, as it turns out, I found something I knew you needed, too," John said.

"Well then," Maggie said with a smile, "let's exchange our gifts in the living room."

"I'll start the fire again," John offered. "Let's sit by the hearth to open them."

"Perfect," Maggie said. "My gift is in my closet. I'll bring it down."

"I hid mine behind the tree," John said.

I looked between them, quivering with anticipation. I adored surprises. Suddenly, this day was looking up.

John got the fire going.

Maggie retrieved her gift from her closet and returned to the living room. She handed him a square box, about the size of a watch box.

John pulled off the red and green plaid bow and tore the wrapping. He chuckled as soon as he saw the manufacturer's logo.

"This is perfect," he said. "I've been wanting one of these for ages."

I hovered over John's shoulder, straining for a better view. It looked like a regular coffee mug, but the bottom was thicker and emitted a pulsing red glow. The mug came with a matching disc. This was one of those newfangled gadgets we didn't have in my day.

"I know," Maggie said. "Everyone who has one of these rechargeable heated mugs swears by it. I figured you could take it to the animal hospital. You're so busy, you never get to finish a cup of coffee. I'm sure it's stone cold by the time you get back to it."

"That's exactly right," John said, his eyes twinkling. "Your turn." He picked up another small box and handed it to her.

Maggie pulled off the stick-on bow easily but then struggled with the layers of tape John used when wrapping packages.

"Honestly, John," she laughed, "I'll need power tools to open this."

"Here, let me get a corner started," he said, tearing a piece of the paper for her.

Maggie finished unwrapping the gift. They both burst into laughter.

"This was a really good gift," she said.

I floated to John's other side for a better look. He had gotten her the same thing—only in rose gold instead of gray.

"I know how focused you get when you're working at your computer," he said. "You ignore your coffee for hours. I figured this fancy new warming mug would be perfect for you."

"Thank you," Maggie said. "When I bought yours, I thought about getting one for myself. The price tag stopped me, but I'm thrilled to have it."

She leaned across the crumpled wrapping paper, took his face in her hands, and kissed him.

How fun was this? They each got the other a gift—when they weren't supposed to—and it turned out to be the same item. If my hands didn't pass through each other, I would've clapped them in glee.

The day had started poorly, but this was a lovely turn of events. I watched as Maggie and John gathered up the wrapping paper and carried their new mugs into the kitchen. Maggie washed them both while John plugged in the charging discs. She set the mugs on the discs and declared she was heading upstairs to bed.

"I'll feed the dogs and take them out, then be right up," he said.

Maggie headed for the stairs, and I trailed behind her.

CHAPTER 6

"Here he comes now." Frank Haynes waved his hand over his head at the lanky teen as he rounded the corner of Forever Friends. Dodger, David Wheeler's midsize mutt and constant companion, trotted alongside his master as they crunched across the frozen ground toward the group of men huddled in the adjacent vacant lot.

Josh Newlon and Tim Knudsen turned to watch David approach.

Frank opened his arms wide to greet the boy he loved like a son. "I picked up the architectural drawings for the new guide dog school yesterday. I'm so glad I got them while you were home on Christmas break."

David stepped into Frank's loose embrace, and they patted each other on the back.

Sean Nash stood next to his stepfather, shifting his weight from one foot to the other, waiting to greet David.

"Hey, man," David said, swinging toward the adolescent boy and greeting him with high-fives.

"This is a big day for you both," said the other man, standing with them in the cold sunshine of the winter morning. Tim extended his hand to David, and they shook. "Founding a school to train seeing-eye dogs is huge, Frank. Going to school to become a guide dog trainer—and to train others to do the same—is incredibly impressive, David."

"It means a lot to me that you could drop everything and join us today, Tim. We've relied on your expertise in real estate since the inception of this project," Frank said. He turned to Josh. "Your education in school administration fills a gap in experience that I don't have. David's knowledge of guide dog training will be at the heart of our venture."

Frank turned his attention to Sean. "And Sean has stepped in to fill the void left by David's absence at Forever Friends. He's been my eyes and ears over there while I focus on making Forever Guides a reality."

Frank tapped the open palm of his left hand with the two-inch-thick roll of architectural drawings he held in his right. "Sean and I took a quick look at these last night. I think you'll be thrilled to see what our dream looks like on paper."

Frank removed the rubber band from the tall cylinder of drawings and carefully unfurled them. He stepped forward to stand in front of the others as they gathered behind him, leaning over his shoulder to view the plans.

"This first sheet," Frank said, "is a rendering of the front elevation."

Tim whistled softly. "Wow. That's impressive," he said. "I love the swoosh of the canopy over the wall of double glass doors at the entrance."

"It's dramatic," Josh agreed. "It looks like you're entering someplace important."

"You are," Frank said. "Forever Guides is going to improve the lives of thousands of people. The walkway up to the doors is twenty feet wide, with lush landscaping on either side. I wanted the architecture to set the tone for the experience within our walls. It needed to look welcoming, with a sense of permanence."

He glanced over his shoulder at David.

The young man's throat tightened. It took him a moment to find his voice. "It certainly does," he said. "I expected this to look like the entrance to Forever Friends."

"Forever Friends is a terrific facility, and I'm proud of it," Frank said. "But it's utilitarian in design and function. The entrance isn't memorable."

"If Forever Guides looks half as good in real life as it does in these plans," Tim said, "you've achieved your goal."

Frank flipped to the second page of the plans. "This shows us the entire Forever Guides campus. I know we had originally talked about one building, but the architects convinced me we would be better served by three buildings."

"The one in the back is going to be the puppy center. We'll house our breeding program there, and the puppies will stay until they go to their puppy raiser families. Our veterinary clinic will be there as well. The larger two-story building on the right will be the dormitory for guide-dog users when they come to campus to train with their dogs."

"I thought we weren't building a dormitory right away," David said. "We were going to put people up in one of the nearby business hotels when they're here for training."

Frank inhaled. "I know that was the plan, but staying off campus isn't ideal for the handler or the dog. You've told me about the residential program at the Guide Dog Center, where you've been working and training. A lot of synergy takes place while people are together, learning to become a handler-guide dog team. It would be a shame for them to miss out on that."

"Where did the money come from?" David asked bluntly.

"I think everyone here knows that Forever Guides has a secret donor—and it isn't me." Frank raised his eyebrows as he looked from face to face.

"You mean Gordon Mortimer?" Tim asked.

"The donor wants to remain anonymous, so I won't confirm or deny," Frank said, smiling. "When I consulted with him after we received the preliminary plans, he insisted that we construct the entire project from the get-go."

"That's incredibly generous," David said. "It *is* important for the handlers-in-training to live on campus with their guides. I'm stoked to hear this."

"The dormitory building will house twenty hotel-style rooms with en suite bathrooms, a fully equipped catering kitchen, a communal dining room, and a large central living room for people to watch television, play games, or talk. There will also be dog relief stations on either side of the building," Frank said. "The last building on this drawing is the one whose elevation you viewed on page one. It will be the administration building. Josh's office and the other administrative staff will be there. We'll have a conference room, another small kitchen, and a gift shop."

David reached over Frank's shoulder and traced his finger along sidewalks that looped between the buildings. "We'll use these in the early stages of our training, before our handler and guide dog pairs are ready to go into the outside world. We'll construct overhead obstacles, sharp turns, inclines, and intersections with roadways to teach our students mobility skills with their dogs."

The sun ducked behind a cloud, and the morning felt even colder. Frank rolled the plans back into a cylinder. "Do you want to inspect the detail drawings?" he asked. "You can see where your offices will be." He smiled at Josh and then at David.

"Sure," David said. "I want to go over all the plans. I've been so excited."

"Me too," Josh said.

Frank studied the expanse of open land in front of him as he replaced the rubber band on the drawings. "Can you imagine it?" he asked, looking at David.

"I can." David nodded. "There's nothing going on here right now, but I can feel the energy in this ground."

Josh agreed, "When this place is built and filled with humans and their guide dogs, it's going to be remarkable."

"I'd like to review every drawing in that stack, too," Tim said.

"Okay, everybody, let's go back to my office at Haynes Enterprises. We'll spread these out on the conference room table and go over them with a fine-tooth comb. I want each of you to consider them carefully. If there's anything that needs to be changed, please speak up."

"Now is the best time to make modifications," Tim said. "Before you send these out for construction bids."

Frank led the way to the parking lot. "Dream big, every-body," he said. "We're creating a magical place."

CHAPTER 7

The bell over the door of Celebrations announced Susan's arrival as she entered the gift shop that was a fixture on the square. Judy was at the register, almost hidden from view by tall stacks of half-priced boxes of Christmas cards, rolls of wrapping paper, and assorted ribbons and bows. She and Susan waved to each other as Susan made her way to the racks of greeting cards.

Judy gave her customer the total for her purchase and swiped the woman's credit card. She placed the items in carrier bags imprinted with Celebrations in a flourishy font and handed them across the counter.

"Thanks for coming in," Judy said. "It's always nice to see you."

"I haven't missed an after-Christmas clearance sale

at Celebrations since your mother had the store," the woman said.

"I appreciate your loyal patronage," Judy replied, smiling as the woman turned and walked to the door.

Susan approached the register. "I'm afraid I'm a small sale compared to that lady," Susan said, placing an engagement card, a package of New Year's Eve napkins, and one of paper New Year's Eve dessert plates on the counter. She gave Judy a rueful smile.

"You're a year-round customer," Judy said. "The woman who just left comes in once a year for our after-Christmas sale. And that's fine. I love all my customers, no matter how much they spend."

"That's why you're so successful," Susan said. "It's so much more fun to shop here than at the big box retailers at the mall."

"From your lips to God's ears," Judy said, scanning Susan's items. "I'm glad to see you today. Does that mean everyone is feeling better at your house?"

"Julia's fever broke yesterday, and she slept through the night. She's fine this morning, so I felt comfortable leaving her with our nanny while I run errands. I took this week off. Luckily, Aaron and I never got sick."

"I'm glad my shop was one of your errands," Judy said. She pointed to the engagement card. "Did you hear about Sunday and Josh?"

"Mom couldn't wait to tell me. I'm thrilled for them! As a matter of fact, I'm meeting Sunday for coffee at Pete's in fifteen minutes. She's on vacation this week, too, and called to see if we could get together. I can't wait to hear all the details."

"I believe they're planning a traditional wedding, probably in spring or summer."

"I love the sound of that," Susan said. "That had always been my dream—until I got so sick after donating my kidney to Nicole. Aaron and I didn't know how long it would take me to recover"—she turned her face away—"or even if I would recover. Getting married in the hospital was an experience I'll never forget. I don't regret not having the big traditional wedding I always dreamed of, but I'm happy Sunday gets to have one."

"Me too," Judy said. "Looks like you're having a New Year's Eve party?"

Susan chuckled. "If you can call it that. Since Mom and John couldn't be with us on Christmas Day, we're having them over for New Year's Eve. We'll have dinner at six, exchange gifts, and they'll be on their way home by nine. Unless Julia keeps us up, Aaron and I are never awake at midnight anymore. I bought those napkins and plates on a whim—as a nod to the festive occasion." She cocked her head and looked at Judy. "Do you and Jeff have fun plans?"

"Actually—we do," Judy said.

"Do tell!" Susan grinned. "Are you dressing up and going somewhere swanky? Maybe dinner and dancing at The Mill?"

Judy laughed. "Nothing of the sort. It's been such a busy

holiday season here at the store, and then we hosted the Christmas potluck. Frankly, we're both pooped. Jeff and I agreed to stay in and have an early dinner. He's quite a cook, as it turns out, and is going to make brisket in the crockpot."

"Really?" Susan exclaimed. "That's what I'm fixing! Did he get the recipe out of last Sunday's paper?"

"I think so," Judy said. "You'll have to compare notes on how it turns out."

"I'll make sure we do," Susan said.

"After dinner, I plan to climb into my flannel pajamas and snuggle on the sofa with him while we watch a romcom. I'm going to suggest *The Holiday*."

"That's my favorite," Susan said. "I've seen it a zillion times. Sounds like the perfect New Year's Eve date to me." She checked her watch. "I'd better get going—I don't want to be late for Sunday."

Judy came around the counter and hugged her friend.

"Happy New Year," they murmured to each other.

SUSAN ADDRESSED the envelope to Sunday and Josh, taking care to render the first letters of their names in an elaborate font. Calligraphy was a hobby she had abandoned when she became a mother. She rocked back in her chair and studied her efforts, pleased with the effect. She placed the card, with a handwritten note from her, into the envelope and licked the tip of the V to seal it shut.

She set the card on the table. Sunday would be here any minute, and she was glad she'd arrived with enough time to sign the card.

Susan felt a rush of cold air as the door opened behind her. She turned to see Sunday stepping inside, out of the cold.

Sunday spotted Susan and hurried across the dining room. "Thank you for meeting me this morning," Sunday said. "I understand you've had a hectic week, what with Julia's illness. It was very important to me to see you before we both get busy with our jobs and our lives after New Year's."

"Of course," Susan said. "I'm always happy to see you."

"You heard our news?"

Susan grinned. "I sure did. If you were hoping to keep your engagement a secret, I'm afraid that ship has sailed. Announcing anything in Judy's presence is the equivalent of publishing it on the internet."

"So I've been told," Sunday said with a laugh. "We aren't keeping our good news secret, however."

"I'm glad," Susan said. "It certainly is good news." She slid the card over to Sunday. "This is for you and Josh—from Aaron and me."

"Gosh, this will be our first engagement card. Thank you, Susan. Do you mind if I save it to open with Josh tonight?"

"Of course not," Susan said. "So, speaking of Judy, she just told me you're going for a traditional wedding."

"That's right," Sunday said. "It'll be small, but we both want a church wedding with all the bells and whistles."

"I love the sound of that," Susan said. "Mom told me you're considering getting married in the Highpointe College Chapel."

"We are," Sunday said.

"Have you seen it?" Susan asked.

"Only from the outside," Sunday replied. "That red brick exterior in the Gothic Revival style is stunning, and exactly what I want."

"You have to go inside," Susan said. "With the sun streaming through that huge stained-glass window behind the altar—well, it's absolutely breathtaking."

"It's open to the public every day this week from eleven until four. I plan to look at it when we're done here," Sunday said. "It sounds like it'll check all the boxes on my wish list for a venue."

Susan checked her watch. "It's almost eleven. Would you like company? I'd be happy to go with you." She looked at Sunday and then gave her a rueful smile. "I'm sorry—I shouldn't intrude and invite myself. This is your decision. You may not want someone tagging along."

"Actually," Sunday said, "I would love to have you with me." She took a deep breath. "That brings me to the reason I asked you to meet me here today." She held Susan's gaze. "As I said, we'll have a small wedding. I was an only child, and my parents are both gone. They were only children, too, so I don't have any aunts, uncles, or cousins. Josh and I each want to invite someone we love to stand up with us." She took another deep breath before continuing. "I was wondering if you would be my matron of honor?"

Susan's eyes widened. "I'd *love* to be your matron of honor, Sunday," she said, her eyes becoming moist. "As the title implies, it would be my honor."

"You have a busy life," Sunday said. "I won't make a lot of demands on your time. I don't expect you to throw me a shower or a bachelorette weekend or any of that. Pick whatever dress and color you want to wear. I just want you with me on that day."

"What if I want to throw you a shower or a bachelorette weekend?" Susan put a hand on top of Sunday's. "I'd love to do all those things and support you however I can. I'm glad you're flexible about what I'm going to wear, but I want you to pick the color." She paused. "There's something I should tell you. We haven't told anyone else yet—we wanted to wait —but, since my news might impact your wedding, I think you need to know."

Sunday raised an eyebrow and nodded for Susan to continue.

"I've been feeling queasy for the past few weeks," Susan said. "We were going to wait after the holidays, but I couldn't stand not knowing. A home pregnancy test tells me I'm expecting again."

"Oh, Susan—that's wonderful!" Sunday cried. "I'm so happy for you. I know how much you and Aaron want a second child."

"We've had two miscarriages since Julia, so we don't want to announce this until after the first trimester," Susan said.

"Your secret is safe with me," Sunday said. "I won't even tell Josh."

"I might be big as a horse by the time you get married," Susan said. "Are you sure you don't mind a very pregnant woman in your wedding photos?"

"Are you kidding? Of course we won't mind," Sunday said. "Have you told your mom?"

"Not yet, but I doubt I'll be able to keep this a secret from her. We're so close, we know each other's thoughts."

Sunday nodded. "I had that kind of relationship with my mom before she passed."

"I'm terribly sorry your mother won't be here to help plan your wedding," Susan said. "I could never replace her, but I'd love to help any way I can."

"If you really mean it, I'd like to run things by you. Josh is so busy completing his coursework for his degree and getting settled into his new job that he isn't terribly interested in the details of our wedding. Whenever I mention something to him, he just agrees and says we should do whatever I decide."

Susan chuckled. "Sounds par for the course for most men. In some respects, I suppose that's nice—but, if you really want a second opinion, you're not going to get one."

"Exactly," Sunday said. "I'd love to have a sounding board."

"Well, now you do," Susan said.

The server approached their table. "Sorry for the wait. What can I get you?" He turned to Sunday.

She placed her order for a mocha latte.

"I'll have a tall black coffee," Susan said. "And can you make those both to go, please?" She winked at Sunday. "We need to be on our way—we've got a wedding chapel to tour."

Sunday beamed. "Yes," she agreed, "we've got places to go and decisions to make."

CHAPTER 8

*A*nita stepped onto the sidewalk outside of Pete's Bistro on New Year's Eve day, her carryout order of a club sandwich and chips secured in a carrier bag. She'd eat half of it now for lunch and save the rest for dinner. She and Gordon Mortimer had agreed to have their New Year's Eve dinner together—on FaceTime. He, of course, would be in New York City, and she would be here. The thought of celebrating with him—even virtually —brought a warm flush to her cheeks despite the frigid temperatures. She stepped away from the door, set her parcel at her feet, and pulled her scarf close under her chin.

Two familiar figures huddled in conversation two doors down. The woman caught sight of her and swung her hand over her head in greeting.

Anita headed in their direction. "What are you two doing out here on this frigid afternoon?"

Tim glanced at the pink bakery box he was holding. "Nancy's birthday is tomorrow, and I picked up her favorite cake for her. I was heading into Celebrations to buy a card. I've also got a gift certificate for a monthly massage."

"I'd give you an A+ on your efforts," Anita said. "I'm sure Nancy will be thrilled."

"I've always felt sorry for people with birthdays on major holidays. They seem to get shortchanged," said Tim. "When I married Nancy, I promised myself I'd never let that happen to her. This cake isn't even on the menu at Laura's. It's a lemon poppyseed pound cake with lemon drizzle icing. Laura makes it using Nancy's grandmother's recipe."

"You're too good to be true," Judy teased him.

"And why are you on the sidewalk outside Celebrations?" Anita asked Judy.

"I removed my front window display this morning," Judy said. "I give the space a thorough cleaning whenever I reset my window. Then I stand here and look at the space while I think about what I'm going to display."

"It's your version of a painter looking at a blank canvas," Anita said. "Your window displays are fabulous. I draw a lot of inspiration for mine from yours."

"That's a nice thing to say," Judy said. "Arranging a display is creative. When this space is clean and empty, I come out here and look at it from every angle. Then I go back into my store and cull through what I've got on the shelves or boxed up in the back that I'd like to feature. I let all of that percolate in my subconscious for a day or two before I fill the space."

"I agree with Anita," Tim said. "You're a real artist."

"Maybe you can help me with my displays at the sewing machine museum I'm going to build," Anita said. "I'd be happy to pay you for your expertise."

"I'd love to and you're *not* paying me," Judy said. "I've already been thinking about it, to tell you the truth."

"What's this about a sewing machine museum?" Tim asked. "I haven't heard about that."

Anita bit her lip.

"It's a terrific idea," Judy said. "Tell him."

"I've got a basement full of old sewing machines that my mother and grandmother used in our shop. I thought they were so pretty and began collecting them. Well, you know how it goes—one purchase leads to another, and pretty soon you have dozens and dozens of them packed away in a basement. I asked Gordon to appraise them for me recently," she said. "Have you met him?"

"I have. He's the man from New York who helped Maggie and John sell the valuable silver they found in Rosemont's attic."

"That's the one. Gordon told me my collection isn't worth a lot of money. He said the machines I have are beautiful and should be out where people can see them. He encouraged me to start a museum with them. Gordon even took me to tour a small appliance museum not far from here.

Anyway, I decided he was right and that I'd open a sewing machine museum right here in Westbury."

"Congratulations, Anita. I think that's one of the coolest things I've ever heard. Nancy loves to sew—I'm sure we'll be lined up to get in on opening day."

"Thank you, Tim. It's early days, yet. I've been making list upon list of things I need to do. The first item is finding a place I can afford to buy or rent. There's not enough space in Archer's Bridal."

Tim spun around, facing the square. "I think it should be located here," he said. "On the square. This is the area we want to enhance to attract tourists to Westbury."

"Spoken like a member of the town council," Judy said. "I think you're right, though. I'd love it to be located on the square. You'd get foot traffic into the museum, too. The square is a busy place."

"It would be convenient for me if it were located close to Archer's Bridal," Anita said. "I plan for the museum to be open on Saturday and Sunday, and by appointment during the week. It would be easy for me to nip over and unlock it if it was on the square."

Tim pointed to the middle of the block on the far side of the square. "What about that building?" he asked. The words Candy Alley on a blue and white sign, faded by the sun and ravaged by the rain, were visible through the bare branches of trees on the square.

"You mean Charlotte's old business?" Judy asked. "The

candy store has been vacant since she passed away four years ago. Is it on the market? I don't see a For Sale sign."

"No, it's not listed," Tim said. "Someone inherited it from her, and it's clear they don't intend to run a candy store—or any other business, for that matter—out of the space. It's not unusual for properties that are owned by a person's estate to remain vacant for years while the heirs decide—"

"Or fight over," Judy interrupted.

Tim chuckled. "Or fight over—what to do with it."

"That location would be ideal," Anita said. "I've been in and out of that store since I was a child. If memory serves me, it's plenty big enough to house my museum. But if the property isn't on the market, I don't know what good that does me."

Tim turned to face Anita, his eyes narrowed in thought. "Would you like me to make inquiries on your behalf?" he asked. "I won't mention you're interested in buying it or what you'd like to use it for. I'll find out who owns the property and contact them. Sometimes people get so overwhelmed with managing an estate that they're gridlocked and grateful to receive an expression of interest."

"It sounds like a lot of work with potentially no reward," Anita said.

"If we can't get that property, I'd be delighted to help you find something else," Tim said. "At any rate, I'm curious about Candy Alley and its future use. As a realtor, I'd like to know what the current owners plan to do with it."

"I'd appreciate it if you'd make some calls, if you really don't mind," Anita said.

"Would you be interested in seeing it, if I can arrange a showing?"

"Definitely," Anita said. "I have nothing on my calendar for the foreseeable future that I can't move. Set up a time and I'll be there."

"I'll do my best," Tim said. "And now I'd better get that card and be on my way."

"Happy New Year to both of you," Anita said, as Tim and Judy entered Celebrations.

~

ANITA CARRIED her takeout lunch through the deserted workroom to the break room at the rear of the bridal shop. Her workroom supervisor and the two seamstresses sat together at a round table in the center of the room.

She smiled at the women who, after over three decades at Archer's Bridal, were more like family than employees.

"We're caught up, aren't we?" Anita asked. "Every dress that was promised for next week is ready?"

"Yes. And the following week too," the supervisor said. "After months of being behind, we're finally up to date."

"It's slow this time of year," Anita said. "Valentine's Day always brings a surge of engagements, so we'll be plenty busy in a couple of months." She faced her employees. "You can go home now and get ready for your evening plans."

One seamstress chuckled. "That would mean putting on my PJs and ordering a pizza."

"Sounds like the perfect New Year's Eve to me," the other woman said.

"Well, you can get an early start on things."

"Thank you, Anita," the two seamstresses replied in unison. They replaced their empty plastic containers into lunch boxes and headed to their lockers along the opposite wall to retrieve their coats.

"The sign I posted on the door earlier in the week says we'll be open until 3:00 p.m.," the supervisor said. "I'll stay until then."

"You don't need to," Anita replied. "I doubt anybody's going to come in. If they do, I'll handle them. I appreciate the offer, but there's no reason for both of us to hang around with nothing to do."

"If you're sure?" the supervisor's voice ended on a question as she rose from her chair.

"Absolutely." Anita placed her Styrofoam container with her sandwich on the counter and took a can of diet soda from the refrigerator. "I'll eat my lunch while I focus on year-end paperwork. An uninterrupted afternoon is exactly what I need to get started on the books."

"Okay," the supervisor said. "Promise me you'll close at 3:00 and head home. New Year's Eve is not a night to get caught up in your bookkeeping."

"Heh—I only did that once, and it was years ago," Anita said defensively. "Believe me, I don't want to be out on the roads tonight. I'll lock up at 3:01 and be home by 3:10."

"See you next year," the supervisor said as she put on her coat and headed out the door.

Anita pulled out a chair, popped the top on her soda, and began eating her sandwich. Her mind drifted to the former Candy Alley building. It would be the perfect location for her museum. A seed of excitement formed in her chest as she contemplated the possibility. It grew and blossomed the more she imagined the museum's potential home.

The brick required a good power washing. She would need to hire a graphic designer to devise a logo and her sign. She closed her eyes and inhaled, picturing it.

Tim hadn't even had a chance to contact the owners yet. Anita knew she shouldn't get her hopes up. She picked up a chip and popped it into her mouth. It had been years since she allowed her dreams unfettered access to her mind.

If the owners were willing to sell, she would need to figure out how much she could afford to spend. Thankfully, she had money to invest. Archer's Bridal provided a steady income over the years. Anita had lived modestly, and routinely saved more than half of her income.

She picked up the Styrofoam box and her soda and headed to her desk in the tiny office off the break room. It was time to check her bank accounts and make a budget for this new venture.

Anita took another bite of her sandwich and logged onto her computer. She spent the next hour and a half nibbling on her sandwich and chips while she scrutinized her financial situation and made a budget.

The sound of her cell phone ringing interrupted her thoughts. Her phone was in her purse in the break room. The ringtone told her Gordon was calling.

She abandoned her paperwork and hurried to answer her phone before it went to voicemail.

"Gordon," she said.

"Hello, Anita," he said. "You sound out of breath. Am I interrupting?"

"Absolutely not. I was in my office and had to race into the other room to get my phone. You're early," she said. "I thought we were going to FaceTime later."

She held the phone to her ear as she returned to her office. The Styrofoam container sat empty on her desk. She'd been so engrossed in her work that she'd eaten the entire sandwich and all the chips without realizing it. *So much for bringing dinner home,* she thought to herself.

"I know," Gordon said, "and we'll still be together for dinner later. I miss you, and I decided to check on you."

"That's sweet of you," Anita said. "I'm fine. I'll be leaving here shortly—I'm closing early. How about you? Did you have a busy day?"

"Well ..." he hesitated before continuing, "you could say that."

"I'd love to hear about it," Anita said, cradling the phone between her shoulder and her ear while she carried her empty soda can and the Styrofoam container to the trash. She paused, waiting for him to continue.

"Gordon?" she said, frowning as she pressed the phone tighter to her ear. "Gordon?"

She pulled the phone away and looked at the screen. They had been disconnected.

"Must be my fault," she muttered, quickly punching in his number and hitting the call button.

"Hello, Anita," came his voice, but, oddly, the phone was still ringing in her hand.

Anita furrowed her brow. Confused, she turned in a slow circle, scanning the empty break room.

"Anita?"

The voice was no longer coming from the phone. It was coming from behind her.

Puzzled, Anita turned slowly … and froze.

Standing in the middle of the bridal showroom, framed by the soft glow of the afternoon sun streaming through the window, was Gordon. He was impeccably dressed in a black wool overcoat, a black turtleneck, and dark green trousers.

"Gordon," she sputtered, taking a stumbling step back. Her free hand flew to her heart as if she could steady the wild thudding in her chest. "What are you doing here?"

A slow, tender smile spread across his face. He shrugged out of his coat and tossed it over one arm, his dark eyes never leaving hers.

Before she could say another word, he crossed the distance

between them with long, purposeful strides and gathered her into his arms. Anita barely had time to inhale the crisp winter air clinging to his clothes before his lips found hers.

Their kiss was deep and unhurried, as if he were memorizing the moment—and she was only too happy to let him.

When they finally broke apart, Anita rested her forehead against his chest, trying to catch her breath. "You ... you're really here," she whispered, the words muffled against the fabric of his sweater.

"I'm really here," Gordon murmured into her hair, tightening his arms around her. "Good thing we're not near your display window," he said, when they finally came up for air. "Our kiss would've steamed up the glass."

Anita rocked back in his arms and put her palms on his chest. "That would give this town something to talk about!" she said with a giggle. "I can't believe you're here!" She pressed her palms against him as if to confirm his presence. "I'm thrilled to see you. When did you get in?"

"A couple of hours ago. I'm staying at The Mill. I checked in and came straight here. And that, my dear, is what I've been doing today—braving long lines, busy airports, and packed flights to be with you on New Year's Eve."

"My goodness," Anita said. "That's romantic! I was about to close the shop. Let's run to the grocery and pick up something for dinner. I was going to bring half of my lunch home, but I ended up eating it all. I'm afraid I don't have much on hand."

"You know me better than that," Gordon chided. "I

wouldn't barge in on you and expect you to prepare me a meal. We've got dinner reservations at The Mill at seven."

"Oh, my gosh! That would be lovely," she said. "I've always wanted to go there for New Year's Eve. They're booked months in advance. How did you get a reservation?"

"Fate is on our side, my dear. They had a cancellation, and I grabbed it. I was hoping you'd like my surprise."

"I *love* your surprise," she said, before taking a step back and putting a hand to her head. "I'm not sure what to wear."

"You always look lovely," he replied. "Don't stress. Wear what you have on."

She rolled her eyes. "Absolutely not. I'll find something in the recesses of my closet."

"I'll walk you to your car and pick you up at your place at 6:15, if that's all right."

"Perfect," she said, crossing to her computer. "I'll log off and tidy up these papers, and then we'll leave."

"What are you working on?" he asked.

"Plans for my new museum," she said, arching an eyebrow at him. "I'd love to tell you about them."

"And I can't wait to hear," he said. Gordon picked up her coat from the back of the chair where she had dropped it and held it for her.

They stepped into the late afternoon sunshine, locked the door, and strolled arm in arm to Anita's car.

CHAPTER 9

*M*aggie secured her seatbelt and twisted to look at the object in the back of John's Suburban that filled the entire space. A moving blanket concealed its identity.

"I can't wait to see what's back there," she said to John. "I didn't know you had a surprise gift for Julia. We've got these two Disney princess costumes for her." She patted the two packages wrapped in Santa Claus paper that she held on her lap.

"I think a grandpa should have a few tricks up his sleeve," John said, clearly enjoying his secret.

"I can't believe you've been driving around town with whatever it is back there since Christmas," Maggie said. "You could have stored it in the garage. I wouldn't have peeked!"

John slid his eyes to hers and raised a skeptical eyebrow before backing out of the garage.

"What?" Maggie asked, laughing. "I wouldn't have!"

"Maybe not. I want everyone to see it at the same time, is all."

"Won't you need a hand moving it into their house?"

"Aaron will help me," John said. "He already knows."

"No way!" Maggie erupted.

"Simmer down," John chuckled. "As I said, I want you and Susan to see it when Julia does."

Maggie squeezed his hand. His obvious infatuation with their granddaughter warmed her heart beyond measure.

They rode in companionable silence until John turned onto Susan and Aaron's street and backed into their driveway.

"I'll go inside to greet Susan and Julia," Maggie said. "I'll send Aaron out here to help you. If that little girl sees her grandpa—her favorite person on the planet—you'll never shake her off long enough to get this thing inside."

"Great idea," John said. "Aaron and I will have it set up in her room in five minutes. Ten tops. I appreciate you running interference for me."

Maggie leaned across the console and planted a kiss on his cheek. "I'm happy to be your wingman anytime." She got out of the car and entered the house through the unlocked front door.

"Hey, everybody!" Maggie called as she stepped inside. She unwound her scarf from her neck and tossed it and her coat on a chair in the entryway. The warm, fragrant aroma of roasting beef and freshly baked bread enveloped her.

"In the kitchen!" Susan called.

"Grammy!" Julia cried from the family room, where she was reading a book with Aaron.

Maggie joined them and opened her arms as the little girl flung herself into them.

"Will you show me the book you're looking at?" Maggie asked, hugging her close. "Reading is one of my favorite things to do." She sat on the sofa and scooped Julia onto her lap.

Maggie and Aaron exchanged a look, and he nodded.

"Daddy's got something to do," Aaron said. "Can Grammy finish reading to you?"

Julia nodded emphatically.

Aaron handed Maggie the book and left the room.

"I'll be with you in a sec," Susan called from the kitchen. "I'm putting the finishing touches on the au gratin potatoes before I put them in the oven."

"Take your time," Maggie said. "We're doing fine."

"*Angelina Ballerina*," Maggie said, reading the cover. "This was one of your mom's favorites. Mine too! Is it okay if we start over at the beginning?"

"Yes!" Julia said, burrowing deeper against Maggie's chest.

They were turning the last page when John and Aaron entered the room. Julia sprang off Maggie's lap.

John set the Christmas packages he was carrying down

by the tree and opened his arms to her. She threw herself into them, and he lifted her high, swinging her around.

"How's my best girl?" he asked, beaming. "Feeling all better and ready for Christmas with us?"

"Feeling better!" she declared.

Maggie smiled at the joyful grandfather-granddaughter reunion. "I'll go get Susan," she said. "We need her out here to open presents."

She found her daughter gripping the counter with both hands, arms rigid and white knuckled. "Honey, are you okay?" Maggie asked, hurrying to her side.

Susan took a deep breath and straightened. "I'm fine," she said. "It was just a wave of nausea. It's passed."

Maggie pursed her lips, swallowing the question that hovered on the tip of her tongue.

Susan met her mother's eyes, and a smile bloomed, wide and radiant. "We couldn't stand not knowing," she said. "I took a pregnancy test two days ago. We're trying to keep it a secret until I'm past the first trimester, but I had to tell Sunday yesterday." She grasped Maggie's hands and whispered, "I'm pregnant!"

Maggie pulled her daughter into a tight hug, both women clinging to each other. "I'm overjoyed," Maggie finally managed to say.

"We are too," Susan replied, tears prickling the back of her eyes. "Despite all the morning sickness and fatigue, we couldn't be happier."

"And you told Sunday?"

"She asked me to be her matron of honor," Susan said. "And I was thrilled to accept. Since they're planning a spring or summer wedding, it's only fair she knows I'm expecting, and that my due date is mid-August."

"That was thoughtful of you," Maggie said.

"I'm so happy for them—and honored to stand up for her."

"You and Sunday are becoming close friends, aren't you?"

"We are," Susan said. "We just click. It's so nice to have a best friend again, besides my mom, of course. You'll always be my BFF."

The patter of little feet interrupted their moment.

"Mom, Grammy—Daddy sent me in here to get you! It's time for presents!"

"Lead the way, sweetheart," Maggie said.

They followed Julia into the family room. Aaron helped the little girl play Santa as she handed out gifts.

"I've always wanted one of these!" Maggie exclaimed when she unwrapped the beautiful Fair Isle sweater in soft tones of cream, beige, and taupe. She hugged Julia, Susan, and Aaron. "I'll wear it tomorrow. Thank you!"

John admired his new watch. Aaron loved the hiking boots he'd been hoping for. Susan wrapped herself in her new plush bathrobe with a delighted laugh.

"I think it's time for someone else now," John said. "Those two big boxes are for you, Julia." He rose from the sofa and handed her one.

Julia tore off the paper and carefully pulled out the fancy

dress with a glittery yellow skirt, blue satin bodice, and red satin cape that tied in a bow at the neck. The box contained a headband with a matching bow and an artificial apple.

"Do you know who wears this?" John asked.

Julia turned questioning eyes to him.

"Snow White!" he said. "Now you can be just like her!"

Julia clapped her hands in delight.

"There's another one, too," John said, handing her the second box.

"Cinderella!" she cried as she pulled a light blue gown with a bejeweled velvet bodice and sweeping tulle skirt, a tiara, and sparkly plastic "glass" slippers from the package.

She jumped up, shimmied out of her red and green plaid Christmas dress, and pulled the elaborate costume over her head. Julia plopped onto an ottoman and thrust her feet out expectantly.

John knelt, fitting the slippers onto her feet like a proper footman. "They fit perfectly! You must be the real Cinderella," he said with a wink.

Julia sprang to her feet and, after an unsteady wobble on the low heels, twirled around the room.

"Thank you, Grammy and Gramps!" she cried.

~

"THAT WAS LOVELY," Susan said. "I'll go finish dinner so we can eat."

"Not so fast," John said, grinning. "There's one more gift."

Susan looked around, puzzled. "I don't see anything."

"Let's go look in your room, Julia," John said.

Susan glanced at Maggie, who shrugged, equally mystified.

Julia grabbed John's hand and led him down the hall. A wooden playhouse fit for a princess stood against the far wall of her room. Rising five feet to a gabled roof, it bore the words "Princess Julia" above a small, child-sized door. Intricate bluebirds perched along the roofline, and silk roses in shades of pink overflowed from flower boxes under arched windows.

John knelt beside Julia. "Do you recognize those birds?"

Julia's eyes widened.

"They helped Cinderella sew her dress," John supplied the answer.

Julia nodded.

"Do you want to go inside?"

Julia flung open the door and walked in.

John crawled inside after her while the other adults peered through the windows, smiling.

Inside, a dressing table with a tufted stool and a gilded mirror occupied one side. A child-size pink velvet sofa sat in the center.

"You can put your brushes, bows, and jewelry here," John said, opening a small drawer in the dressing table.

Julia plopped onto the stool, gazing at her reflection.

On the other side, a clothes bar held two sparkling hangers.

"And here," John said, "is where you hang your princess dresses."

Julia flung her arms around his neck. John chuckled and hugged her close.

Maggie and Susan exchanged a look full of affection.

"This is incredible," Susan whispered. "Where did he find this? It looks handmade."

"It is," Aaron said. "John designed it and had it custom-built."

Susan pressed a hand to her chest. "Mom, you had no idea?"

"None," Maggie said, shaking her head. "That man can keep a secret."

"He most certainly can," Susan said, grinning at Aaron. "Should we tell him?"

Aaron nodded.

John backed out of the little house, Julia right behind him.

Susan's eyes shimmered with emotion. "We have one more gift," she said. "It's not a physical gift—at least not yet."

John looked at her, puzzled.

"You love being a grandfather. Would you like to do it again?"

CHAPTER 10

*Gordon pulled back Anita's chair and offered her his elbow. The elegant couple, she in loden green velvet that kissed her ankles and he in a tailored black suit with a black shirt and tie, exited the dining room of The Mill. Other diners followed their progress with admiring glances.

"What a fabulous meal! That's the best beef Wellington I've ever had," Anita said. "Though I'm sure it pales when compared to what you've had in New York."

"I was about to say the same thing about the Wellington," Gordon said. "The service was impeccable, too, and the chef handled every dish perfectly."

"So Westbury isn't the sleepy backwater I think it is?"

"Not in the least," Gordon replied. He placed his free hand over hers as they strolled toward the lobby. "Have I told you how stunning you look? That green velvet dress is perfect with your eyes. And to think you were worried about having nothing to wear."

"I'd forgotten about this dress," she said. "To tell you the truth, this is the first time I've worn it, and I've had it for years. Someone brought it into my shop for alterations and never returned to pick it up. Those items typically go on the sale rack, and if they don't sell, we donate them. But I thought this dress was so pretty, I kept it for myself."

"You must've had a premonition that you'd need it one day." His eyes twinkled as he looked at her. "That swirly skirt looks like it's perfect for dancing."

"It's called a fit-and-flare style," Anita said. "And, yes—it would be fun to dance in this."

"They have dancing in the ballroom tonight," Gordon said. "The Mill has hired a ten-piece orchestra to play big band music from nine until midnight."

Anita squealed. "You're kidding me!"

"I didn't know if you like to dance," Gordon said with a smile. "But I reserved a table for us in case you'd like to check it out."

Anita stopped walking and tugged on his elbow, pulling them both to a halt. "Pinch me," she said. "I must be dreaming."

Gordon chuckled. "I'll take that as a yes."

"It's a yes times a thousand," she said, her voice trembling with joy. "My ideal man? That's you, Gordon."

He led her to the ballroom.

Anita peered around Gordon's shoulder while he gave his name to the host. The band was playing "One O'clock Jump" by Count Basie. At nine thirty, the dance floor was already crowded.

The host checked off Gordon's name on his list and led them around the outskirts of the dance floor to a small round table on the far side of the room. Gordon slipped the host a folded bill and pulled out Anita's chair for her.

A server arrived with water and asked for their drink order.

"Champagne?" Gordon looked at Anita and raised an eyebrow.

She turned both palms up and looked around the room, wide-eyed. "Yes," she said. "This whole evening is straight out of central casting for a fantasy New Year's Eve date. I'm certain they'd be drinking champagne."

"Do you have a favorite?" he asked her.

Anita sputtered with laughter. "I rarely drink champagne. I'm afraid I don't," she admitted. "Pick whatever you'd like."

Gordon placed the order with the server, who nodded with a look of appreciation in his eyes.

"Very nice choice, sir. I'll be right back."

Gordon and Anita turned their attention to the dance floor. A couple in front of them executed West Coast swing moves with flawless precision.

Anita leaned toward Gordon. "They're fabulous," she said.

He nodded, eyes scanning the room. "As a matter of fact, ninety percent of the people out there are really good. I had no idea there were so many talented dancers in Westbury. I'll bet people come from all over to enjoy this," Gordon said. "The Mill puts on a first-rate New Year's Eve."

The server returned with a silver champagne bucket on a stand, rivulets of condensation snaking down its ice-cold sides. He plucked the bottle from the ice, wrapped it in a towel, and gripped the cork while twisting it off. A fragrant, wispy cloud of champagne followed the soft pop. He poured a small sample into a tall flute and handed it to Gordon.

Gordon took a sip and nodded.

The man filled a flute for Anita and topped off Gordon's. "If you'd like anything else, please let me know," he said, pointing to a card leaning against the bud vase in the middle of the table. "We offer coffee and dessert if you'd like something later."

As the server moved away, Gordon turned to Anita. He picked up his glass and held it out.

"To us," he said. "To the excitement that next year holds for us."

Anita tapped his glass with hers. "Hear, hear."

They both sipped their champagne.

"Ready?" Gordon asked. He set his glass on the table, stood, and extended his hand to her.

"If you're sure we won't embarrass ourselves," Anita said. "I used to dance, but that was years ago. I'm terribly rusty."

"Nonsense," Gordon said. "The only thing that really matters is that we have fun."

She placed her hand in his, and he led her onto the dance

floor as the band began playing "In the Mood" by Glenn Miller. Gordon took her hands and pulled her close.

"Something tells me," he said, "we're going to give the rest of these couples a run for their money."

He leaned back and led her into a basic sugar push sequence.

Anita followed his lead, and everything she'd ever learned came rushing back.

Gordon and Anita danced the night away, returning to their table only occasionally for a sip of champagne or a drink of water.

When the orchestra played Irving Berlin's "Cheek to Cheek," Anita melted into Gordon's arms. As the song suggested, she lifted her chin and pressed her cheek against his, drinking in the lingering scent of his aftershave.

"You smell divine," Gordon whispered in her ear.

"I was thinking the same about you," Anita replied.

Gordon pressed a kiss to her temple.

As the song ended, the orchestra leader proclaimed it was almost midnight. He encouraged the dancers to raise a glass. The orchestra leader announced that the orchestra would conclude with "Auld Lang Syne," and invited everyone to the lobby for The Mill's fireworks display over the river.

"Would you like to stay for the fireworks?" Gordon asked.

Anita nodded. "They're famous. I'd love that." She didn't say what she was really thinking—that she didn't want this night to end.

Gordon retrieved their champagne flutes from the table

and handed Anita her glass. They looped their arms around each other and swayed to the sentimental tune as they drained their glasses. A loud pop sounded overhead, signaling the stroke of midnight.

Gordon pulled Anita to him, lowered his mouth to hers, and they greeted the New Year with a lingering kiss.

CHAPTER 11

*J*osh pressed the off button on the remote and tossed it onto the ottoman. He brought his feet to the floor and turned to Sunday.

"That was a great movie," he said.

"I can't believe you'd never seen *The Holiday* before," Sunday replied. "It's the *perfect* holiday movie—friendship, romance, a gorgeous California mansion, a charming English country cottage, and actors with English accents. What more could you want?"

Josh chuckled. "I suspect the houses are a big part of the attraction for you."

"I have to admit," Sunday said with a grin, "I am a bit house crazy."

Josh's expression softened. "Speaking of houses … where do you want to live when we get married? Should I

84

move in with you? I assume my place is too small for the four of us. Heck, it's even too small for me and these two dogs."

"That's the practical solution, but I'd love to find a new place for us. A home where all the memories will include both of us from the beginning."

Josh nodded. "My lease is up at the end of the semester. How about yours?"

"I've been month-to-month for the last year," Sunday said. "I've been saving for a house and waiting for the right one to come on the market." She sighed, adding, "We're incredibly busy with wedding plans, your graduation, and your new jobs at Forever Friends and Forever Guides. We don't really have the time or energy to look for a house right now. I guess moving in with me is our best option."

"We'll go house hunting this summer," Josh agreed, his voice warm. "When things calm down."

Cara, Josh's petite German shepherd, and Dan, his easy-going black Lab, lay stretched out on the rug, their backs against the sofa. When Josh put his feet on the floor, both dogs stirred. They yawned, stretched, and rose to their feet. Dan's tail swished lazily while Cara padded over to the back door.

"I think these two need to go out," Josh said, pushing himself off the sofa. "I'll be right back."

"I'd like to stretch my legs too," she said, glancing at her watch. "We've got another hour before midnight. By the end of the movie, I was struggling to keep my eyes open. A brisk walk in the night air is exactly what I need—or I'll never stay awake to welcome the new year with you."

"We don't have to stay up," Josh teased. "New Year's Eve is no big deal. Kissing someone at midnight doesn't bring good luck."

Sunday gave him a playful bop on the arm. "You don't know that," she said with a smile. "This is my first—and hopefully only—time being engaged on New Year's Eve. We'll be married by the next one. I certainly intend to make the most of this year."

She swung her legs off the sofa and stood, stretching. "I've got an idea," she said, following Josh and the dogs to the back door. "Let's take these guys for a walk—like we did when we got engaged."

"That's a terrific idea," Josh said. "I'm sure they'd like more exercise than just a quick trip to the backyard. Do you want to stroll around this neighborhood, or pile into the car and go somewhere?"

"I'd love to drive to the streets behind the square," Sunday said, her eyes lighting up. "All those mansions are so gorgeous, decorated in Christmas lights. It'd be fun to see them one last time this season."

"We'll head to the house where you agreed to make my dreams come true," Josh said.

"Oh, that'd be perfect," Sunday said, her voice catching slightly. "We can park and walk the dogs up and down the street to give them some exercise." She leaned toward the dogs and addressed them in a singsong voice. "What do you think?"

Both dogs turned toward her, tails thrashing in response.

Josh smiled as he clipped the harnesses onto Cara and Dan. He and Sunday slipped into their coats, bundled up for the crisp night, and the foursome headed out the door—two humans, two dogs, and hearts full of anticipation for the year ahead.

~

Josh drove slowly down the residential street. Cars lined both curbs, and the charming storybook cottage where he'd proposed to Sunday was at the epicenter. Every light inside the small home was on, and the front door stood open. People spilled out of the house and clustered in lively groups on the lawn that extended to the sidewalk. A catering truck was parked in the driveway, and through their closed car windows they heard '90s pop music pulsing.

"What a contrast to the quiet, peaceful night I proposed," Josh said, his voice touched with nostalgia.

"Yes, it looks like they're having quite a party," Sunday replied, watching the laughter and commotion with a small smile.

"Do you want to get out and walk the dogs here, anyway?" Josh asked.

"No," Sunday replied. "It would seem like we're gate-crashing. Let's drive around the block to the Olsson House and park there. I love that street. I'm sure there'll be plenty of Christmas lights to look at, and we can walk the dogs without them getting distracted by partygoers."

"Good thinking," Josh said as he turned the corner and made his way to the middle of the block, pulling to a stop in front of the Olsson House.

They got out of the car and paused at the curb, taking in the grandeur of the Olsson House. It was bathed in soft white lights and adorned with a garland-wrapped railing and bows of burgundy velvet.

"What a beauty," Sunday said softly.

"That it is," Josh agreed. "Would you like to own a home like this one day?"

Sunday stepped forward and tilted her head as she admired the Victorian mansion. "Living in a beautiful old home is a dream of mine, but, with our librarian and nonprofit administrator salaries, it's not likely. And that's perfectly fine with me. I'm sure we'll find something we both love—and can afford."

"I'm glad to hear it," Josh said. "I'd hate to think you'd be pining your whole life for something you'd never own."

"I already have the most important thing in life—a loving and kind partner," she said, turning her gaze to him. "The rest doesn't matter."

They turned away from the Olsson House and walked along the street, the dogs trotting contentedly at their heels as they admired the twinkling Christmas decorations on the homes they passed.

"Do you want to cross and walk back on the other side of the street?" Josh asked.

Sunday nodded, and she and Cara led the way. The houses on this side were two-and three-story red brick structures with intricate trim and architectural detailing that reflected the grandeur of their original owners—all except one of them.

A few houses down and across the street from the Olsson House sat a one-story structure with a warm stone exterior. The steeply pitched roof culminated in a dramatic point. An arched front door with a speakeasy window and a large, diamond-paned window were nestled below the peak. Twin chimneys rose from either side of the sharply slanted roof.

Sunday slowed her pace as they approached. "I can't see how far back this house goes, but it looks much smaller than the others on the street."

"Someone could have torn down one of the big ones and replaced it with this," Josh suggested.

Sunday stopped where a curving brick walkway met the sidewalk. She studied the roofline and the craftsmanship around the window and door. "I don't think so. This all seems authentic to the period. They simply built this house smaller than the rest."

"Maybe the person who owned the lot didn't have enough money to build a mansion," Josh said.

"That's possible," Sunday replied. "Or it was built as a mother-in-law suite. Who knows? If I owned it, I'd research to find the answer."

Josh slipped his arm around her waist and pulled her close as they both stared at the house.

"There aren't any Christmas lights on it," he noted. "They may not celebrate Christmas, of course, but the snow hasn't been plowed off the driveway or the walkway. Do you suppose it's vacant?"

Sunday shrugged. "That's possible." She wrapped her arm around his waist, and they leaned into each other.

The dogs sat obediently, waiting for their people to finish taking in the scene.

"Would you be happy living in a house like this?" Josh asked.

Sunday nodded without hesitation. "I love the house where you proposed. And the mansions on this street. But for all their grandeur," she said, glancing up and down the street, "this one has a warmth and coziness to it that's … compelling." She inhaled deeply and smiled up at him. "It's almost like the *There Was an Old Woman Who Lived in a Shoe* house" she said. "Do you know that Mother Goose book?"

Josh laughed. "Of course I do. What kid hasn't heard that story?" He grinned. "It makes sense that my favorite librarian would describe a house with a literary reference."

"I'm glad you understand me so well," Sunday said, her voice full of affection.

Cheering and whistling reached them from the next street over. A few small fireworks exploded in bright sparks against the night sky.

"It must be midnight," Josh said, turning to face her.

Sunday tilted her head back and lifted her chin. "Happy New Year, darling. The only thing I need for the home of my dreams is you."

Josh brought his lips to hers.

She slid her arms up his back to his shoulders, and he held her close as they welcomed the new year together, under the stars.

CHAPTER 12

The movie credits rolled. Jeff scooted to the edge of the sofa and picked up the almost-empty popcorn bowl. He held it out to Judy. "Want any more of this?"

Judy shook her head.

"Should I save the rest?"

"No," she said, standing up and stretching. "It's never good leftover. We'll make more the next time we want popcorn."

"It's almost midnight," Jeff said as he headed toward the kitchen with the bowl. "We timed things well."

Judy collected their soda cups and followed him. "Let's leave this on the counter until morning," she said. "I'd love to go upstairs."

"I'm ready to turn in," he replied, "but don't you want to ring in the New Year?"

"I meant let's go up to the third-floor turret room. Maybe we can see the fireworks from The Mill because of that high vantage point."

"The Mill is at least fifteen miles from here, isn't it?"

"Something like that," Judy said. "I know it's unlikely, but I'd like to find out. Growing up across the street, I used to wonder whether you could spot them from this turret. On a clear day, parts of the Shawnee River by The Mill are visible."

"Let's find out," Jeff said, placing the bowl beside the soda cups.

Jeff and Judy climbed the wide, gracious staircase to the second floor. They walked past six bedrooms to the plain door that concealed a narrow flight of stairs leading to the third floor. Jeff flipped the switch, and a bare overhead bulb lit their way.

They climbed the stairs and stepped into the round room, fitted with generous leaded-glass windows on every side. The only furniture was a circular, wrought-iron bench.

"It's almost a full moon," Jeff said. "There's plenty of light in here. Want me to switch off the stairway light?"

"Yes, please," Judy said. "It'll be easier to see the outside if it's dark in here."

Jeff flipped the switch at the top of the stairs to turn off the bulb.

Judy moved to the windows overlooking the front and

right side of the house. "I think The Mill is this way," she said, pointing into the distance.

"That would be my guess," Jeff agreed. He wrapped his arms around her and pulled Judy's back against his chest, looking over the top of her head at the quiet scene below.

"It's really pretty from up here, isn't it?" Judy asked. "All the twinkling lights along the street ... it's like these old houses have dressed for dinner."

Jeff chuckled. "That's a good way to put it. It's impressive, that's for sure."

Judy snuggled into his arms, and they stood in silence, soaking in the beauty of the night.

"Won't be long now," Jeff said, twisting his wrist to look at his watch. "It's ten minutes until twelve."

"I should've put Christmas lights on my old house," Judy said, glancing across the street. "It sticks out like a sore thumb."

"You were busy with the store, and we were getting ready for the Christmas potluck," Jeff said. "I never thought about it. We'll put lights on it next year—if you still own it."

"I'm not ready to sell it. Not yet," Judy said. "I know it's silly, and I'll never live there again, but that house has been in my family for three generations. I hate the thought of selling it to someone who'll park a dumpster in the yard the minute they close escrow and start ripping out the beautiful old woodwork and trim. I won't allow the charm to be stripped from my beloved little house, only to become some soulless, clean-lined, modern monstrosity."

"My goodness," Jeff teased gently. "Tell me how you *really* feel."

She turned her head toward him, and he kissed her forehead.

"I understand," he said gently. "It would be a shame to force a modern vibe onto that very traditional house. But when you sell it, the buyers have the right to make it their own. You'll have to come to terms with that."

"If I could find someone who loves it the way I do, I might be okay with selling it. I'd love the new owners to be a young couple, just starting out. It was my grandparents' first home—first and only, actually. They raised five children in that house. Nobody needs to change it."

"Hang on to it as long as you like," Jeff said. "I promise I'll put Christmas lights on the house next year. It looks a little forlorn."

They stood, gazing at the street below, waiting for the stroke of midnight.

A couple walking two large dogs stepped into view. Jeff and Judy watched as they strolled past the Olsson House, crossed the street, and stopped in front of Judy's old home. They slipped their arms around each other's waists and stood gazing up at the house as the dogs sat calmly at their sides.

The woman pointed to the chimneys on the roof, then to the diamond-paned window and the arched front door. The man nodded, inclining his head toward the woman.

Cheers and whistles erupted from partygoers on the next street. A few small fireworks popped nearby.

The man on the sidewalk stepped in front of the woman. She tilted her head back, and he wrapped her in his arms.

"I think I'd like a buyer like that couple," Judy whispered.

A muffled series of booms echoed in the distance.

Jeff and Judy scanned the horizon, but didn't see any fireworks. They turned their attention back to the couple below.

The woman stepped deeper into the man's embrace, and they melted into a kiss.

"I think they've got the right idea," Jeff said, gently turning Judy to face him. "A year ago, my current life would have been unimaginable to me. I'm so happy here—with you, Judy. I hope I make you as happy as you make me … and that all your dreams come true."

"You do—and they have," Judy said. She reached up, caressed his cheek with her hand, and rose on her toes to kiss him.

CHAPTER 13

Gordon cupped his hands around his face and pressed them against the plate-glass window.

"They've papered over the inside of the window," Anita said. "You won't be able to see anything."

"I know," Gordon murmured. He didn't move. "There's a tiny tear in the paper, and I was hoping to get a glimpse inside—but it's too dark."

They stepped to the edge of the sidewalk and looked up at the building formerly occupied by Candy Alley.

"It's a handsome old façade," Gordon said. "With a thorough cleaning, repairs to the window trim, and a fresh coat of paint on the front door, this building will be beautiful. I understand why you'd want to open your museum here."

"I'm happy you agree," Anita said. "I can't wait to get

inside and see what shape it's in, now that it's been vacant for so many years."

"I'm sure Tim will contact the owners after the holidays," Gordon replied.

"I don't want to wait that long," Anita said with a sigh. "I wish Tim would call me."

The phone in her purse rang before she'd even finished speaking. She retrieved it and swiped to answer the call.

"Tim!" she exclaimed, pivoting to face Gordon as a grin erupted across her face like last night's fireworks.

"Oh my gosh," Anita said, laughing. "Gordon and I are standing in front of the building! I was just saying how anxious I am to take a look."

She listened for a beat, then tapped the screen to place the call on speaker.

"That's right," she continued. "Gordon came in on New Year's Eve to surprise me. Tell us—how did you get in touch with the owner so quickly?"

"I'm in Rotary with the attorney handling Charlotte's estate," Tim explained. "I called him on New Year's Eve, right after I saw you. He said he'd contact his client before he left for the day. Turns out, the owners got back to him first thing this morning. He called me straight away. I knew you'd be happy to hear the news. Our kids and grandkids are coming over soon to celebrate Nancy's birthday, but I had time to let you know first."

"I'm glad you did," Anita said. "Thank you so much."

"I'll have the keys in hand first thing tomorrow morning,"

Tim continued. "The fact that the owners got back to their attorney so quickly tells me they're motivated sellers. This could be good for you."

"I need to open the shop at ten tomorrow morning," Anita replied. "I'm available any time after ten thirty."

"Let's meet in front of Candy Alley at eleven," Tim said. "Will you both be there?"

"Gordon has to leave first thing in the morning—" Anita began.

"I'll change my flight," Gordon interrupted. He looked directly at Anita. "That is—if you'd like me to be there. I don't want to intrude."

"Are you kidding?" Anita said, eyes shining. "I'd *love* for you to see the place with me. I value your opinion. Without your encouragement, I wouldn't have even thought of opening a sewing machine museum."

In the background, the sound of barking dogs rose from Tim's end of the call.

"That's our family," he said with a chuckle. "I'd better go. I'll see you tomorrow at eleven."

"Thank you, Tim," Anita said warmly. "And wish Nancy a very happy birthday from us."

GORDON SWUNG his rental car onto the long, sweeping driveway leading to Rosemont.

"It's awfully nice of Maggie and John to invite us to stop

by for dinner," he said. "How in the world did they know I was in town? I didn't tell them."

"There's no such thing as a secret in Westbury," Anita replied. "Someone must've seen us at The Mill last night."

"But today's a sleepy holiday," Gordon said. "Nobody's been out and about to spread the word."

"In these days of social media and text messages, sweetheart, news spreads like wildfire. Unlike many places, I think good news spreads fastest here."

He pulled to a stop in front of Rosemont's imposing stone façade. Leaning forward, he gazed out the windshield. "Every time I see this place, it takes my breath away," he said. "The chimneys, the gabled roofline, all those mullioned windows ... they're perfectly proportioned. The architect created a masterpiece."

"I couldn't agree more," Anita said. "But for all the grandeur of those three stories, my favorite thing about this house is the arched mahogany front door. It's massive and impressive—but it's also homey and welcoming. Just like the people living there."

"I agree with that too," Gordon said. He got out of the car and walked around it to open her door.

"I wish we had something to bring them," Anita murmured. "My mother and grandmother would be furious if they knew I was going to dinner without a hostess gift."

"I grew up the same way," Gordon said.

Anita looked up at him, her lips pressed into a thoughtful line. Then her eyes lit up. "I've got it," she said. "I'll offer to give them a private guided tour of the new museum before it opens."

"They'll both love that," Gordon replied. "More than any flowers or bottle of wine we could bring. That's an excellent idea."

They exchanged a smile and climbed the wide steps to the front door.

Gordon struck the brass door knocker against the plate, sending a crisp whack into the quiet afternoon.

They heard a momentary outburst of barking that was quickly silenced. The door swung open, and John ushered them inside. Eve and Roman waited patiently to be released.

Maggie crossed the living room toward them, untying a festive holiday apron and pulling it over her head.

"Hello, you two!" she said, throwing her arms wide and hugging Anita, then Gordon.

"Happy New Year," Anita said warmly.

"The same to you both," John said, shaking Gordon's hand with a smile.

Maggie turned to Gordon, arching an eyebrow. "What's with sneaking into town without telling me? Have I done something wrong? Are you trying to avoid us?"

Gordon flushed. "Nothing of the kind. I made a snap decision to ring in the New Year with Anita. Everything happened so fast, I didn't have time to tell anyone. Since I had initially planned to go home tomorrow, I figured there was no point."

"You *were* going to go home tomorrow?" Maggie asked,

intrigued. "I'd like to hear more about that. Come into the library—I've set out a few nibbles before dinner."

They followed her into the generous room, its wood-paneled walls glowing in the firelight. Late afternoon sunshine filtered in through the French doors, casting a golden hue across the polished floors.

John released Eva and Roman from their stays. After a warm greeting for the guests, the dogs settled into their beds by the hearth.

John gestured toward an open bottle of chardonnay on a tray. "We've also got red, if you prefer."

Anita and Gordon both pointed to the chardonnay and nodded their approval.

Maggie motioned them to chairs flanking a low coffee table. A charcuterie board filled with cheeses, crackers, mixed nuts, and seedless red grapes sat at the center. She handed each of them a small plate and cocktail napkin.

"What's keeping you here another day?" she asked Gordon.

Gordon looked at Anita. "I think it's your story to tell, honey."

He helped himself to a cracker and a cube of aged sharp cheddar.

"I plan to open a small sewing machine museum," Anita began, "with the beautiful antique machines that have been gathering dust in the basement of Archer's Bridal."

Maggie nodded. "I had heard that."

"I'd like it to be located on the square," Anita continued.

"Being close to Archer's Bridal would be convenient for me, and Tim Knudsen thinks it would be a tourist attraction."

"I agree with him," John said. "It'd be something unique for Westbury."

"Tim suggested the old building that housed Candy Alley. He contacted the owners, and they're interested in selling. He's arranged for me to view it tomorrow morning. Gordon was kind enough to postpone his flight so he could check it out with me."

"I'm as excited to get inside that place as she is," Gordon said. "It was boarded up before I ever came to Westbury."

"I spent most of my paper route money in Candy Alley when I was a boy," John said with a grin. "I have a lot of happy memories of that place—just like you do, Anita. It's exciting to think you might be the new owner."

"I was only in it once, before Charlotte passed away," Maggie said. "That was the year I moved into Rosemont. I was posting notices for the Easter carnival. I can't say I remember anything about the place." She clapped her hands together. "This is so exciting! You'll have to let us know the minute you open escrow."

"We haven't signed a contract yet," Anita said. "I'm trying not to get my hopes up."

"I have a feeling it's going to work out for you," John said. "This will be another chapter in the building's colorful history."

"What do you mean?" Anita asked.

"I'm not really sure," John admitted. "It was before my

time, but I think that building had a shady past." He narrowed his eyes in thought, then shook his head. "I really can't remember any specifics."

"My goodness," Anita said. "I'll have to look into that." She selected a small bunch of grapes and began plucking them off one by one.

"Who knows what secrets you'll find buried there," Maggie chimed in. "Rosemont's attic has been full of surprises—and Judy found the ornaments in the Olsson House that led her to Jeff."

"Now that you mention it," Gordon said, "I recall a rusty filing cabinet in the corner of the attic upstairs under Rosemont's eaves. I took a quick look months ago when I was assessing the furniture stored there. If I remember correctly, it's full of newspaper clippings from the '20s through the '70s. That might be a good place to start our research."

Maggie and John exchanged a knowing glance at his use of the word "our."

A buzzer sounded from the kitchen.

Maggie picked up her wineglass. "That's me. We're having lemon lasagna. It's a recipe from this morning's paper. Meatless, and supposed to be lighter fare for the new year." She smiled from Gordon to Anita. "I should've told you when I invited you—you're going to be my guinea pigs. There's also a green salad and garlic bread. If the lasagna is horrible, we'll order a pizza."

"It smells delicious," Anita said.

"I've never known you to make anything that isn't fabulous," John added.

"I love you for saying that, John," Maggie replied. "But you know that's not true."

She turned toward the kitchen. "At any rate, I'm headed in to finish up. You three stay here and enjoy your wine. I'll let you know as soon as everything's ready. We're eating in the kitchen, family style—because both of you are like family to us."

CHAPTER 14

*A*listair

Maggie and John went to bed as soon as they got home last night. In bed before midnight on New Year's Eve? I've been living in the Rosemont attic as a ghost for years, but even I thought that was ridiculous.

I drifted up to my attic in a bit of a funk. This hadn't been the holiday season I'd hoped for. I floated over to the window that faced the old mill. The night sky was clear and cloudless. In the distance, muffled pops and cracks signaled the arrival of midnight. I strained my eyes and caught glimpses of a few high-arching fireworks. I suppose I'll have to be satisfied with that level of frivolity.

New Year's Day began in a leisurely fashion. Maggie and John both slept in and spent a quiet day at home. I wafted restlessly up and down the stairs, longing for something to break the monotony. Late in the afternoon, a car pulled into the drive. I immediately recognized the tall, trim gentleman who emerged from the driver's seat.

We'd spent a fair amount of time together in Rosemont's attic—although he was unaware of my presence. I had watched him examine our hotel silver, antique paintings, and priceless furniture with a connoisseur's eye. He was knowledgeable and treated our treasures with a reverence I found refreshing. He was dressed neatly in a turtleneck and slacks, even on this day off. I approved.

He opened the passenger door for the woman with him. I wouldn't have expected anything less.

Maggie and John were expecting them. I'd seen Maggie arranging hors d'oeuvres in the library earlier, and wondered why, but now it made sense—we were having company. I love when we host at Rosemont. My spirits were picking up.

I followed them into the library and hovered in a corner, eavesdropping on their conversation.

When they got to the part about Candy Alley, my ears perked up. John was right—that building had a sketchy past. Shady dealings had taken place there, indeed. I could've told them a thing or two.

I was pleased to hear that Gordon remembered the filing cabinet in the attic. The documents stored there contained much of what they needed to know. I could add a few juicy details myself, but there was no way for me to share them.

I drifted after them into the kitchen and listened with

half an ear as the conversation wound down over dinner. My thoughts remained firmly fixed on the events of years ago.

Later that evening, I watched as Gordon and the woman climbed back into the car. What an interesting adventure they were about to embark on.

CHAPTER 15

*J*osh pulled into the employee parking lot of
Forever Friends at six the morning after New
Year's Day. As he'd expected, Frank Haynes was
already there.

Josh let himself in through the employee entrance. The
morning crew, busy feeding and exercising the dogs and cats,
offered waves and warm greetings as he passed. The occasional happy bark drifted out from the wing that housed the
kennels.

Josh's usual routine involved walking those corridors,
greeting familiar animals, and learning the names of new
ones. He loved those few minutes spent scratching muzzles
through the cages and offering encouragement to the souls
still waiting for their forever homes. Today, he continued on

to the short hallway where the administrative offices were located. He was on a mission.

Except for Frank's, all the office doors were closed. Josh's new boss sat with his back to the door, focused intently on a spreadsheet open on his desktop monitor.

Josh knocked on the doorframe. "Morning, Frank," he said.

Frank spun around in his chair. "Josh! Good morning. I thought you were working at the college this week."

"I am," Josh said, stepping inside. "We're posting the notice for my replacement as Maggie's administrative assistant today. I promised to help her sort through the applicants. There are also a few projects I'd like to finish before I train my replacement."

Frank nodded. "Good. I don't want to leave her in the lurch—Maggie's been too good to me. I can keep the plates spinning here for a few more weeks." He raised his eyebrows. "So, why are you here?"

"You know I got engaged before Christmas."

"Yes!" Frank's face lit up. "Loretta and I are thrilled for you. She knows Sunday from her book club and says she's terrific. Loretta thinks you two make the perfect couple."

Josh's cheeks turned crimson. "Thank you. I'm really glad to hear that. I came by because I wanted you to know we've decided to get married on the last Saturday of March."

"Excellent," Frank said. "I'm sure you'll want time off—both before and after the wedding. That's fine. Have you decided where you're going for your honeymoon?"

"We haven't gotten that far yet," Josh admitted. "In all honesty, Sunday is completely swamped with wedding planning. We reserved the Highpointe College chapel for the ceremony, and the reception will be in the surrounding garden."

"I've lived here my entire life and have never been in that chapel," Frank said. "I hear it's beautiful." He glanced back at his spreadsheet, then looked up again. "Thank you for letting me know. Take as much time as you need."

"Thanks," Josh said, stepping fully into the office. "There's something else I'd like to ask you."

"Please," Frank said, gesturing to the chair across from his desk. "Is anything wrong with your new role here?"

"No, nothing like that. I'm incredibly excited to be managing Forever Friends and overseeing the educational side of Forever Guides." He took a deep breath before continuing. "This is personal. I know we haven't known each other that long, but I feel like we're on the same wavelength. I admire how you run your businesses—and the way you've taken David under your wing. You're a good family man, Frank. I respect that."

Frank's complexion deepened with each word Josh spoke. "You evidently don't know much about me." His voice was hoarse. "My backstory isn't one to be proud of." The shame he carried clung to his words like a shroud.

Josh held his gaze. "I know about your past, Frank. The man sitting across from me today isn't that guy."

"You're not ashamed to be associated with me?" Frank asked quietly.

"Of course not," Josh said. "In fact, I came here to ask if you'd stand up with me at my wedding."

Frank rocked back in his chair, stunned.

"We're having a small ceremony," Josh continued. "Susan Scanlon is Sunday's matron of honor. And, if you're willing, I'd like you to be my best man."

Frank remained motionless, as if flooded by a surge of emotion. Then, his expression cracked, and he stood, coming around the desk and extending his hand.

"I would be honored," he said, his voice thick. "I've never been anybody's best man before."

"Thank you," Josh said, taking Frank's hand and pulling him into a one-armed hug. "Sunday will be excited to hear this. She said to tell you we don't know what anyone's wearing yet. I'll let you know as soon as we decide."

"I'm fine with anything you want," Frank said, still visibly moved.

"Great," Josh replied. "Mark that Saturday off on your calendar—and be sure to tell Loretta."

"Will do," Frank said with a smile.

Josh moved toward the door. "I'd better get to Highpointe. Maggie and I have a big day ahead of us. And I think you've got a spreadsheet calling your name."

Frank nodded. "You've made my day, Josh," he said, watching as the younger man disappeared down the hall.

CHAPTER 16

*T*im waved at the couple exiting Archer's Bridal on the other side of the street. He noted the time on the clock embedded in the sign above Burman Jewelers. It was 10:45. As he expected, Gordon and Anita had arrived early for their scheduled showing.

"It's a cold one today," he called, holding out his hand to shake hands first with Anita and then Gordon. "I'm glad you're dressed warmly. It feels even colder in there." He gestured toward the door of Candy Alley with his head. "At least out here there's sunshine."

"Did you go through it already?" Anita asked.

Tim nodded. "I prefer to tour a property on my own before taking a client to see it."

"Well," Anita asked, "first impressions?"

Tim grimaced. "Are you afraid of mice?"

"Oh gosh," Anita said. "They're not my favorite. Do you think they've got a mouse?"

"I'm certain of it," Tim said. "And not just a mouse—but a nest of them. Maybe even a mischief."

Anita gave him a puzzled look. "I take it that means more than a nest."

"I'm afraid it does," Tim said. "When Charlotte passed away, her heirs locked the door and walked away. None of the inventory was cleared out. It's obvious that food attracts mice—or rats. I'm honestly not sure which. Could be both."

Anita shuddered.

Tim put his hand on her elbow. "The place is full of trash, debris, and scat. I've already called the executor's attorney about the deplorable state of the property. He promised they'd send an exterminator in immediately and have the debris hauled away, but it might take days to schedule someone. Would you like to wait until the premises have been treated?"

"I'll book another trip out here," Gordon said, "if you want to postpone this viewing."

Anita shook her head. "Nope. I don't want to wait. I've been thinking about nothing else for the past two days. Let's go inside."

Tim smiled. "I thought you'd say that." He reached into the bag he was holding. "I nipped into Westbury Hardware and picked up these masks for us. We don't want to contract hantavirus." He handed one to Anita and one to Gordon before putting on his own. "Let's get started," he said, opening the door and ushering them inside.

The shop walls were lined with honey-colored wooden shelves. Original wood and glass display cases stood two deep, back-to-back, in the center of the room. Behind their grimy glass was a mountain of shredded paper boxes and wrappers, once vivid with the colors of the candies they had protected. A vintage National cash register sat at the end of a wooden counter, its brass badly tarnished. Cobwebs hung from the rafters. A glass apothecary jar, supporting an accumulation of dust like unblemished snow, contained peppermint sticks. The tag hanging from the lid bore the price: five cents or three for a dime. In sharp contrast with everything around them, the red and white candies looked pristine and inviting.

Anita took two steps into the room, her shoes pulverizing the scat beneath her feet.

Tim switched on small LED flashlights and handed one to each of them. "The electricity hasn't been turned on for ages," he said.

"You didn't exaggerate, Tim. This is pretty bad," Anita said.

"I'm sorry to say this room is in better shape than any of the others. Are you sure you want to continue?"

"I do," Anita said. She turned to Gordon. "This is *way* worse than we thought. If you don't want to keep going, I completely understand."

"There's no chance you're proceeding without me," Gordon said.

"Follow me," Tim said, opening a wooden door at the back of the shop. Cartons that had once held candy were piled high along the walls. Some lay strewn across the floor. All of them had been attacked by rodents. Tim trained his flashlight on the far corner of the room. "This was where she stored her inventory. Can you make out that odd-looking door in the corner?"

Anita and Gordon both nodded.

"That's a dumbwaiter," Tim said. "It may be broken, but I think it's repairable."

"It looks like a large dumbwaiter," Gordon said.

"I agree," Tim said. "That might be a good thing if you wanted to put in an elevator. The space would probably be big enough."

"If we use the second floor as part of our museum, I'd like to put in an elevator," Anita said. "I want my museum to be accessible."

"Whether that space works or you need to install an elevator somewhere else, I think this property could be modified to include one," Tim replied. "Would you like to see the second floor?"

"Lead the way," Anita said.

They backed out of the storage room. Tim led them to a partition that concealed a stairway leading to the second floor.

"Look at the beautiful carving on this banister," Gordon

said. He trained his flashlight on the wood and brushed off a thick layer of dust. "This is mahogany, for heaven's sake. I wasn't expecting that."

"The stairs are extra wide too," Anita said. "I'd still want to put in an elevator, but this would be a lovely way for visitors to get to the second floor."

"Are the steps sound?" Gordon asked.

"They seem to be," Tim replied. "I used them this morning."

They climbed to the second floor and entered a room heaped with junk from floor to ceiling. The foot of a rusty iron bedstead and a molding mattress peeked out from stacks of newspapers, cardboard boxes, clothing, broken furniture, and more.

Anita gasped.

She and Gordon stood next to Tim as they surveyed the scene.

"Charlotte appeared to be a hoarder," Tim stated.

"I had no idea," Anita said. "This makes me so sad. I wish I had known."

"People keep that quiet," Tim replied. He pointed to the exposed mattress and then to an old refrigerator obscured by bags of trash. "I believe Charlotte lived up here."

"I think you're right," Anita said. "I seem to remember that she resided above her shop."

Gordon elevated his tall frame onto his tiptoes and pointed to the far wall. "It looks like there's a door over there. Maybe that's a bathroom."

Tim said, "That makes sense."

Gordon pointed to a dark stain running the length of the ceiling along the outside wall. "That's water damage and possibly mold. I think the roof leaks."

"I figured I'd need a new roof," Anita said.

"If that's mold," Gordon said, "it'll have to be remediated, and the plaster repaired." He pointed to another area of the ceiling. "There's an opening that I'd guess conceals access to the attic."

"I'll bet that's where the mice or rats are," Anita said.

As if on cue, scratching greeted her words as rodents ran from one end of the attic to the other.

"Eek," Anita said. "I'm not going up there."

"You won't have to," Tim said. "But the roofers will need to get in there. If you make an offer, we'll include an inspection contingency in our contract. The building inspector will evaluate it."

"Good," Anita said. "Should we hire the inspector now? I want an estimate of the cost to make this space usable before I make an offer."

"The building inspection comes after you open escrow," Tim replied. "Before we make an offer, though, you should hire someone knowledgeable about old buildings, and the cost of repairs in our area, to go through this place. I suggest Sam Torres," Tim said. "He's a licensed general contractor and has experience restoring older buildings."

"He's who I would ask," Anita said.

"I talked to Sam and Jeff at the Christmas potluck," Tim

said. "They said they'd learned tons about restoration doing the Olsson House. They were kidding each other about finding another project. I think they'd both jump at the chance to work on this with you."

Anita looked at Gordon. "What do you think?"

"I've been extremely impressed by Sam's work at Rosemont. He'd be *my* choice," Gordon replied. "We still don't know the extent of what this building needs to make it habitable," he said. "The bones are good. There appears to be plenty of space for your museum. We haven't been able to see enough of the floors to determine if they can be refinished or if you'll need to replace them. Those wooden display cases are lovely, and would fit right in to your museum once they're restored. There are a lot of positives about this space," he said. "The key is going to be buying it for the right price. You need to make sure you have a generous budget for repairs. Sam can probably do most of the work, and he'll know who to hire for the things he can't. He also knows the going rates for labor and materials in this area. I'd hire him before putting together an offer."

Anita made a full turn around the room. "This space will beautifully showcase my sewing machine collection. I want to own this building and bring new life into it."

"Sounds good," Tim said.

The herd of rodents in the ceiling made another thundering pass to the other side of the room.

Anita crossed her arms over her chest and hugged herself. "Yuck."

"Let's get out of here and call Sam," Tim said.

They retraced their steps to the first floor.

"What's behind this door under the stairs?" Gordon asked.

"That's a basement," Tim said. "All these old buildings have them. I didn't look down there." He stopped walking. "Would you like to take a peek?"

"Let's save that for Jeff and Sam," Anita said. "I want to go through the space again after the exterminators have finished and the detritus has been hauled away."

They stepped out the front door into the cold sunshine and ripped off their masks in unison.

Tim held out his hand. "Here. I'll take those. We don't want to reuse them." He walked to a nearby trash barrel and deposited them.

Anita looked up at Gordon. "What do you think? Am I being foolish in wanting this location? Is my heart getting the better of my head?"

Gordon put his hands on each of her forearms. "What does your gut tell you?"

"That my museum belongs here." She glanced over her shoulder at the door to the former Candy Alley. "This is where it's meant to be."

"Then I think you should pursue it," he said. "Get input from Sam and Jeff and negotiate a good price. Everything we've seen can be fixed. It's only a matter of money. Your offer can reflect the cost of repairs."

Her shoulders straightened, and she stood a little taller, like a flower after a spring rain.

"Who knows?" Gordon said. "Hidden treasures may lurk inside."

"Just like Maggie and John suggested," Anita said. She turned to Tim. "Let's call Sam and get the wheels in motion. The sooner I own the building, the sooner he and Jeff will have their next project."

CHAPTER 17

*S*unday stood in front of the full-length mirror in the library's third-floor women's bathroom. She held her phone in her left hand, scrolling through photos of wedding dresses she'd bookmarked. It was easier to imagine what they might look like on her if she visualized in front of a mirror. Sunday wanted to order her dress as soon as possible. She felt guilty doing this at work, but classes hadn't resumed yet after the winter holiday, and she wasn't busy.

After answering the smattering of emails in her inbox, Sunday had spent the morning combing through vintage wedding dresses offered by a plethora of online retailers. She knew what she wanted—the dream dress that had lived in her mind since adolescence had never changed. She longed for a creamy-white lace gown with long sleeves, a fitted V-neck bodice, a full skirt, and a train.

Looking through the online bridal shops, she realized what she wanted was no longer in fashion. She told herself she should consider some of the newer styles, and then swiftly rejected the thought. Being a rare book librarian, she appreciated old and vintage things in every aspect of her life. She would have to find her dress in a vintage shop. That someone had already worn it didn't bother her in the least. Sunday liked to think that a dress that had launched a prior happy marriage would bring her luck.

The restroom on the third floor, near her office, was rarely used. She could peruse her choices to her heart's content. She was toggling between her two favorites— looking from her phone to her reflection in the mirror and back again—when the restroom door opened and Lyla stepped inside.

Sunday looked at the woman who had gone from colleague—as the library's bookkeeper—to best friend, and now soon-to-be mother-in-law. The story of how Lyla had given up Josh for adoption at birth, believing his father had died of cancer, only to reunite with her son years later after his adoptive parents had passed away, still brought a lump to Sunday's throat. That Robert Harris— her counterpart rare book librarian at another university —had turned out to be Josh's very much alive biological father, and now Lyla's loving husband, always made her weepy. It all sounded like a romance novel, except it was true.

"Looking for me?" Sunday asked.

"I am," Lyla replied. "You weren't in your office, so I decided to track you down. What are you doing?"

"Wedding dress shopping," Sunday said. "Don't tell on me, okay? I'm caught up on my work."

"Your secret is safe with me," Lyla said. "You work rings around the other librarians. If you want to take a few minutes to shop for your wedding dress—well, I think you'd be like *every* bride in America. It's fine by me. Have you found anything?"

Sunday tapped her screen and held it out. "These are my two finalists. I came in here to look at the dresses and then at myself in the mirror to see what I think." She scrolled to the second one.

"Oh, they're both lovely," Lyla said. "You wouldn't go wrong with either one. They're very different—the lace one is demure and detailed while the satin one is much simpler. Do you have a favorite?"

Sunday nodded. "The lace one has been the dress of my dreams my whole life. I was thrilled when I found it first thing this morning, but I've been second-guessing myself ever since—telling myself I shouldn't buy the first dress I see."

"Nonsense," Lyla said. "When you know, you know."

She took the phone from Sunday and stepped back, studying the image, then turning to picture it on Sunday.

"I think the lace one will be perfect. It's very Kate Middleton, you know."

"The train isn't anywhere near as long as hers," Sunday said, "but it's got the same vibe."

Lyla handed the phone back and watched Sunday's face as she looked at the photo.

"You know how a cloud covers the sun," Lyla said, "and then suddenly moves away—and it's as if God has shone a spotlight on the earth?" She met Sunday's eyes in the mirror. "That's what you look like when you scroll from the other dress to this one. You've got your answer. I think you should order it."

Sunday grinned at her friend and pulled her into a hug.

"Thank you for helping me make this decision," she said. "I'll order it as soon as I get back to my desk."

"Any other wedding news to share?" Lyla asked.

"We filled out the forms to reserve the Highpointe College Chapel for the last Saturday in March," Sunday said. "A few minutes ago, they confirmed our reservation. We'll have a late morning wedding with lunch in the chapel gardens."

Lyla clasped her hands together. "Oh, that sounds fabulous!"

"Unless we have rain," Sunday said. "Then it'll go from fabulous to disastrous."

"Let's not think that way," Lyla said. "We'll keep an eye on the weather forecast and we'll have a Plan B—just in case. Anything else?"

"Susan Scanlon has agreed to be my matron of honor, and Frank Haynes will be Josh's best man," Sunday said.

"Excellent!" Lyla said. "You're making tremendous progress."

"There's one more thing I'd still like to resolve," Sunday said. "I was going to ask you about it."

"I'm here right now. What is it?" Lyla asked.

"The ladies' room isn't the nicest place for this conversation…" Sunday hesitated.

"Don't stand on ceremony with me," Lyla said gently. "What can I do to help?"

"My folks have both passed. I was an only child and so were both of my parents, so I don't have anyone to walk me down the aisle," Sunday said. "I can walk by myself, but you know what a traditionalist I am. This isn't the norm—but you are my best friend and will soon be my mother-in-law. Would you walk me down the aisle, Lyla?"

The words reverberated off the tile and porcelain. The silence crackled with emotion.

"I'd love to," Lyla said, her voice brimming with emotion.

The two women stepped together and hugged.

Lyla was the first to pull back. "I can't tell you how much this means to me," she said. "I waited decades for a family I never thought I'd have—and look at me now."

She turned toward the mirror, grabbed a paper towel from the dispenser, and dabbed at the tear tracks of mascara under her eyes. Their eyes met in the mirror.

"If you don't have lunch plans tomorrow, let's go out somewhere so we can really talk," Lyla said.

"I'd love that," Sunday said. "And now—I'm off to order that dress before someone else snags it."

CHAPTER 18

*Anita rose from her desk and strolled through the workroom to the window at the front of her shop.

"You're going to wear a path in the floor," her workroom supervisor teased.

Anita chuckled. "I know," she said, tapping the face of her smartwatch. "I'm getting in my 10,000 steps every day, pacing between my desk and the window." She stared across the square at Candy Alley.

As promised, the executor of Charlotte's estate had responded to the request Tim had made on her behalf. A van had appeared the day after she, Gordon, and Tim toured the premises. Lettering on the side of the vehicle proclaimed: *Junk Removal Pros — We Handle All Your Refuse Removal Needs.*

Anita had seen the van pull up first thing in the morning.

She'd watched from her shop window as a crew of four workers entered Candy Alley. A dumpster had arrived at the curb by midmorning. She'd grabbed a cup of coffee and stood at the window as the workers deposited trashcan after trashcan of refuse into it.

The supervisor joined her at the window.

"I never would've guessed there was so much junk in that place," she said.

"Right?" Anita replied. "I was shocked when I went through the premises the other day. I'm glad to see they got started on this so quickly."

"Are they taking everything out of the space?" her supervisor asked.

"I hope not," Anita replied. "We asked that they leave the old display cases and the cash register. Those are vintage items that would be a great addition to my museum."

"What happens after all the junk is gone?"

"Exterminators will arrive—the place is infested with mice or rats. Probably both."

"Yuck!"

"When that's done, they've promised to bring in a commercial cleaning crew to remove the layers of dust, grime, and rodent scat."

The supervisor placed her hand gently on Anita's elbow. "You really want this space, don't you?"

Anita nodded. "I'm afraid so. As bad as it is, I see its potential."

The supervisor took one last look over her shoulder at the active scene across the square.

"Our seamstresses know how badly you want this," she said. "We're rooting for you."

Anita turned to face the workroom. "Thank you," she said. "I appreciate your support."

The six women gathered around the worktables nodded in acknowledgement.

"I'd better get back to it," the supervisor said.

"Me too," Anita sighed. "Standing in front of this window isn't hurrying things along over there. I can't seem to help myself. I'm like a moth to a flame." She returned to her desk and busied herself with the week's payroll. When she was done, she refilled her coffee cup and resumed her surveillance.

～

Anita manned her post behind the shop window for the next several days. She pulled her cardigan close around her and stepped out the door to take a better look at the action across the square.

The pest control company had cleared the property of rodents, and the crew from Ace Janitorial Services had begun work the previous morning. A team of six had entered the building with buckets, mops, a shop vac, stacks of microfiber cloths, and a trolley of cleaning supplies. She had seen them leave the building at 11:47 a.m. for lunch and return promptly at 12:45 p.m. They'd departed for the day at 5:00 and returned at 8:30 that morning. Although she'd kept a close eye on Candy Alley, there had been nothing for her to see.

Until now.

The crew was stowing the shop vac, the trolley of cleaning products, and green vinyl trash bags filled with dirty microfiber cloths into the back of their van.

Anita clasped her arms over her chest, hugging herself. Her breath crystallized into tiny droplets as she exhaled. *I'll catch my death,* she told herself, *but I want to be sure of what I'm seeing.*

The cleaning crew finished packing up, locked the door of Candy Alley, climbed into their van, and drove away.

Anita swung around and hurried inside Archer's Bridal. She crossed the workroom in five quick strides. Her phone lay on her desk, and she lunged for it.

She held it in her hand, debating whether to text Tim or call him. He'd assured her she could tour the premises again as soon as the work the executor had promised had been completed. Cleaning was the last step. She practically vibrated with excitement at the thought of getting inside the newly sanitized space. Anita was tapping out a text to Tim when her phone rang with a call from him. She abandoned her message and swiped to answer.

"Hello, Tim," she said. "I was just texting you."

"I bet I know what was on your mind," Tim replied, his tone teasing.

"Try me," Anita said.

"You were going to tell me the cleaning crew is done, weren't you?"

"They just left!" Anita said. "How did you know?"

"They called the attorney who represents the executor, as they were preparing to leave," Tim said. "Have you been monitoring the progress at Candy Alley these past few days?"

"You know me too well," Anita said. "I have a bird's-eye view of the place from my shop. Other than processing this week's payroll, I've done nothing else but watch the comings and goings of the various service companies."

"I'd have done the same if I were in your position," Tim said. "So, you know the place is ready for another look?"

"I sure do," Anita said.

"That's why I'm calling. When would you like to tour the property again?"

"I'm ready right now! I'll put my coat on and be there in under a minute."

Tim chuckled. "I need a bit more time than that. Actually, I was going to propose we meet there later this afternoon. I talked to Sam yesterday, and he confirmed that he and Jeff can meet us there any day this week after three. Would you like me to ask them to stop by to help assess the property?"

"I'd love nothing more," Anita said. "If I still feel the way I felt after seeing it the first time, I'd like to make an offer as soon as possible."

"They've given me their asking price," Tim said, and disclosed it to her.

"Oof," she groaned. "That's at the top end of my budget."

"They're throwing a number out there," Tim said. "It's too high. I analyzed the comps. The price they're asking is for a property in pristine, move-in-ready condition. As we've seen, Candy Alley will require major refurbishment. That's why we need Sam and Jeff to get in there as soon as possible. We'll use their estimates for the required work, with a generous cushion for cost overruns, to come up with our offer."

"That makes sense to me," Anita said.

"I'll call Sam now," Tim said, "and we'll meet you there."

"Oh, I can't wait!" Anita said, her voice as giddy as if the captain of the football team had asked her to the senior prom.

"One last thing," Tim said. "I don't want to rain on your parade. I know how excited you are about this property and your museum. But I want to caution you—rein in your enthusiasm and look at this building with clear eyes. The sellers may not accept a reasonable offer."

"Why are you saying this?" she asked softly.

"Because I want you to buy the right property for your museum," he said. "That means the right location at the right price. Emotions often play a large role in choosing real estate, but it's never wise—especially when acquiring a business location—to let your heart overrule your head."

Anita took a deep breath. "I don't want to make a bad financial decision," she said. "I'll try to control myself. And I give you permission to tell me if you think I'm making a mistake."

"Good," he said. "Because I represent you—and that's my job."

"Understood," Anita replied. "See you at three."

"Despite what I just said," Tim added, "I believe the sellers will be reasonable. I want to make this deal happen for you."

CHAPTER 19

*a*nita stamped her feet against the cold sidewalk to keep warm while Tim fumbled with the key.

"This old lock is cantankerous," he said over his shoulder. "If you buy this place, one of the first things I'd do is change the lock."

"Duly noted," she said, trying to keep the impatience from her voice. Now that she was here, standing on the threshold, she wanted him to hurry up. The cleaning crew had replaced the brown paper covering the inside of the window. Passersby still couldn't see into the shop. She had tried.

A small pickup truck pulled to the curb and parked. She greeted Sam and Jeff as they climbed out to join her.

The tumblers in the lock clicked into place, and Tim pushed the door open. "After you," he said.

She bounded through the door, with Sam, Jeff, and Tim

close behind. Anita walked to the middle of the room and turned in a circle, taking in the cleaned space.

"Gosh, this looks so much different," she said. "If I close my eyes, I can imagine the magical candy store of my childhood."

"I'd say they did a fine job," Sam said. "Based on what Tim told us, it was a complete mess."

"That's an understatement," Anita said. She pointed to the display cabinets and cash register. "I'm glad they left those, as requested."

"The attorney said the only other things they left in place were a dozen wooden crates in the basement," Tim added.

"What's in them?" Anita asked.

Tim shrugged. "Don't know. He said the owners wouldn't tell him. They think a buyer might want the contents. If the buyer doesn't, the seller will arrange to have them removed."

"Have you ever heard of anybody doing that?" she asked.

"I've been in this business for over thirty years," Tim said, "and this is a first for me."

"Should I be worried about it?"

"The attorney said the sellers assured him there's nothing hazardous or dangerous. They think the contents will be a fun surprise for someone."

"Now I'm really intrigued," Anita said. "Could I take a teeny peek at them when we're in the basement?"

"I'm under strict instructions not to open them," Tim said. "Think of it this way: when people put their houses on the market, they sometimes lock a closet and don't let buyers see inside. They secure valuables too large for a safe deposit box. The sellers regard these crates the same way."

Anita looked at Sam and raised her eyebrows.

He shrugged. "I don't see any reason to worry about it. You've got bigger issues to deal with." He scraped the floor with his foot. "This is beautiful old wood, but it's badly worn from years of foot traffic. You'll want to either refinish it or put down new flooring."

"I definitely want to refinish it," she said. "Visitors should feel like they've stepped back in time when they enter my museum. It'll be like a journey to the past."

"I love the sound of that," Tim said.

"Let's start on the second floor." Tim moved to the partition that obscured the stairway. Once again, he handed small flashlights to each of them. "The attorney said they also removed the refrigerator up there. The door had been left open, and it had become a rodent hotel."

"Oh gosh." Anita pressed a hand to her chest. "That's so revolting. I'm glad they got rid of it."

They climbed the stairs, Jeff lagging behind to assess the integrity of the handrails and the soundness of each step.

The cleared second-floor space revealed a six-foot section of kitchen cabinets along one wall. The door to the bathroom on the opposite wall stood open. They each stepped into the small room that included a porcelain pedestal sink, a toilet, and a tiny cast-iron bathtub. A medicine cabinet, its door askew on its hinges, hung above the sink.

"I thought there'd be a sink in those cabinets," Anita pointed to them. "Since Charlotte lived up here, I'm assuming that was her kitchen."

"She must've done her dishes in the bathtub," Sam said. "People did that sort of thing in the old days."

"I can hardly imagine," said Anita. "Charlotte ran that candy store until she was in her mid-nineties. I hate to think of her going up and down those stairs at that age—and doing dishes in the tub."

"I knew Charlotte longer than you did," Sam said. "A more independent person you've never met. She lived how she wanted and wouldn't have welcomed charity—or pity—from anyone."

Anita nodded. "That's comforting. I hate the idea of buying a place where someone was unhappy."

"You won't be," Sam assured her.

Jeff joined them, having completed his inspection of the stairs. "Everything appears to be structurally sound," he said, "but, like the flooring below, the stairs will need to be refinished." He looked down. "This floor is in even worse shape than downstairs."

Sam pointed to the ceiling. "Gordon was right. There's water damage on the ceiling and along the outside wall. The plaster on the wall is dark. That has to be mold."

"I agree," Jeff said. "It'll have to be torn out, and either replastered or replaced with drywall." He looked at Anita. "Plaster will be more expensive. You'll save money by using drywall."

"If you install display cases along that wall, no one will know what's behind them," Sam added.

"That's a good way to save money," Anita agreed. She took a deep breath. "We know I'll need to replace the roof, refinish the floors, remediate mold, and replace the wall up here."

"I'd plan on replacing the wall on both floors," Sam said.

"I want to remodel that bathroom," Anita said, "so it can function as a public restroom. It feels unhygienic now."

"I agree," Sam said. "Will you install an accessible public restroom on the first floor, too?"

"Yes," Anita said. "And I'd like to rip out the dumbwaiter and put in an elevator."

Sam and Jeff took measurements of the existing dumbwaiter at the second-floor opening.

"That'll work," Sam said. "We'll add that to our list."

"What else?" Anita asked.

"The seller hasn't turned the utilities back on, so we can't test anything, but I would replace the electric knob and tube wiring," Tim said.

"The heater and air conditioner are probably decades old, too," Jeff said. "If they are, you'll want new units."

"Wow," Anita said. "It feels like we're going to be taking the place down to the studs and redoing everything." She looked from Jeff to Sam, her expression glum.

"It's always best to do things right from the get-go," Sam said. "You'll probably need new plumbing and a new sewer system."

"By the time we're done, my offer will be less than half the asking price," Anita said. She looked at Tim. "Do you think there's any chance they'll accept that? Is there any point in going forward?"

Tim rested a hand between her shoulders. "If I didn't think there was a good chance we'd be successful, we wouldn't be here."

"But you warned me things might not work out," Anita said.

"I did," Tim replied. "But only because I don't want you to overpay."

He looked at Sam and Jeff. "I realize you've only been inside for a few minutes and haven't done a thorough inspection, but, based on your professional experience, do you think this place can be restored?"

"Absolutely," Jeff said.

"Sure," Sam agreed. "None of this is difficult. We faced much bigger challenges at the Olsson House."

Jeff nodded.

"Jeff and I want to make sure you know how much money you'll need to make that happen," Sam added.

Anita shut her eyes and inhaled a calming breath. "Thank you for that," she said. "When I get the numbers from you, Tim and I will put together an offer. I'll hope for the best but be prepared for the worst. If I have to find another place for my museum, so be it."

"That's the spirit," Tim said, patting her on the back.

"Let's look at that basement," she said. "I'm not leaving without seeing it."

They returned to the first floor and crossed to the plain door obscuring the narrow stairs. Using flashlights, they went down to the hard-packed dirt floor. Someone had whitewashed the raw planks on the walls long ago. The space was empty except for a row of wooden crates, six across and stacked two high.

Anita crossed to the crates and trained her flashlight across every inch of each one. She looked over her shoulder at Tim.

"I'm not trying to open them," she said, "but if there's a crack in the boards and I can see inside—well, that's not breaking any rules."

"I agree," Tim said.

Tim, Jeff, and Sam added their flashlight beams to hers as they all tried to see the mysterious contents.

Anita surreptitiously brought one hand to the top of a crate and pushed it gingerly. The top remained firmly in place.

"I guess we'll have to wait until I own this place before we find out what's in these," she said. "I'm so curious, I can hardly stand it." She turned to Tim. "For heaven's sake, don't let me get carried away and offer too much just so I can find out what's in these crates."

"I promise," Tim said. "Let's head to my office. We can start writing the offer while Sam and Jeff work up the numbers we need."

Jeff looked at Sam. "Judy and Joan are at book club tonight, so we're on our own for dinner. Let's go to Pete's and put a pencil to all this." He waved his hand around him.

"I was going to suggest the same thing," Sam said.

They all stepped onto the street, and Tim locked the door.

"We'll email you our suggestions by the end of the evening," Sam said. "That way, you can make your offer first thing in the morning."

Anita clasped her hands and brought them to her chest. "Thank you so much for dropping everything to help me. I know it'll be a daunting task to whip this place into shape, but, if anyone can do it, it's you. I've got a wonderful feeling about what's to come."

CHAPTER 20

*J*osh's cell phone pinged with two incoming texts in rapid succession. He pulled his eyes away from the application for his replacement he was reviewing, and picked up his phone. Both messages were from Sunday.

Can you step away from your desk for 30 minutes?

Now?

He checked the time and was surprised to see that it was almost eleven. He'd been reviewing applications without interruption since seven thirty. Josh raised his hands over his head and stretched. A break would be welcome. He tapped at the screen of his phone.

Sure. Want to grab lunch?

The three dots beneath his message undulated.

Won't have time. I'll pick you up in front of the admin building in five.

He responded with a thumbs-up emoji and rose from his desk. Maggie's door stood ajar, and he stuck his head around the corner.

"I'm taking an early lunch," he said as she looked up from an industry journal.

"Sure," she replied. "Take as much time as you want. We still have a few calm days until classes resume."

Josh grabbed his jacket from the back of his chair and stepped into the bright sunshine of the winter day. Sunday pulled to the curb at the bottom of the wide stone steps that led to the impressive façade of the Highpointe College administration building. He trotted down the steps and slung himself into the passenger seat.

They leaned across the center console for a quick kiss.

Josh studied her profile as she pulled away from the curb. "There's an intensity about you this morning. We're on a mission, aren't we?"

Sunday flashed him a smile. "You're right. I wanted us both to tour the college chapel."

"I'd like to see our wedding venue too," Josh said, "but we've got plenty of time for that, don't we?"

"Actually, no. If we're getting married there in two and a half months, I need to order the wedding invitations now."

"Doesn't everyone send them online these days?"

"Not for weddings," Sunday said, her tone prickly. "At least I'm not doing online invites for our wedding. I'm getting ours from Celebrations. I have an appointment with Judy later this afternoon. Do you want to come with me and help select them?"

Josh raised both hands, palms out. "Nope," he said. "That's all you. I'm happy with anything you pick."

Sunday nodded. "I know we've already selected the chapel as our venue, but I wanted us to see it together—before I order the invitations. We'll get married at eleven, followed by a brunch reception."

"I thought we agreed to that," he said.

"We did, but I want to see what the chapel looks like at that time of day. It's why I texted you. We've been in a rush to get our wedding planned, and I want to make sure we don't make any mistakes."

"That's smart," Josh said. "I'm sure it'll be perfect, but I'd love to see it with you before our big day." He lifted her right hand from the steering wheel and planted a kiss on it.

She smiled again and turned into the chapel parking lot.

The red brick Gothic Revival structure nestled among the bare limbs of winter trees like an egg in a nest. The crenellated parapet along the roofline stood in sharp relief against the deep blue of the cloudless sky. A prominent rose window, reminiscent of the one at Notre Dame, dominated the façade.

"The altar is in front of that window," Sunday said as they approached the entrance, "and the morning sunshine coming through it should be spectacular."

"I've walked by this building dozens of times and always

admired it. I don't know why I never went inside." He took her hand in his. "I'm glad I'm seeing it for the first time with you."

Josh opened the right half of the arched wooden door for Sunday, wincing as the frozen iron hardware stung his bare hand.

They were alone in the chapel. Morning sun streamed through the stained-glass window, casting rivers of crimson, ochre, and sapphire across the polished wooden pews and pooling in glowing color on the slate floor.

Josh and Sunday joined hands. The air held the faint scent of beeswax and the lingering aroma of evergreens from the Christmas holiday. Hand in hand, they moved slowly, reverently, down the center aisle toward the altar. They stood in silence, soaking in the quiet grandeur of the space.

Sunday turned toward him, her eyes bright as if lit from within. "What do you think?" she whispered in the solemn stillness.

Josh swept his gaze across the face of the woman he loved. "Breathtaking," he said.

She smiled up at him. "Isn't it?"

"I was referring to you," he said, "but, yes, the venue is perfect." He bent to kiss her.

Sunday took a step back. "Nope," she said, grinning. "The first time you kiss me in this space will be when we're married."

CHAPTER 21

*A*nita ran from the lunchroom to her desk and snatched up her phone just before the call went to voicemail.

"This is Anita," she said, huffing and puffing.

"It's Tim, Anita," he said, and the tone of his voice already told her what she longed to hear. "They've accepted your offer."

She stood at her desk, clutching the phone to her ear, too emotional to respond.

"Anita, they accepted your offer," Tim repeated. "Candy Alley will be yours."

She forced herself to find her voice. "Did they ask for more money or anything?"

"Nope. I think the fact that you're a cash buyer and

willing to close escrow in ten days did the trick. Your only contingencies are the inspection and a clean title report."

"How soon can we get the inspectors in there?"

"I'll call the firm I use for commercial projects as soon as we hang up. I'll stress that we need a fast turnaround. You'll probably have the report in three days—four at the most."

"Wow," Anita said, bringing her free hand to the side of her head. "I almost can't believe this."

"Congratulations," Tim said. "What are you going to do to celebrate?"

"I've been thinking about that," she replied. "I'd like to invite a few people to the space once I have the keys. We'll christen the place with a toast and open those crates in the basement. I think it'll be fun to have a public reveal."

"That's a terrific idea," Tim said. "I hope Nancy and I are on the guest list."

Anita chuckled. "You're at the top of the list. I thought I'd invite Jeff and Judy, Sam and Joan, Sunday and Josh, and Maggie and John—plus Gordon, of course. He's been on Long Island this week doing an appraisal for an estate, and we haven't spoken for a few days. He knows I made the offer, and he'll be thrilled they accepted it. I need to find out when he's available to come to Westbury."

"It might be wise to wait until they remove the damaged walls and remediate the mold. Sam doesn't want anyone spending more time in that space until those things are done."

"Did he say how long that will take?"

"He told me they'll be able to get it done within a week. He also suggested the new roof should go on right away."

"Can they do that during the winter?" Anita asked.

"The extended forecast shows temperatures slightly above average—and, most importantly, no rain or snow," Tim said.

"Everything is going my way with this project," Anita said. "I'll call Sam as soon as we hang up, so he can start work as soon as the deed transfers to me. I'll ask when he thinks it'll be safe for me to throw my party. Once I have a date, I'll let you know."

"Nancy and I aren't going anywhere this winter, so we'll be available," Tim said. "But do you really intend to wait that long to find out what's in those crates?"

Anita bit her lip. She'd been wondering the same thing. "If I invite my dearest friends for the great unveiling, I'm not going to peek ahead of time. If it's disappointing, I'll have my friends around me, but, if it's something cool, it'll be more fun to share my joy with all of you."

~

ANITA KEPT her cell phone in her pocket for the rest of the day. She had texted Gordon her news as soon as she'd finished her conversation with Sam and asked him to call her when he had a chance.

He'd mentioned the day before that the heirs were becoming increasingly contentious with each other. The old mansion had been in the family for decades, filled with items that were fine when acquired and were now extremely valuable. Gordon said he loved seeing people enjoy their prized possessions almost as much as he hated seeing them fought over by greedy heirs, who only appreciated them for their financial value, not their intrinsic beauty.

Bursting with excitement to share the news and get his input, she waited for his call. She was on her way to bed when her phone finally rang.

"Gordon," she said, "I'm so glad to hear your voice."

"Congratulations, sweetheart," he said, his voice thick with fatigue. "I'm sorry it's so late."

"Don't worry about me," she replied. "It's an hour later where you are, and you sound exhausted."

"I had dinner with the family tonight. My appraisals are finished, and the plan was for them to divide the furnishings they wanted to keep and sell the rest. I was prepared to offer my recommendations for various auction houses."

"You said that was the plan," she replied. "What actually happened?"

"We were in a private dining room at a restaurant," Gordon said. "I've learned from experience to hold these meetings outside the home. Public spaces tend to encourage better behavior."

"Uh-oh. I don't like the sound of this," she said.

"We made it through the salad course easily enough, but things got testy during the entrée. By the time they handed out dessert menus, the discussion had become heated. A shouting match turned into a shoving match over coffee, and the restaurant finally asked us to leave."

"Good heavens," Anita said. "Aren't these heirs wealthy in their own right? What in the world are they doing fighting over chairs and carpets?"

"I've seen this happen many times before," Gordon said. "It doesn't matter how much people have—they want more. I love my job because I get to handle some of the most beautiful things in the world, but the downside is that I'm forced to interact with greedy people in high-stress situations."

"I'm so sorry to hear this," she said. "When will you finish out there?"

"We decided—in the parking lot after the restaurant ejected us, no less—to meet for breakfast tomorrow morning. If they reprise last night's scene, I'm packing up and heading back to Manhattan."

"I'll be thinking about you the whole time," Anita said. "Please let me know how it goes, one way or the other."

"I will," Gordon replied. "Anyway, that's not why I called. Tell me your good news."

She gave him the *Reader's Digest* version. "The details can wait until you're back home and have had a good night's sleep. The only thing I'd like to know from you now is if you would like to come to my party where we open the mystery crates?"

"Are you kidding? Of course I want to come," Gordon said. "I don't want you to open those without me."

"Wouldn't dream of it," she said. "What does your schedule look like?"

"I'm tied up for the next couple of weeks," Gordon said. "Even if I return to my office tomorrow, it'll take another three or four days to complete the appraisal documents. After that, I'm accompanying a client to an auction at Sotheby's in London for a few days."

"Gosh, Gordon," Anita gasped. "You lead such a glamorous life."

Gordon chuckled. "You wouldn't say that if you'd seen me getting thrown out of that fancy restaurant tonight."

"Now that you mention it, I would like to have seen that," she teased. "I'll make sure my party is after you get back from London. I'll text you several dates to choose from."

"That's very nice," Gordon said, stifling a yawn.

"And now," she said gently, "I've taken enough of your time. I can hear how tired you are. I don't want to impose any further."

"Talking to you about the frustrations of my day has helped me," he said. "If I hadn't spoken to you, I would've been ruminating about them until the wee hours. Now that we've talked, I can set them aside and go to sleep peacefully. You're like a tonic for my soul."

Her knees went weak, and she sank onto the side of her bed. "I'm happy to be your sounding board any time," Anita said softly. "You'll be in my thoughts tomorrow. Sweet dreams," she said.

CHAPTER 22

S unday hovered at the edge of Lyla's desk. Her friend, hunched over her keyboard, hammered numbers into a spreadsheet. Sunday cleared her throat, and Lyla finally looked up.

"You're focused on what you're doing," Sunday said. "I'm sorry to disturb you."

Lyla pushed herself into the back of her chair. "Year-end reports," she said. "I'll be at these for weeks. What's up?"

"I wanted to let you know I'm leaving early today," Sunday said.

"Wedding plans?" Lyla asked.

"Absolutely," Sunday replied. "I'm headed to Celebrations to order our invitations."

"You're sticking with the chapel?"

Sunday nodded. "Josh and I went there at lunchtime. It's going to be perfect."

"I'm glad," Lyla said. "I think so too. Did you order your dress?"

"Yes," Sunday said. "I received an email saying it has shipped. I can't wait for it to arrive, so I can get it to Anita for alterations."

"Since you'll be close to Archer's Bridal this afternoon, I suggest you stop in to see Anita," Lyla said. "Show her a photo of the dress. One look and I bet she'll be able to tell how straightforward it will be to adjust."

"Great idea," Sunday said. "I'll do that."

"I don't want to stick my nose in," Lyla added, "but I'm interested in every detail. I'd love to see the invitations you select."

"Of course," Sunday said. "I'll take photos on my phone. You're still my BFF, and I want to share everything with you."

Lyla chuckled. "Have fun."

"Will do. I'll fill you in tomorrow," Sunday said, and walked away.

She made the drive to the square in record time and found a parking spot in front of Celebrations. The square wasn't busy in the middle of this weekday afternoon. Sunday checked her watch—she was twenty minutes early for her appointment with Judy. A visit to Anita wouldn't make her late.

Sunday entered Archer's Bridal a few minutes later. The

workroom supervisor welcomed her, and Sunday asked if Anita was available.

Anita heard Sunday's voice from her desk in the next room and came out to meet her. They exchanged greetings, and Anita inquired about how the wedding plans were coming along.

"I'm working through my list," Sunday said. "It feels daunting, but I know I'll get through it. I stopped in today to show you a photo of the wedding dress I ordered online."

"I'd love to see it," Anita said.

Sunday pulled her phone out of her purse and scrolled through her photos. "Here," she said, turning the screen toward Anita. "It's this one."

Anita looked from the photo to Sunday and back again. "This style will be stunning on you," she said. "Very graceful. The skirt should move beautifully as you walk down the aisle."

Sunday placed her hand on her heart. "I love hearing that," she said. "I didn't even think about how it would move."

"You've made a great choice. Do you know when you'll receive it?"

"I received an email saying it has shipped. They provided the tracking number, so I'll check every day. I came here to show you the photo and ask if you think it'll be feasible to alter it."

Anita took the phone and expanded the photo with two fingers, studying it carefully. She removed her reading glasses and handed the phone back. "Yes—as long as the dress isn't more than a size or two off, this will be easy to alter. The only issue will be if it's way too short."

"I don't think it will be," Sunday said. "The listing included the length, and, if anything, it should be too long."

"A full skirt like that takes time to hem, but it's very doable," Anita said. "I think you're set." She smiled at Sunday.

"That's a relief. I'm nervous, ordering a dress this close to my wedding. I need this one to work."

"I'm sure it will," Anita said. "Bring it in the moment you get it. In fact, I suggest you wait to try it on until you come in —getting yourself into that dress will be a two-person job."

Sunday laughed. "I never would've guessed. I'll call you as soon as it arrives."

Anita put her hand on Sunday's elbow. "Even if it's delivered on the weekend, call me. I'll open the shop so you can try it on. I know how anxious you are."

"That's so nice of you," Sunday said. "But I don't want you to come to the shop on your day off."

"About that," Anita said, smiling. "I'm spending most of my time here these days. You'll hear about it soon enough—I purchased the old Candy Alley building."

"The one across the square?" Sunday asked.

"Yep," Anita said. "I bought it for my sewing machine museum."

Sunday clapped her hands. "That'll be the perfect place for it. When do you plan to open it?"

"The building's in sad shape," Anita said. "We've got months of renovations ahead of us."

"Do you still want to display some of your machines in the exhibit space at the library, like we discussed before Christmas? It's cleaned up and ready to go."

"I've been so wrapped up in buying this property and planning the renovations that I forgot about your kind offer," Anita said. "I'd love to have a mini display at the library."

"We'll put up a sign that announces the museum is *Coming Soon*. When you have an opening date, we'll redo the sign to include the date."

It was Anita's turn to press her hand to her heart. "I'm so grateful," she said.

"You haven't toured the space," Sunday reminded her. "Come to the library, so you get an idea of how many machines you'll be able to display. If you give me basic info on the machines, I'll make placards to post by each one. When can you stop by?"

"Are you headed back to the library now?" Anita asked.

Sunday shook her head. "I'm on my way to Celebrations to order my invitations. That shouldn't take too long. I'd be happy to go to the library with you when I'm done."

"I don't want you to hurry your decision," Anita said. "If you're working tomorrow, I'll stop by first thing in the morning, before I open the shop."

"That'll be perfect," Sunday said.

"I'll see you then," Anita said, walking Sunday to the door.

"And please keep me posted about your dress. I can't wait to see you in it."

~

THE PERSON STAFFING the information desk called Sunday to let her know she had a visitor. Sunday grabbed a notebook and pen and headed downstairs. She and Anita greeted each other with a hug.

"Did you get your invitations ordered?" Anita asked.

Sunday nodded. "They're so pretty! The background is a pale peach that mimics a watercolor finish. An inset border of pale green vines frames the text, which is printed in a scrolly—but not too fancy—font. There was so much to choose from that it took me almost two hours to decide."

"Believe me," Anita said, "that was fast. Since Judy and I both work with brides, we compare notes. She's told me stories of brides and their mothers who spend hours looking through invitation books and come back to the store several times before they make a decision."

"Good grief," Sunday said.

"That you finished in two hours may make you the most decisive bride of the year. I'll bet Judy even closed the shop on time and was home for dinner."

"Not quite," Sunday said with a laugh. "We had so much fun chatting that I spent another hour and a half talking with her after she closed up."

Anita smiled. "Judy's a good listener. That's why she

knows everything going on in this town— she's genuinely interested in what people have to say. People sense that in her and open up to her."

"Honestly," Sunday said, "I felt like she was the big sister I never had. We went over my wedding plans, and she offered some terrific suggestions."

"I'm glad to hear it," Anita said. "She's very knowledgeable. I'm sure she gave you great advice."

"We also segued into where Josh and I are going to live after the wedding."

Anita cocked an eyebrow at her.

"He's going to move in with me until we have time to look for a place near the center of town. That location will be close to both of our jobs. We'd love an older home, like the ones behind the square. There's a house across the street from the Olsson House that appears to be vacant. Josh and I strolled past it on New Year's Eve, and now I drive by it every day on my way to work." She sighed. "It's not for sale, and we won't have enough saved for a down payment for at least a year, anyway. Even the fixer-uppers are out of our price range, so we need to find someplace to rent."

Anita tilted her head. "What did Judy say to that?"

"She told me she grew up in her grandmother's house on one of the streets behind the square and inherited it when she died. She shared the story of how she bought the Olsson House on a whim at a tax foreclosure sale—and how the hand-carved wooden ornaments in the attic led her to her husband. If that isn't a Hallmark Channel Christmas movie script, I don't know what is!" Sunday laughed. "Anyway, Judy told me she loves their neighborhood and would never consider living anywhere else. She encouraged us to keep saving our money. She said a real estate miracle might happen for us, just like it did for her when she was the successful bidder at that sale."

Anita chuckled. "That sounds like her—and it's solid advice. My mother used to say, 'You never know where your good is going to come from.'"

"I like that," Sunday said. "But you didn't come in here to talk about my wedding invitations and our real estate woes. Let's look at the exhibit space." She led Anita to a large open area off the main reading room. "This is where we're going to house our rotating exhibits."

Anita stepped into the space. The vaulted ceiling of the first-floor room was illuminated by a ring of windows. Wrought iron and glass pendants hung from the ceiling. The hardwood floors added warmth to the space. Three plexiglass display stands stood in the middle, surrounded by enclosed display cases.

Anita swiveled to face Sunday. "This will be perfect. I already know which three machines I'll place on the display stands." She studied the cases. "How much display space is there in those three cases?"

"Eighteen feet," Sunday said.

"I'll need to go home and measure my machines, but I think I'll need eighteen inches of space for each one."

"That's twelve machines," Sunday said, "plus the three

that will be in the center. How soon do you want to begin setting them up?"

"I'll look at the machines in my basement today and decide what I want to display," Anita said. "Are you sure you have time to make the information placards for me?"

"Absolutely," Sunday said. "I love doing that sort of thing. Send me a photo of each machine, together with any information you have, and I'll work up the placards. I'll send everything to you for approval before I print them."

"That's so helpful," Anita said.

"Lyla Kershaw is an artist, and she's designing the signs for the front of the library and the one that will go at the entrance to the exhibit in the main reading room."

"You're making this so easy for me," Anita said gratefully.

"I think it's going to be a very popular attraction," Sunday said. "It'll draw people into the library." She snapped her fingers. "I've had another idea—we'll set up a QR code to the museum's website on the signage."

Anita looked at her with a blank expression.

"The website will include a sign-up link for your newsletter," Sunday explained.

"My newsletter?" Anita asked, wide-eyed.

"Of course! You'll need a newsletter to stay in touch with museum patrons. We'll also link to your social media accounts."

Anita placed her hands on either side of her face. "Social media? I didn't even think of that. Can't I just open my museum, put out a sign on the sidewalk, and leave it at that?"

"Not if you want it to be successful in this day and age," Sunday said with a smile. "Don't worry about all that. I'll help you get everything set up and teach you what and how to post. Once you get going, it'll only take a few minutes a week."

"This is way more work than you bargained for, Sunday. You've got a wedding to plan. I can't ask this of you."

"You didn't ask me," Sunday said. "I offered. And I'm glad to help."

"But—" Anita began.

Sunday held up a hand to silence her. "Your job is to select what you want to display. Mine is to make the rest of this happen."

Anita blew out a breath and turned in a slow circle. "I'm going to make a beautiful exhibit for you," she said. "The library will be proud."

"And we're going to make yours the must-see new museum in the state."

CHAPTER 23

Frank opened the front door as Josh approached along the walkway.

"Thanks for coming on such short notice," Frank said, stepping aside and motioning Josh over the threshold.

Sean hovered behind Frank, shifting his weight from foot to foot.

"You know my son, Sean?" Frank asked.

"We've seen each other at Forever Friends," Josh said, "but we haven't officially met." He held out his hand to the young teen.

Sean stepped forward and shook his hand.

"Follow me," Frank said. "Loretta set out a spread of hors d'oeuvres that could suffice for a meal."

"Mom's been in the kitchen the entire day," Sean added. "She's been singing, so we know she's having fun."

The three entered the kitchen. Trays of caprese skewers, bacon-wrapped dates, and toasted baguette slices topped with warm brie and fig jam were placed at the end of the island. A tiny crockpot containing bubbly crab dip sat next to a basket of crackers.

Loretta slid a casserole dish of scalloped potatoes into the oven, brushed a damp tendril of hair off her forehead, and turned to greet Josh.

Josh held out a bouquet of roses and stargazer lilies that Sunday had suggested as a hostess gift.

"Thank you," Loretta said. "But you didn't have to do this."

"It's very nice of you to have me over for dinner," Josh said.

Frank handed Josh and Sean small plates and gestured toward the hors d'oeuvres.

"This looks wonderful," Josh said, eyeing the offerings.

Loretta gave him a thousand-watt smile as she pulled a vase from the cabinet above the refrigerator. "Have you heard from David?" she asked Frank.

Frank covered his mouth as he spoke around a mouthful of warm, gooey date. "No—and it's not like him to be late."

Sean pulled his phone from his pocket. "I've got a text from him. David had trouble getting his car started, but he's on his way. He says he'll be here in ten minutes."

Loretta picked up a plate and helped herself to a caprese skewer. She turned to Sean. "Would you go tell your sisters the appetizers are ready if they'd like some?"

Sean headed toward their bedrooms.

"I'm going to feed the twins before we sit down," Loretta said, setting her plate on the counter.

"Do you need any help?" Frank asked.

She shook her head. "Don't forget to offer Josh something to drink," she added over her shoulder as she left the room.

"It's been so long since we've had company for dinner. I'm rusty on my hosting duties," Frank said with a sheepish shrug. "What can I get you?"

"I know it's boring," Josh said, "but I'm a water drinker."

Frank filled a glass with ice water and handed it to him.

"I'm happy to meet your family," Josh said. "I understand you've been a father figure to both David and Sean. It's so cool you allowed David to fulfill his community service obligations at Forever Friends."

"David's attention-seeking theft from his school following his father's suicide was a cry for help," Frank said. "That experience led him to his life's purpose—working with guide dogs."

"Now Sean appears to be interested in service dogs, too," Josh said. "You should be very proud."

"Those two boys—young men—are remarkable. They'll be successful in life, no matter what. I'm lucky to watch them grow into their full potential." He smiled at Josh. "Loretta and I were talking the other night, and she suggested having you and David over, so you could become better acquainted. She pointed out that the two of you don't really know each other yet. You'll eventually work closely together. David heads back to California and his studies at the Guide Dog Center in a few days, so tonight was our last chance for a while."

"David seems terrific," Josh said. "I'm looking forward to working with him, and I'm glad we have this chance to connect before he goes back. I also want to spend more time with Sean."

"Sean's always asking about the plans for Forever Guides, but I haven't included him in meetings," Frank said, his tone growing serious. "He's only thirteen. I feel bad that he spends so much time at Forever Friends. He's a kid, and I want him to enjoy his childhood."

"From what I've seen, Sean is serious and focused. I think he genuinely cares about the rescue animals," Josh said. "If you're worried about pushing him into a family business— like sometimes happens with family-owned restaurants— you don't need to be. Sean's interest is real."

The worry lines around Frank's eyes vanished, like ice that's just been cleaned by a Zamboni.

Loretta and Marissa returned to the kitchen, with Bonnie and Branson in tow. Nicole was close behind. Sally, Daisy, and Snowball stormed to the front door, barking.

"That'll be David," Frank said, heading down the hall.

Loretta inserted a sheet pan of chicken thighs in the oven and followed him to the front door.

~

"THERE'S one last piece left. Who'll take this off my hands?" Loretta carried the cake into the dining room. "I want to wash this plate and put it away."

Josh drew back in his chair. "It was absolutely delicious— the whole meal was—but I couldn't eat another bite."

Loretta looked from David to Sean. "Surely one of you boys would like this."

"Sure," they both said in unison.

Loretta chuckled. She cut the piece into two smaller slices and served one to each of the teenage boys. "The twins are asleep, and I'm going to help Marissa and Nicole finish cleaning the kitchen. Stay here as long as you like," she added. "But someone come get me before you leave. I want to say goodbye."

Frank pushed back his chair from the table. "You did all the cooking. Leave the cleanup to me. I'll get it later."

Loretta passed behind him on her way to the kitchen and rested her hand on his shoulder. "You're always good about cleaning up when I cook," she said. "I don't mind doing it tonight. It sounds like you're in the middle of a serious discussion." She patted his shoulder and disappeared into the kitchen.

Frank looked at the three young men around his dinner table. "This has been a very productive evening. Construction of the new guide dog school will take two years. That seems like a long time, but it'll be ready to open before we know it. There's a lot of work ahead of us. I'm glad to have you on my team."

"Running either a nonprofit or an educational institution were my two dream jobs," Josh said. "I can't believe I've found a position that lets me do both, straight out of grad school."

"I believe they call that kismet," Frank said, smiling. "I'm as delighted as you are."

David finished his slice of cake and set down his fork, eyes lowered to the table.

"You've been awfully quiet," Frank said. "Anything bothering you, David?"

David sucked in a breath. "During these last few months at the Guide Dog Center, I've realized I have so much to learn about training a seeing-eye dog, let alone teaching others how to do it." He looked up at Frank, his eyes clouded with doubt. "So many people have donated time and money to my dream, and I'm beyond grateful. But I don't have the skill required to run the technical side of the school. It'll probably take me years to acquire it." Misery poured from him like water over a dam. "I can't do this, Frank," he said. "I'm a fraud."

Josh leaned across the table toward David and started to speak, but Frank raised a hand to stop him.

"No one ever expected you to be in charge of guide dog training when Forever Guides opens, son. I hope you'll want to return to Westbury to work at the school, but I wasn't even sure of that. You're young, and things are going to change in your life. Heck, I'm even halfway expecting you to fall in love and stay in California." He leaned forward, his voice warm. "The point is, David, you sowed the seeds for this remarkable facility, and they've taken root. Forever Guides will become a reality, thanks to you. I'd love for you to be part of it—but, if you're not, it's still going forward."

"Really?" David asked.

"Absolutely," Frank replied. "I'm sorry you've been carrying such a heavy weight on your shoulders. If you decide you don't want to come back, say the word. Don't be afraid to tell me. I won't be mad."

"It's not that," David said. "California is great, but Westbury is home. I'll come back when I finish my training. I was worried you were expecting too much from me when I returned."

"We're looking forward to having you as an integral part of our team," Josh said, "but no one expects you to be the chief technical expert on guide dog breeding, training, or handler assignments. Part of my job as school administrator will be to hire the staff. One of my first tasks will be to prepare an organizational chart and job descriptions. We'll begin our recruitment process the year before Forever Guides opens."

"You've already thought of all this?" David asked.

Josh nodded, smiling. "We have. And because you're employed by one of the premier guide dog schools in the country, I'd love your input on the job descriptions and staffing levels—if you have time."

"I'll make time," David said. "Whatever you need, I'm

there for you. How will you find the right people? There aren't that many guide dog trainers."

"We'll advertise on social media," Josh replied. "And I'll post jobs in industry magazines. Westbury is routinely rated as one of the top 20 small cities in the U.S. That'll help us. Many people in big cities are looking for a quieter lifestyle."

"Sherry Parker has also offered to help us recruit," Frank added. "She was a veterinary intern at one of the East Coast guide dog schools. Sherry still has lots of contacts. She and John are also going to serve as our vets until we hire staff in-house."

David rocked back in his chair. "You've got this."

Frank and Josh both nodded.

"I've been worrying about nothing," David said. "I feel so much better."

"I'm glad," Josh said. "You've got enough to think about with your studies."

"That's right," Frank agreed. "Josh and I know nothing about training service dogs. Heck, I can't even train my own household pets. Josh and I will handle the business end of Forever Guides."

Josh nodded his agreement. "When do you head back?"

"I plan to leave by the weekend," David said. "Dodger and I drove, and it's a two-day trip. My mom insists that I take my car into the shop first, to make sure everything's okay."

"That's smart," Frank said. "You don't want to break down en route. It's a long drive."

Sean, who had been listening, finally spoke up. "You said it was hard to start your car tonight. That's why you were late."

"It's the first time that's happened," David said. "I think it'll be okay."

"I hope you have a safe trip back," Josh said. "And now I'd better go—I have to work in the morning."

They rose from the table.

"I'll go tell Loretta you're leaving," Frank said.

Josh, David, and Sean headed to the front door.

"Could you bring Dodger over before you go?" Sean asked. "I miss him."

"Sure," David replied. "I was going to bring him tonight, but my mother wanted him to stay with her."

Loretta and Frank joined them at the front door.

"Everything was delicious, Mrs. Nash," Josh said. "Thank you so much."

Loretta pulled him into a hug. "You're most welcome," she said. "And it's Loretta, please."

Josh shook Frank's hand and walked to his car.

"Did I hear that we'll see you again before you leave?" Loretta asked.

"If that's okay," David said.

"Of course it is," she replied. "You're welcome here anytime."

She and Sean stood in the open doorway as Frank walked David to his car.

David got in and inserted the key. He turned it, and a click-click-click echoed into the night. He tried again, with the same result.

Frank walked around the back of the car, bending to examine the tread on the tires as he came alongside the driver's door.

David opened the door a crack.

"You can roll down your window," Frank said.

"It doesn't work anymore," David replied. "I have to open the door—even at a drive-through."

Frank nodded. He was rich now but remembered the beat-up old cars of his youth. "You're going to need a new starter, son," Frank said, "and maybe an alternator. Your tire tread is low. I'd recommend a new set before you take off."

David stared at him.

"If you need money to help with that—" Frank began.

"I've saved money from my wages at the Guide Dog Center," David said. "I should be able to pay for those things myself."

"Okay," Frank said. "But just in case, I'm here for you."

David shut his door and turned the key again. This time, the engine caught. He pulled out of the driveway, leaving a faint smell of burning oil in his wake.

Frank walked back to the house, shaking his head.

Sean retreated to his room.

Loretta slipped her arm around Frank's waist as he came inside. "I know what we need to do tomorrow," she said. She lifted her face to his, her eyes twinkling with excitement.

"Are you going to tell me?" Frank asked.

Loretta planted a kiss on his cheek. "I think you'll figure it out."

CHAPTER 24

*A*nita took a step back to admire the charcuterie board she had ordered from Pete's Bistro. The long wooden rectangle took center stage on a display cabinet. The arrangement featured cured meats, sliced and cubed cheeses, mixed nuts, dried fruits, and an assortment of crackers, artfully placed along its length. A wheel of baked brie rose on a pedestal stand, flanked by small bowls of honey and jam. Bottles of both alcoholic and nonalcoholic champagne stood in buckets of ice on the counter next to the cash register, along with a silver tray of fluted glasses.

Gordon came up behind her and wrapped his arms around her waist. "It looks beautiful, sweetheart."

She nodded in agreement and glanced at her watch. "People will arrive any minute. I can't wait to thank them for believing in my vision."

"You've got a remarkable group of friends, that's for sure," he replied. "But that's how you roll here in Westbury."

She swiveled in his arms and planted a kiss on his cheek. "I have you to thank most of all for this," Anita said. "I wouldn't have thought of opening a museum if you hadn't suggested it."

"Pfft," he said, brushing off the compliment. "I don't know about that."

She glanced up at the overhead pendant lighting. "Thank goodness they still work. It'd be too dark for people to roam around in here without them. It's awfully chilly, though—the old heater isn't keeping up."

"It definitely needs to be replaced," Gordon said.

"Should we run over to Archer's Bridal and borrow the space heater we use in the workroom?" she asked.

"If people leave their coats on, they'll be fine," Gordon said. "I'd be hesitant to plug in that heater. It might blow a fuse."

"Hadn't thought of that," Anita said.

"Besides, once a few more people are here, it'll warm up. Are you excited to open those crates?" he asked. "I certainly am."

"And how," Anita replied. "I thought about suggesting the two of us take a peek when you arrived yesterday, but, since I've asked people to a 'great reveal' party today, I thought that would be cheating."

Gordon chuckled. "I admire your self-restraint."

Motion outside the shop window drew their attention.

"That'll be your guests," Gordon said, stepping forward to open the door.

Tim and Nancy were the first to arrive. Close behind were Joan and Sam, followed by Judy and Jeff. The women hugged Anita and greeted Gordon warmly.

"I'm so glad you're here," Anita said to her friends. "The renovations are just getting started, but already things feel so much better in here. Having the mold remediated and the walls repaired goes a long way toward making me comfortable in the space."

"I can't believe I'm saying this," Sam said, "but we're ahead of schedule. The roofers are coming back tomorrow to finish up. They said they'll be done before noon."

"That's wonderful news," Tim said. "They're predicting heavy snow and record cold by the end of the week. I'm sure they want to finish before that hits."

The door opened again, and Sunday and Josh joined them. Anita and Sunday hugged like old friends.

"So, this is the site for Westbury's newest museum?" Sunday asked, stepping back and surveying the space, her eyes wide. She turned to Anita. "This could not be more perfect. I'm so excited for you."

"You're too sweet," Anita said, blushing. She turned to Gordon. "Will you open the champagnes and pass out glasses?"

"I was about to suggest that," Gordon said, moving toward the beverages.

"While we're waiting for Maggie and John to arrive,"

Anita said to the group, "please help yourselves." She pointed at the food. "It's happy hour, and I'm sure everyone's hungry. We don't know what we'll find in those crates in the basement, so I suggest everyone fortify themselves first."

"This looks so pretty," Sunday said, admiring the spread.

"It's from Pete's," Anita replied.

"That's who's catering our wedding reception," Josh supplied.

Everyone took an appetizer plate and began filling it. Gordon passed out drinks, and soon conversation hummed as everyone nibbled. The offerings on the board began disappearing.

Anita glanced toward the door. "It's not like Maggie to be late," she said to Josh. "Do you know if something came up at the college?"

"I don't think so," he replied. "We talked about coming here tonight. She and John are—"

The door opened, and a gust of wind pushed Maggie and John inside.

"Sorry we're late, everyone," John said, holding up his hands. "It's all my fault—I got tied up at the animal hospital."

"It's not a problem," Anita said. "We're glad you're here now."

"You're more understanding than my wife has been," John said, winking at Maggie. "She's so eager to get into those crates, I thought she was going to explode."

Maggie cuffed him playfully on the shoulder. "I *am* looking forward to seeing what's inside. I kept texting, asking when you'd be home because I didn't want to delay everyone else." She smiled at the group. "If we were going to be much longer, I was going to tell Anita to proceed without us."

Anita threw her arms wide and hugged them both at once. "I'm so glad you're here. We would've waited. The reveal wouldn't be the same without you."

Gordon took their drink orders, and Anita insisted they help themselves to food. She then walked to the far end of the room. "I have a few words to say before we go downstairs."

The group quieted as she spoke.

"I want to thank each of you for your friendship and encouragement." She turned to Gordon, her smile landing on him like a spotlight. "I'm especially grateful to Gordon for suggesting this museum and insisting I could pull it off. I'm so happy that each of you could join me tonight."

She raised her glass. "Here's to all of you."

"Hear, hear," Gordon said, raising his glass and tapping it against hers.

Her friends raised their glasses. Everyone took a sip.

"And now," Anita said, eyes shining, "I think it's high time we found out what's in those crates in my basement!"

Anita walked to the door leading to the basement and flung it open. The battery-operated lanterns Gordon had placed on the steps and hung from hooks in the ceiling illuminated their path. Sam and Jeff brought up the rear.

Each person gasped in astonishment as they stepped off the bottom step and into the basement for the first time. They lined up along the far wall, facing the unmarked, rough-sawn oak crates.

Maggie leaned into John, bringing her lips close to his ear. "I feel like I did the first time I stepped into Rosemont's attic. This is so exciting."

John nodded.

"You've remembered something, haven't you?" she whispered, studying his face.

John shrugged, raising his hands, palms up.

Sam and Jeff crossed the room to stand beside Anita.

"This is exactly what we saw when we came down here—twelve identical crates, six across and stacked two high." She opened her arms wide to encompass the crates behind her. "They were nailed shut, and the seller refused to let us open them before the building's purchase. We tried to see inside using flashlights, but there are no openings to give us even a glimpse." She looked at Sam and then Jeff. "Believe me—we tried."

A titter of laughter passed around the room.

"So, without further ado," Anita said, "Sam and Jeff will now open the crates."

She stepped aside as each man approached a crate, wielding a hammer and crowbar. They got busy loosening nails. Jeff's crate came open first. He waited until Sam loosened his lid. They looked at each other, nodded, and lifted the lids.

Anita peered into Jeff's crate. A thick layer of sawdust covered the contents. Jeff pulled a pair of work gloves from the back pocket of his jeans and handed them to her. She slipped them on and sculpted a divot in the sawdust.

"My hand's connected with something," she said over her shoulder. "It feels like a wooden divider." She continued digging, her brow furrowed in concentration. Her hand hit another object, and she used both hands to feel along its outline. Slowly, she pulled it an inch from its perch, shielding it from view with her body. Holding it with her left hand, she brushed away more sawdust with her right. Anita stared at the object, then threw her head back in delighted laughter.

Her friends leaned in like stalks of wheat bent by a strong wind.

Anita looked over her shoulder. "The history of this place just got a whole lot more interesting," she said. She pulled an amber glass bottle from the crate. Shaped like an oversized flask and made of ornate pressed glass, it featured a capital W outlined by a circle in its center. Wax sealed the corked bottle. "I believe this place was home to moonshiners—back in the day," she said.

Maggie spun toward John. "Is that what you remembered?"

He nodded. "I knew I remembered something salacious about this place. But I couldn't recall what until we stepped down here and saw those crates. They'd be the perfect way to store and transport moonshine."

"Is there still booze in them?" Judy asked.

Anita nodded as she held up the bottle. "It appears to be full." She handed it to Judy.

"It's a beautiful old bottle," Judy said, passing it to Josh.

"It's definitely full," Josh confirmed, turning it upside down. "The seal has held all these years—nothing's leaking." He handed it to Sunday.

Anita moved to the next compartment and confirmed it contained an identical bottle. She felt across the top of the open crate. "There are twelve bottles in this row." She removed one and held it against the side of the crate. "They could fit two rows per crate, so that's 24 bottles times 12 crates ..." Her voice trailed off.

"Two hundred eighty-eight bottles of hooch," John supplied the mathematical answer.

"Wow," Anita said with a laugh. "I guess we could have quite a party with this stuff."

Sunday handed the bottle to Maggie. "You won't want to drink this," she said. "Not until we test it. Unopened whiskey from a commercial manufacturer might be fine, but moonshine? That's risky. Moonshiners often added toxic additives such as methanol or industrial alcohols to increase their output. These toxins can cause blindness—or worse, even death."

The bottle made its way back around to Anita, who gently returned it to its slot.

"Let's see if the next crate contains the same," she said. She moved to Sam's crate and found another bottle. Newspaper wrapped this bottle, but its contents appeared identical to the first.

"Well," Anita said, "this is … interesting." She looked at Tim. "Since I'm not going to do anything with these, should we ask the seller to haul them away?"

"Just because you won't drink the whiskey," Sunday said, "doesn't mean it isn't valuable. These bottles are beautiful. They may be worth something. Another option is to display them on shelves down here. Save the newspaper that the bottles are wrapped in, too. It'll provide contextual historical clues. This room could become part of your museum—a nod to a thriving bootleg business in the 1930s."

"That's a fun idea," Judy said. "Some of your sewing machines are from that era. It fits."

Anita tapped her lip with one finger. "I'll have to think about it." She turned toward the stairs. "I guess the mystery's been solved."

"Not so fast," Maggie said. "Aren't we going to open the rest of the crates?"

"They probably have the same thing in them," Anita said.

"I think we need to find out," Maggie insisted. "Sam and Jeff can open them, and we can each search a crate to verify the contents. That would save you time, wouldn't it?"

"Sure," Anita admitted. "But you don't have to—"

Maggie turned to the others. "What do you say? Do we want to open these crates and see what's in them?"

"Yes!" came the resounding reply.

Sam and Jeff opened the remaining crates, and everyone dug in. As expected, 24 bottles of whiskey were nestled inside each one.

"That's a lot of inventory to leave abandoned," Tim said. "I wonder why it got left behind. This must've been worth a fortune back in the day."

"They might have been interrupted," John said.

"Maybe the sheriff found out and arrested them," Judy offered.

"If that were the case," Gordon said, "why wouldn't the officers have removed the inventory?"

"The bootlegger could have been gunned down by the mob," Nancy suggested.

"This story is getting more interesting by the minute," Anita said. "I hope I can find out what really happened."

"I'll look in the college archives," Sunday said. "We have a comprehensive collection detailing Westbury's history."

Gordon snapped his fingers. "If Maggie and John will permit me, I'd like to go through that filing cabinet in Rosemont's attic—the one I mentioned on New Year's Day."

"And I'll poke around the attic at the Olsson House," Judy said. "There are stacks of old newspapers up there I haven't touched."

"That's a lot of work," Anita said. "Are you sure you want to do that?"

"Yes," Sunday, Gordon, and Judy replied in unison.

"There's nothing better than a historical mystery," Judy

said, grinning, "especially when we've got connections to people from the past."

"You are the best," Anita said, beaming. "Who knew this place would bring its own mystery to my project? Perhaps I should rename this place the Westbury Sewing Machine and Moonshine Museum!"

CHAPTER 25

*A*listair

I was dozing in the library with Roman, Eve, and the three cats. Maggie and John had gone out early, and the six of us had settled in together to await their return.

Upon their arrival home after dark, John typically joins our library gathering. He turns on the TV, stretches out on the sofa, and tunes into a game. It doesn't matter which—he follows all sports. Maggie usually heads to their bedroom to change out of her work clothes before joining him. He then switches the channel to a drama they both enjoy, and we spend a pleasant evening before going to bed.

I knew the moment they walked through the kitchen door that tonight would be different. I heard the rapid pace of their conversation from the library as they headed to the stairs.

I stirred myself and floated after them. Instead of turning toward their bedroom, they headed to the stairway leading to my attic.

I came to full attention. This was definitely out of the ordinary.

I zoomed to catch up with them as they reached my attic and turned on the naked overhead bulb.

"Wait there," John told her. "I'll pull that filing cabinet out. It's dusty and you'll get your clothes dirty."

Maggie hovered at the top of the steps.

John crossed to the filing cabinet under the eaves. He put his shoulder against the front and leaned into it, grabbing it from behind and giving it a mighty shove to the right. He repeated the process two more times, then stood back, brushing dust from his hands and trousers.

"There," he called to Maggie. "Now Gordon can easily open the drawers all the way."

"Thank you," Maggie said. "He plans to be here first thing in the morning, before I leave for the office. He's eager to find information about the bootlegger who operated out of Anita's building."

This news sent me flying upward, and I smacked my head on an overhead beam. Maggie and John didn't hear me cry out in pain.

I brought myself back down to a safe height. The prospect of having that nice Gordon Mortimer in my attic for a day made my spirits soar. With any luck, I'd find what he was looking for before he arrived in the morning. I'd dog ear pages or place papers askew to draw attention to them. I liked all of Maggie and John's friends, but I had a special fondness for Anita and Gordon. They appreciated old things. If I could help them, it would be a night well spent.

CHAPTER 26

*J*osh and Sunday stepped onto the sidewalk outside of Laura's Bakery. He leaned in to kiss the corner of her mouth.

"You had a smudge of icing on your lip," he said.

She wiped the area with her fingers. "Did you get it all?" she asked.

"Sure did," he said. "Your kisses are always delicious, but this one was even more so."

She rolled her eyes. "That's corny—even coming from you."

He took her hand, and they walked toward his car.

"Do you think we made a wise choice?" she asked.

"About what?"

"The flavor of cake we want. What else?"

"Frankly, I liked all three of them," he said. "They were each delicious."

"I agree. The Earl Grey cake is trendy, but I thought it might be too exotic. Amaretto is nice, but I loved the combination of coconut cake with lime filling. I was also drawn to the photos she showed us of decorations using coconut." She glanced at him. "Do you think we'd be better off going with traditional piping and rosettes?"

"I have no idea what that is. We're going to have a happy marriage, no matter what our cake looks or tastes like. Piece of advice?"

Sunday cut her eyes to his.

"We've made a good decision. Let's not second-guess ourselves. We've got too many things to think about. You'll drive yourself to exhaustion that way—especially since you've taken on these added research projects for Anita's museum."

Sunday was silent as they continued to walk.

"I know you're right," she finally said. "I need to let things go."

They crossed the street and passed by Archer's Bridal. Sunday slowed her pace.

"Do you mind if I pop in to see if Anita's there?" she asked. "I'd like to tell her that I'm not done hunting through the archives, but so far I've found nothing that connects her new building with a bootleg operation."

Josh checked his watch. "I don't need to be back for another twenty-five minutes. We have time. It's a nice day.

I'll go for a walk in the square and be back here in ten minutes."

Sunday kissed him on the cheek and headed into Archer's Bridal.

Anita was tying a large white box with a satin ribbon. She handed it to the young woman standing on the other side of the counter. "Your dress is clean and packed in archival tissue," she said. "If your daughter wants to wear it to her wedding, it'll be in perfect condition."

The woman smiled her thanks and exited the shop.

Anita looked at Sunday. "Do you have news about your dress?"

"Not really," Sunday said. "I check the tracking app every morning, and it keeps showing that it's in transit." Worry lines zigzagged across her forehead.

"That's good," Anita said, coming around the counter to place a reassuring hand on Sunday's back. "Winter weather may cause delays. You've still got plenty of time before your wedding. Don't worry about it."

Sunday took a deep breath. "You're right."

"What brings you to the square today?"

"Josh and I were at Laura's for a cake tasting."

"Everything Laura makes is fabulous," Anita said. "What did you choose?"

Sunday told her.

"It's my very favorite," Anita said. "That would have been my wedding cake if I'd ever gotten married."

Sunday said, "That might still happen. I've seen how you and Gordon are together."

Anita turned crimson from her collar to the top of her head. "What an idea," she said. "I think I'm beyond all that."

"Nonsense," Sunday said. "No one is ever too old to be a bride. When you find your person—your soulmate—that's the time to get married."

Anita swallowed hard and cleared her throat. "Thanks for keeping me updated on the status of your dress," she said.

"You're welcome," Sunday replied. "But I stopped in for another reason. I wanted to let you know I've uncovered nothing about Candy Alley to connect it to a bootleg operation. I haven't finished going through the archives at the college, but it appears your new building was home to a store called Candy Alley starting in 1903. It was owned and operated mainly by women. Charlotte's grandparents started it, and her grandmother kept it going as a young widow. Her daughter took it over when she died. Charlotte was an only child and inherited the candy store from her mother in the late 1960s."

"That's disappointing," Anita said. "I wanted something more spectacular and eye-catching."

Sunday chuckled. "Me too. My hope was to find out that Al Capone was a regular midnight visitor."

"Gordon texted me this morning to say he found something interesting in the Rosemont attic," Anita said. "But he wouldn't tell me what."

"Oh, that sounds promising," Sunday said. "You'll have to let me know."

"He's going to the Olsson House after dinner to look at what Judy found in her attic," Anita said. "The two of them were texting up a storm last night. I stuck my head in Celebrations earlier this morning to see if Judy would spill the beans. Neither of them is talking. I think they want to put the entire story together before they share it."

"That's fun," Sunday said. "I'm eager to learn what they've discovered. It might give me a new direction for my research."

"Why don't you join them at the Olsson House tonight?" Anita said. "I'm sure they won't mind. You're part of the research team, too."

"I'd like that," Sunday said. "I'll call Judy to make sure it's okay with them."

Anita leaned toward her. "If you find out anything, will you let me know?"

"And spoil their surprise? Not a chance," Sunday said. "Some things are worth the wait—and I have a feeling this will be one of them."

CHAPTER 27

*a*nita answered Gordon's call on the first ring.

"I know it's almost nine," he said. "Is it too late for Judy and me to stop by? We think we've unraveled the mystery of the Candy Alley bootlegger."

"That's exciting!" Anita said. "I can't wait to hear all about it. Of course you can come over, but I'm still at the bridal shop."

"I didn't know you planned to work late tonight," Gordon said. "I thought business was slow right now."

"I'm not working on bridal shop business," she said. "I'm dumping bootleg whiskey down the drain."

"What?"

"We don't know if the whiskey is safe to drink, so I won't want it hanging around. I asked Sam and Jeff to have one of their crew bring the crates up from the basement and over here to the shop. They did that this afternoon. I got busy right after closing time."

"You've been uncorking bottles and pouring the contents down the drain for almost four hours?" he asked.

"I took a break and ran over to Pete's for dinner. To tell you the truth, the repetition has been cathartic. I pulled up my favorite playlist of Broadway show tunes, and it's actually fun."

"Are you almost done?" he asked.

"I've got three more crates to go," she said.

"How about if Judy, Sunday, and I come to the bridal shop to present our findings?" he said. "I'll stay and help you finish up."

"I wouldn't say no to either of those," she said.

"We'll see you in about five minutes," he replied.

Anita finished emptying the bottles in the crate she'd been working on before her friends arrived. She locked the front door behind them and escorted them to one of the high, rectangular worktables that sat empty beneath a bright overhead light.

"Oh, this will be perfect," Judy said. "Much better than my kitchen table."

Gordon opened his satchel and spread its contents across the table: dog-eared newspaper clippings, a receipt book, a cloth-bound diary stained with age, a packet of handwritten letters tied with a frayed velvet ribbon, and a folded telegram.

"I believe these supply the answers we've been seeking," Gordon said, gesturing to the items on the table.

Sunday and Judy perched on tall stools, while Anita leaned against the edge of the table, peering down at the items like they were puzzle pieces.

"Candy Alley was started in 1903 by Charlotte's grandparents," Gordon began. "Her grandmother's parents were successful candy makers in Boston, and her grandmother's older brother was set to inherit the business. Charlotte's grandparents moved to Westbury as newlyweds with her family's blessing and the recipes from the Boston store. They bought the building, set up shop, and were off to a fine start in the prosperous, turn-of-the-century community of Westbury."

He picked up the bundle of letters.

"These are from Charlotte's great-grandmother to her daughter. At first, the tone is light and breezy. The newlyweds were happy, the store was thriving, and the birth of Charlotte's mother is discussed with great affection. They wrote about planning a trip for the Boston relatives to visit Westbury and meet their granddaughter. That's where the letters end."

He lifted the fragile telegram and handed it to Anita.

She scanned the brief message and gasped before reading it again. "I take it this is from the brother who stayed in Boston and ran the original store?"

"It seems so," Gordon said.

"How tragic," Anita murmured. "That elderly couple got

diphtheria and died within a week of each other—before they could make the trip."

Gordon pointed to the date. "1910. At that point, the Westbury candy store was still prospering. The trail goes dark until 1917."

He lifted the newspaper clippings.

"Here's the obituary for Charlotte's grandfather. He died in a hunting accident. There are several news stories about it, too."

"Oh gosh," Anita whispered.

"You'll want to read these," Gordon said. "There was speculation at the time that it wasn't accidental, but the police couldn't prove anything. Hector Martin—Silas's son—was the close friend who allegedly shot him. There were rumors that Silas used his influence to clear his son's name."

"I guess some things never change," Anita said grimly. "How awful for Charlotte's grandmother."

"She continued to run the candy store after his death. World War I broke out in 1914, and the U.S. joined the fight in 1917. While general food rationing didn't hit America, sugar was in short supply. The government restricted imports from the Caribbean, and overseas demand soared."

"That would've been devastating for a candy maker," Anita said.

Gordon nodded. "Our next clue is in this receipt book. It appears Charlotte's grandmother turned her culinary skills to whiskey making. The first entry shows a sale of twelve bottles of high-proof whiskey to Silas Martin in 1921."

"When was Prohibition again?" Anita asked.

"1920 to 1933," Sunday supplied.

Gordon flipped more pages. "Her biggest customers were Silas Martin and the Olsson family. She made regular sales to both. My guess is they kept her and the candy business afloat."

"Then why was all that inventory left in my basement?" Anita asked.

"We may have found the answer in my mother's diary. My mother and Charlotte were great friends," Judy said, rising to take over. "But first, more of the backstory. Charlotte's grandmother died right after Prohibition ended. Her mother took over the shop, and, by then, liquor was legal again. Those twelve crates were probably bottles she couldn't sell. Charlotte's mother may have feared being arrested if anyone knew she had them, so she locked them away in the basement."

"Why didn't Charlotte get rid of them later? Why hang onto them for decades?"

"Here's the clue from the diary. My mom wrote that Charlotte was bitten by a poisonous spider in the basement as a child and nearly died. She never went down there again —not once. She probably didn't remember those bottles were still there."

Anita took a step back and gestured to the table. "What a story. Did you find anything about where the still might have been?"

Gordon, Judy, and Sunday shook their heads.

"This secret was very well kept, it seems," Sunday said. "I'm not sure we'll ever learn more."

Anita bit her lower lip. "This is a story of women doing what was required to survive."

"In a way, it fits the theme of your museum," Sunday said. "Women using their intelligence and ingenuity to get by."

"I like the sound of that," Anita replied. "Now, more than ever, I want my museum to incorporate this history."

Gordon walked from the table to the open crates lining the perimeter of the workroom, their lids leaning nearby. He picked up one of the empty bottles and held it to the light.

"I have an idea," he said. "Have a plexiglass partition made with shelves for these bottles. It might work as a room divider. You could include a few of the crates to honor the building's past."

"That's a genius idea," Sunday said. "These bottles are beautiful. If you positioned the partition to catch the light, it would be stunning."

"I love it," Anita said. "But I don't know where I'd find something like that."

"You'd have it custom-made," Gordon replied. "Art galleries do this sort of thing all the time. I have sources. And it's not terribly expensive."

Judy blew out a breath. "I can't believe how interesting this building has turned out to be. Who would've thought?"

Sunday stood and pointed to three crates set apart from the others. "Do those still contain full bottles?"

Anita nodded. "Gordon said he'd stay and help me finish emptying them."

"I'll lend a hand too," Sunday said, stepping over and removing four bottles. "Where do I dump these?"

Anita pointed toward the break room.

"Many hands make light work, as my grandmother used to say," Judy added, joining them.

Within half an hour, the remaining whiskey had been poured down the drain. They washed the bottles and returned them to their crates to dry.

Gordon and Anita said goodbye to Sunday and Judy. He packed the papers back into his satchel, and he and Anita linked arms as they walked to his car.

"I'm tired," she said, resting her head on his shoulder. "But my thoughts are racing. I don't know how I'll ever get to sleep."

"Sleep is overrated," he murmured, bending to kiss her.

CHAPTER 28

"They're here!" Sean cried, racing Sally, Daisy, and Snowball to the front door. Dodger's excited barking soon joined the familiar voices of the three dogs.

David and Dodger stepped into the chaos inside the front door. David commanded Dodger to be quiet and dropped to one knee to greet and calm the other dogs. Sally, Frank's older border collie mix, backed out of the thrashing tangle of tails, keeping her dignity intact. Snowball rose onto her hind legs and placed her front paws on Dodger's shoulders. He turned toward her, and they bumped noses in greeting. Daisy, Sean's Australian shepherd–cattle dog mix, stood taller than Dodger and waited patiently for his attention.

"Mom said we should take the dogs into the backyard," Sean said. "To let them run."

"Good idea," David replied. "It feels almost like spring

today, but the weather forecast is calling for record-breaking low temperatures starting tomorrow night. It'll be too cold for them to do anything but go out for a quick bathroom break."

Sean led the way down the hall and through the kitchen to the back door. The four dogs burst outside, racing around the perimeter of the yard like thoroughbreds erupting from the starting gate.

"Look at them go," Sean said.

"I know," David replied. "Snowball has the shortest legs, but she's in the lead. That little dog has wheels."

"Does Dodger like working at the Guide Dog Center?" Sean asked.

"He's not allowed to come with me," David said. "My landlord has a small dog, so Dodger has company during the day and someone to play with. But I think he really loves afternoons like this, when he gets to run with a pack."

They watched as Sally stopped to sniff something under a bush. The other three dogs noticed she'd fallen behind and joined her.

"Are your mom and Frank home?" David asked.

"They're in the garage doing something," Sean replied. "Mom said they'll come inside to say hello when they're done. Did you see our new car?"

"You mean that huge SUV in the driveway?" David chuckled. "I could hardly miss it."

"We got it yesterday," Sean said. "I didn't even know we were looking for a new car. Mom told Frank they both need cars that hold seven passengers. Frank's Mercedes SUV didn't have a third row, so that's why they got this one."

"It sure looks fancy," David said.

"Did you get a new car?" Sean asked. "The one you pulled up in isn't yours."

"No, mine is still in the shop," David said. "It needs a lot more work than we thought. That's my mom's car."

Sean nodded. "I heard Mom and Frank talking about you needing a safe car."

"I know," David said. "I want to leave tomorrow because the storm bringing freezing temperatures to Westbury is also supposed to dump heavy snow between here and California. Driving through snow isn't my favorite thing to do. My mom offered to let me take her car back to school. She'd drive mine once it's fixed, but I don't think that's fair to her."

The dogs continued romping and playing in the sunshine.

"I've taught Daisy how to jump through a hula hoop," Sean said. "Wanna see?"

"Of course," David replied. "That's great. Are you going to work on agility skills with her?"

"I am," Sean said. "There's a class starting this spring. As long as I keep my grades up, Daisy and I can enroll."

He whistled for Daisy and picked up a hula hoop leaning against the side of the house. "Sit," he commanded.

Daisy's bottom hit the ground, her gaze never leaving the hoop.

Sean walked ten paces away, held the hoop vertically six inches off the ground, and said, "Okay, girl."

Daisy bounded forward and cleared the hurdle with inches to spare.

David clapped. "Nice going, you two! I'll bet she'll be a natural at agility. I can't wait to see her when I come home for Easter."

Dodger spied his doggy friend and came trotting over.

"Does he remember how?" Sean asked.

"Only one way to find out," David replied.

Sean held the hoop out to David, but David shook his head. "Give it a shot. Let's see whether or not he can do it."

Sean repeated the commands with Dodger, who sailed through the hoop with easy grace. He continued the game with each dog, raising the hoop a little higher each time.

Snowball eventually joined them but retreated when offered a chance to jump, electing instead to curl up in the sun beside Sally for a nap.

Loretta opened the kitchen door and stepped outside. "I thought that was you when we heard the dogs barking," she said to David. "Looks like you two and the dogs are making the most of this beautiful afternoon."

"We are," David said. "It's hard to believe it'll be below zero in forty-eight hours."

"Right? I hate to think about it. Spend as much time out here as you can," she added. "Before you leave, Frank and I need your help with something in the garage—if that's okay."

"Of course it is," David said. "Is Frank still in the garage?"

Loretta nodded. "But it can wait. Enjoy your time outside."

"No, I'll help him now," David said.

Sean looked from David to his mother. "Do you need me, too?"

"Of course we do," Loretta said, opening an arm to him. "We want both of you there."

The two boys followed her around the side of the house to the garage. Loretta tapped the key code into the garage door opener and stepped aside.

The door rose slowly. Loretta's large SUV sat in its usual spot. Next to it was Frank's compact Mercedes SUV. The metallic paint gleamed in the sunshine streaming through the open door. A wide red ribbon encircled the newly detailed vehicle, and a gigantic red bow sat on top.

Frank stood next to the driver's side door, key fob in hand, smiling so broadly it looked like it hurt.

David glanced from Frank to Loretta and back again.

Sean clamped a hand over his mouth to suppress a giggle.

"What do you need help with?" David asked, eyes narrowed in confusion.

"We got a new car yesterday," Loretta said. "I'm going to take the new one, and Frank's getting my old car. That means we have one too many cars."

"You know how much I hate parking a car in the driveway or on the street," Frank said. "We were wondering if you'd take this one off our hands."

David took a step back. "I ... I can't afford a new car—much less your Mercedes."

"We're not selling it to you, son," Frank said. "We're giving it to you."

"That's why they put the bow on it," Sean interjected, grinning at David.

David placed his hands on either side of his head. "You can't do that. This is far too valuable."

"I already talked to your mother," Frank said. "It took some convincing, but she finally said it's okay."

He and Loretta stepped closer to David.

"We want to do this," Loretta said. "You're like a second son to us. I would've worried myself sick about you on the road to California in that old car. You know how hectic our life is with the twins and the three big kids? The last thing I need is one more thing to fret about—especially something I can fix."

"We've been talking about getting a new car for weeks," Frank added. "Loretta's telling the truth. Instead of trading mine in, we gave ourselves peace of mind by giving it to you. There's an extended warranty that goes with it, too."

Like a time-lapse video, David's expression shifted from confusion to disbelief to joy.

Frank pressed the key fob into David's hand. "Ready to take it for a spin? It has a few more gizmos and gadgets than your old car. I'll explain everything, so you're comfortable driving it back to California."

David exclaimed, "Oh my gosh, that would be wonderful! This means I can leave in the morning and avoid the storm."

"That's what your mother and I thought," Loretta said.

Frank opened the driver's side door for David.

"What should I do with my old car?" David asked.

"Sell it. I'll bet the repair shop will give you a fair price," Frank said. "I've dealt with them for years."

"I'll give you whatever money I get for it," David said.

"You don't need to do that," Frank said. "Keep the money. There'll be something you need."

"If you won't take the money, I'll donate it to Forever Guides," David said.

Loretta wrapped him in a hug. "You are a dear," she said.

Frank clapped him on the back. "We'll gratefully accept it." He walked around to the passenger side and opened the door. "Hey, Sean, want to come with us?"

"Sure!" Sean said. He slipped into the back seat.

Loretta pulled the oversized bow off the car. She waved as David shifted into reverse and pulled his new vehicle out of the garage.

CHAPTER 29

*A*nita backed her SUV to the rear door of Archer's Bridal. She glanced at Gordon in the passenger seat. "This is as close as I can get to the door. I'm not sure if all fifteen sewing machines will fit in one trip."

Gordon looked at the cargo space behind him. "Let's try," he said. "We'll put padding around them so they don't knock against each other on the drive to the library."

"I've already wrapped them in blankets or towels," Anita said. "They're waiting on the floor inside the back door." She placed her gloved hand on his elbow. "It's 6:45 in the morning and twenty below zero. Are you wondering what you've gotten yourself into? I'm so sorry, Gordon."

He put his hand over hers and gave it a reassuring squeeze. "The weather isn't ideal," he said, "but there's nowhere I'd rather be. At least it's dry and we won't have to

BARBARA HINSKE

be out in the cold for long. Other than loading the machines here and unloading them at the library, we'll be inside while we're setting up the display."

"Are you ready?" Anita asked.

Gordon nodded. "Let's pull our scarves up over our noses. We'll talk once we've finished transferring the machines to your car."

"I'll leave it running and the heater on full blast," Anita said.

They each pulled their knitted caps down over their ears and wrapped their scarves over their noses. Both of them wore down-filled gloves and puffer coats.

Anita unlocked the shop while Gordon opened the hatch-back. Working together, they quickly stowed fourteen sewing machines in the back of Anita's SUV. She began repositioning them to make room for the fifteenth.

Gordon waved her off, pulling his scarf down to speak. "I'll hold the last one on my lap," he said.

She nodded, and he hoisted the final machine. Anita locked the back door to Archer's Bridal, and they each reclaimed their spot in the front seat.

Anita turned to face Gordon and laughed as she pulled off her fogged-up glasses. She dug a tissue from her coat pocket to wipe away the condensation that formed the moment she stepped from the frigid air into the warm car.

"Can I have one of those?" Gordon asked, extending a hand. "My nose hairs froze in the short time it took me to say that one sentence to you." He blew his nose.

Anita pulled out of the parking area and headed toward the Highpointe College Library. "I'm glad they got the roof at my new building done when they did," she said. "Sam told me the roofers won't work in this weather."

"Having a new furnace is helpful, too," Gordon said. "The interior work can now move forward."

"They're supposed to start refinishing the wood floors next week."

"How long will that take?"

"Sam thinks it'll be a week, give or take."

"Remodeling that space is coming along fast," Gordon said. "Other than a delay in getting the air-conditioning unit, you've completed everything on schedule."

"And under budget," Anita added. She gestured toward the temperature display on the dashboard. "A delay in installing the air conditioning won't be a problem for a long time."

Gordon chuckled. "I think good luck has blessed your project from start to finish—and nobody deserves that more than you."

"I have to admit," Anita said, "I'm encouraged. I was worried about what was in those crates in the basement, but that turned out to be something interesting to add to the museum. With that drama behind us, I believe everything will go smoothly from now on."

They pulled into the employee parking lot behind the library. Sunday's car was the only other car there. Anita backed up to the loading dock, just as Sunday had directed.

We're here, Anita texted.

The metal double doors swung open, casting a bright rectangle of light into the pre-dawn darkness. Sunday stood outlined against the glow. Clad from head to toe in sturdy rubber boots and a thick down jacket with the hood tied close to her head, she looked like a miniature Michelin Man.

Anita and Gordon leapt from the car, and the three of them quickly transferred the sewing machines onto rolling carts waiting inside. Sunday slammed the double doors shut behind them, cutting off the icy air.

"Should I move my car?" Anita asked.

"It's fine," Sunday replied, stamping her feet to warm them. "I checked with Lyla—we're not expecting any deliveries until this afternoon. I don't want to send you back out in that weather if I don't have to."

"Thank you," Anita said.

"Let's roll these carts to the exhibit space," Sunday said. "With the three of us, it'll only take two trips. Follow me."

Sunday led them through the deserted library to the exhibit hall. The room was warm, and they shed their outer layers.

"I've never been in a library before it opened," Anita said, glancing around as they returned for the second group of carts. "It's so peaceful."

"I was thinking the same thing," Gordon said. "It's also got an anticipatory energy. Like the moment the conductor taps his wand on the music stand before the orchestra begins to play."

"That's exactly how I feel," Sunday said. "As soon as the doors open, the magic begins. Knowledge is the most powerful force for good in the world. I know we have the internet now, but libraries are still the worldwide repositories of information. The written word has contributed to the formation of the middle class." She stopped abruptly. "Sorry. I'm going on and on."

"I agree with you one hundred percent," Gordon said. "It's obvious you love this place and your part in it. Highpointe is lucky to have you."

Sunday flushed with pleasure. "I've got a staff meeting in a few minutes," she said. "The library will open in half an hour. Is it okay if I leave you here to set up?"

"Of course," Anita said. "Gordon and I have got this."

"If you need anything, text me. I'll have my phone with me."

"Thank you, but we won't," Anita said. "Don't worry about us."

Sunday gazed at the lumpy shapes wrapped in blankets and towels. "I'm excited to see what you've got under there," she said, pointing at the carts.

"We'll let you know when we're done," Anita said. "You can tell us if you think we need to move anything or make adjustments."

"Sounds good," Sunday said. She turned toward the stairwell that led to her office on the third floor, but paused and looked back. "Lyla needs to know what you've named the museum. She's got the graphics ready to go except for the one that says *Coming Soon.* She needs the name for that."

"I'm sorry it's taken me so long," Anita said. "I've been waffling. It doesn't seem like the name I came up with is quite right."

"I like the name you chose," Gordon said.

Anita shrugged. "I guess I'm being too picky, but it seems like something is missing from it. Anyway, I'm being silly. The name I've chosen is Stitches in Time: A Museum Celebrating Vintage Sewing Machines."

Sunday clasped her hands together. "I love it! That's a terrific name. I'll tell Lyla. She'll have that sign finished by the end of the day."

CHAPTER 30

*M*aggie stepped out of the entrance of the administration building and pulled the hood of her arctic parka over her head. Susan's car waited at the curb. She clutched the hood closed at her throat and hurried down the wide stone steps to the car.

"Thanks for picking me up," she said as she climbed inside.

"Of course," Susan replied. "It's far too cold for you to walk to the library." She reached over and ran her hand along the quilted arm of Maggie's coat. "This is nice and warm, isn't it?"

"It sure is," Maggie said. "I didn't think I'd ever need it here in Westbury, but I'm glad you gave it to me as a 'just because' gift."

"Aaron bought me one for Christmas, and I thought the

same thing," Susan said. "Then it got so cold a couple of weeks ago, and I was thankful to have it. When I saw the forecast for another record freeze, I decided to buy you one."

"You are the best daughter," Maggie said. "Thank you—and happy Valentine's Day."

"Same to you, Mom. What are you doing the rest of the day?"

"John made reservations for us at Stuart's Steakhouse tonight. After the grand opening of the sewing machine exhibit at the library, I thought I'd head home and finish my day there. I've worked late every night for the past week. I don't have any meetings today. If it hadn't been for Anita's exhibition opening, I would've worked from home the entire day."

"I like the sound of that," Susan said, pulling into the library parking lot. "And instead of working when you get home, I suggest you do something you enjoy. You're entitled to an afternoon off."

"What are you doing today?" Maggie asked, changing the subject. "You're awfully chipper. Are you feeling better?"

Susan parked the car. "It's like I'm a new person," she said. "I haven't had morning sickness for the past two days. It's like someone flipped a switch—no more nausea, and my energy level is back to normal."

"That's wonderful, honey," Maggie said. "You must be past the first trimester."

Susan nodded. "Last time, I was sick my whole pregnancy. I hope this one is different."

"Are you and Aaron going out to dinner?"

Susan shook her head. "We didn't make reservations because I was so sick. We'd never get them now, anyway," she said. "Plus, we don't have a babysitter."

Maggie cocked her head to one side. "You remember that you just told me to take the afternoon to do whatever I want?"

Susan looked at her mother and nodded.

"The thing I'd most like to do is spend time with Julia. Can you bring her to Rosemont after we're done here?" Maggie's eyes sparkled. "Since you're finally feeling good again, why don't we keep her overnight? You and Aaron can take our reservation at Stuart's, and I'll make something at home."

"Oh, Mom, that's so nice. But I don't want to interfere with John's plans for your Valentine's Day."

Maggie rolled her eyes. "You know as well as I do that there is no person on the face of this earth he would rather spend an evening with than his granddaughter. We can go to Stuart's anytime." She took her daughter's hand. "I know how miserably sick you've been, honey. I'd love to give you and Aaron a chance to enjoy yourselves without worrying about Julia."

Susan pressed back into her seat, a smile spreading across her face like kindling catching flame. "Honestly, Mom, I can't think of anything we'd like better."

"It's a plan, then," Maggie said. "Now let's get inside. I don't want to miss Anita's remarks. I hope this cold weather doesn't keep the turnout down. She's put in a lot of effort."

"I had the same thought," Susan said. "So I called our book club members the day before yesterday. All of them are going to attend."

Maggie grinned at her daughter. "I adore the way the women of Westbury support each other."

CHAPTER 31

*A*nita stopped at the information desk inside the main entrance to the Highpointe College library.

The young woman behind the desk greeted her with a warm smile. "You're Miss Archer, aren't you?"

"Yes," Anita said, surprised. "How did you know?"

"I recognize you from your photo in the exhibit hall."

"Oh," Anita replied. "I didn't think anyone would pay attention to that."

"Lots of people have gone through the exhibit. I went on the first day. It was absolutely fascinating! I told my mom about it, and she brought my grandmother and my aunt. We all loved it."

Anita placed a hand on her chest. "That's nice to hear," she said.

"Everyone who works here has seen it. And lots of other people, too. You must be here for the grand opening."

"I am," Anita said, unzipping her heavy coat and pulling the scarf from around her neck.

"If I didn't have to work at the desk, I'd attend your talk."

"Will your family be here, do you think?"

"Mom and Grandma had planned to come," the young woman said, "but it's too cold for Grandma to go outside. She lives with us, and Mom can't leave her alone for that long."

Anita cast a worried glance over her shoulder at Gordon.

"I'm sure plenty of people will come out to hear you speak, sweetheart," he said.

"The library set up chairs and a podium," the young woman added. "Someone delivered snacks this morning, too. Normally those aren't allowed in the library, but Sunday okayed it. She said they're a surprise for you."

Gordon placed his hand on the small of Anita's back. "Let's go see that surprise," he said, steering her toward the exhibition space.

A red velvet rope cordoned off the entrance. Five rows of ten chairs faced a wooden podium. The only person inside the exhibit was Sunday. She leaned over a rectangular table covered with a black tablecloth. A crystal vase filled with red roses sat at the center of the table. Sunday was removing decorated sugar cookies from bakery boxes stamped with the Laura's Bakery logo and placing them onto silver trays.

Gordon unhooked the rope, and Anita preceded him into the exhibit.

Sunday turned to them. "Good morning! Are you excited about today?" She walked over and held out her hands for their coats and scarves. "I'll stash these in a closet near the staff break room. My goodness—you look fabulous," she said to Anita. "That red dress fits you to a T."

Anita smiled. "Given the business I'm in, my clothes have to be perfectly tailored."

"I guess that's true." Sunday chuckled. "It's an excellent advertisement for your services." She turned to Gordon and took in his black suit, white shirt, red tie, and red pocket square. "You're dapper, too. You both look like you're straight out of an advertisement for a swanky restaurant on Valentine's Day."

"Thank you," he said. "I've got a tough act to keep up with." He winked at Anita.

"Come look at these cookies," Sunday said, leading them to the table. "Laura toured the exhibit last week and asked if she could furnish them. I thought it was a wonderful idea and approved the exception to our no-food rule."

Anita and Gordon leaned in to look. The cookies were shaped like sewing machines and elaborately decorated with black, red, blue, and green icing. The word Singer was piped in gold.

"My goodness," Anita said, studying one. "These look like the Singer Model 15K that sits at the entrance to the exhibit!" She looked at Gordon, her eyes wide.

"They're miniature works of art," he said. "I'm amazed by Laura's skill. This must have taken her a very long time."

Sunday chuckled. "Laura dropped them off about an hour ago. She said she stayed up very late last night to finish them. She wanted them to be nice for you."

"I don't know what to say," Anita said. "The roses on the table are gorgeous, too."

"Josh sent them to me for Valentine's Day. I brought them down from my office to dress up the table."

"That was extremely thoughtful of you." Gratitude warmed Anita's voice.

Gordon took a photo of Anita and the cookie table, followed by close-ups of the individual cookies.

"Laura set a dozen cookies aside in individual cellophane bags for you to take to your shop," Sunday said. "She wanted you to share them with your crew."

"Laura's the best. I know what I'm going to order for the grand opening of the museum itself," Anita said. "These cookies are just the thing."

"It's twenty minutes before noon," Sunday said. "People will arrive soon. I'll put your coats away and be right back. We'll set you up with a lapel microphone so you can get comfortable at the podium."

Gordon and Anita took one last turn around the exhibit before Sunday returned. She clipped a lavalier mic to the collar of Anita's dress and showed her how to turn the power on and off.

"I'll introduce you," Sunday said. "Even though everyone in town already knows you, it's the thing to do."

Anita forced herself to swallow.

"Are you nervous?" Gordon asked.

Anita nodded. "I've never done public speaking. I woke up this morning in a panic, thinking, *What in the world am I doing?*"

"That means you'll give an excellent speech," Gordon said. "A touch of stage fright sharpens your focus."

Anita slanted her eyes to his. "You make speeches in your line of work all the time. Is that how it works for you?"

"Absolutely," he replied.

"Have you got notes?" Sunday asked.

Gordon reached into the breast pocket of his suit coat and handed Anita a 3x5 card.

"I put bullet points on here," she said, lifting the card. "Gordon said it's a good way to remind myself of what I want to say, and it prevents me from reading my speech. That would be boring."

"Well done, you," Sunday said, leaning over to peek at the card.

Anita turned her back to the podium and faced Sunday. "I'm going to talk about learning to sew on the very machine that's at the front of the exhibit," she said. "My grandmother used that machine in the bridal shop until 1980. I'll briefly describe the machines the bridal shop acquired over the decades and used through the three generations Archer's Bridal has been in my family."

Sunday smiled, encouraging her to go on.

"Rather than talk about the technical aspects of the machines themselves, I'll explain the impact that owning a sewing machine had on a woman's daily life. The sewing machine became popular before premade clothes were readily available. Using a sewing machine slashed the time needed to make clothes and household textiles. Women used their newfound free time for housework, studying, relaxing, and even paid employment. That's what happened to my grandmother. She started her alterations business and grew it into a bridal salon because she owned her own sewing machine."

Sunday clasped her hands together. "This is going to be a fabulous presentation. People will love hearing that."

"A sewing machine was a highly coveted item," Anita continued. "They were often given as engagement gifts instead of diamond rings. It was a status symbol to have one. That's why these early machines are so exquisitely designed and decorated. My museum will showcase some of the furniture cabinets that housed them, too. The Singer Sewing Machine Company was once the largest cabinetmaker in the country. If you had one of these beautiful machines, you wanted to show it off—in your living room."

"Brilliant," Sunday said. "I can't wait to hear more. But I think it's time we start." She took Anita's elbow and turned her toward the audience.

Anita gasped. The seats were all full, and people stood behind the last row.

"I was so focused on talking to you, I didn't hear anyone come in," she whispered to Sunday.

Maggie, Susan, and the eight other women from their book club filled the front row.

Gordon squeezed Anita's elbow. "You're going to be brilliant," he said quietly before joining the group standing at the back.

Sunday stepped to the podium and began her introduction.

Anita spotted Gordon in the crowd. He gave her a thumbs-up.

Sunday concluded her remarks, and Anita took a deep breath. She squared her shoulders and began her talk.

CHAPTER 32

Alistair

We've had a busy day. The mail carrier just left, and three packages were delivered to the front door this morning. Roman and Eve—obviously—had leapt out of their warm beds to race to the door, barking their heads off. Household security was one of their primary jobs, and I appreciated their attention to it.

I knew we still had hours to go before Maggie or John got home. The cats coiled on the sofa, looking like someone had stitched them into a furry throw. Eve and Roman were in their baskets by the hearth. Because my attic was so cold recently, I stayed downstairs.

The dogs and I were getting drowsy when the click of the opening garage door roused us. Eve and Roman lifted their heads from their paws to listen. Someone opened the door from the garage, and they bolted from their beds. I followed at a more decorous pace.

Maggie came through the door, depositing her satchel on the floor. She bent and greeted her faithful companions, then hurried through the house and raced up the stairs to her bedroom.

The three of us followed at her heels.

Maggie slipped off her business suit and tossed it onto the bed. She kicked off her heels and removed her expensive gold watch and fine jewelry, depositing them on a tray atop her jewelry chest. She entered her closet, pulled on a sweat-shirt and sweatpants, and shoved her feet into fuzzy slippers.

Before we even had time to make ourselves comfortable, she tore out of the room and back down the stairs.

The mistress of my house was a creature of habit. Her bedroom routine always included hanging up her clothes and storing her jewelry. Today's behavior was most out of character. Something was up.

I was at her side when she stepped off the bottom stair onto the first floor. I expected her to retrieve her satchel and begin typing away at that silver rectangle that unfolded. That was what she did when she came home in the middle of the afternoon. But Maggie did no such thing.

She lit fires in the library and the living room while humming "My Funny Valentine." She was in fine spirits, so I knew nothing was wrong, but I couldn't figure out what was going on.

I didn't have long to wait.

The doorbell rang, and Maggie was there so fast she beat both Eve and Roman. She flung open the door, and there stood two of my favorite people.

Susan was on the threshold, holding the hand of a small person I knew had to be Julia, although she was so thoroughly bundled up against the cold, I could barely see her face.

Maggie drew them both inside and shut the door behind them.

"Grammy!" Julia's excited cry was muffled by her scarf.

Maggie dropped to her knees and helped the little girl out of her protective outerwear. Julia flung her arms around her grandmother, almost knocking Maggie to the floor. Maggie rocked her granddaughter from side to side, then steadied the little girl and got to her feet.

Susan placed a bright pink backpack decorated with Disney princesses by the stairs. "Did you check with John?" she asked. "Is this really okay?"

"Oh, please," Maggie said, rolling her eyes. "You'd think that man had won the lottery. He's picking up a cheese pizza on the way home and promised to be here by five thirty."

"Julia loves cheese pizza," Susan said. "I hope you didn't order that only because she likes it. You should get what you want."

"It's fine," Maggie replied. "John and I didn't even talk about it. He simply texted me that he'd ordered it."

"He certainly wins Grandpa of the Year—again," Susan

said, grinning. "I hope he understands how grateful Aaron and I are."

Maggie took her daughter's elbow. "He does," she said warmly. "And now, I think you'd better turn around and get out of here. You've got a dinner date with your husband— and enough time to relax in a bubble bath before you go out."

"That sounds like heaven," Susan said. "I can't remember the last time I did that." She placed her hand on the door-knob. "If anything goes wrong, or if you need us to pick up Julia, say the word. We'll come get her anytime."

"You won't need to," Maggie said. "Enjoy yourselves. I'll drop her off at your house on my way to work tomorrow."

"Thanks, Mom. Aaron and I couldn't have asked for a better Valentine's Day gift." She opened the door only wide enough to slip out, but the cold air still gusted in and blew me back into the living room.

Maggie and Julia spent the afternoon drawing hearts on pink construction paper as a Valentine card for John. When Julia grew tired of that, Maggie read her an excellent rhyming book about a llama, and then they watched a show about a blue heeler puppy. I was so entertained, I didn't notice until John came home that the sun had set.

Not only did he have the pizza, he entered the house carrying a teddy bear the size of Julia.

"Gramps!" Julia sprang from the sofa and ran full tilt into his arms.

They ate dinner, and Maggie reminded John that Julia's bedtime was approaching. It had been an unexpectedly engaging day. I was greedy and couldn't stop myself from wanting more.

"I'll put away the leftover pizza and wipe the counters," Maggie said. "It'll only take five minutes. I know Julia's excited about playing her favorite game with her grandpa."

I whipped my head around to look at John.

He took Julia's hand and led her into the living room. John went down on all fours. "Ready for the animal guessing game?" he asked.

Julia cheered and clapped her hands.

It *was* going to happen. I executed three fast spins out of sheer joy.

John raised one arm in front of his face and let out a trumpeting sound.

"El-fant!" Julia screamed.

John grinned. "Very good." He rocked back on his heels, bowed his arms, and scratched at his sides with his fingertips, while making a who-who-ha-ha sound.

"Monkey!" Julia shouted.

"Can you show me the monkey?" he asked.

Julia leapt to her feet and threw herself into her impersonation.

John's grin stretched so wide it almost turned him inside out. I grasped the mantel to steady myself.

The game continued through a wide range of zoo animals, farm animals, and domestic pets. Julia knew them all.

Maggie, who had slipped into a chair by the hearth,

finally spoke as John was searching his brain for another animal. "We may have a future veterinarian here," she said, smiling at them.

John grinned. "That'd be fine by me. But I want her to pursue whatever career interests her as an adult."

Maggie got up and rubbed his shoulder. "I know you do," she said softly. "And, right now, we don't need to think about it—because it's time for a bath and bed." She held out her hand to Julia.

Julia grabbed the giant teddy bear John had given her and stumbled toward Maggie.

"I'll carry that upstairs for you," John said, taking the bear from her.

The three of them joined hands and walked together up the stairs.

I hung back and savored the sight of these people who brought so much love into my house.

CHAPTER 33

"This was the most interesting presentation," the woman said. "I'm going straight to my attic when I get home and pulling out my great-grandmother's old machine. I can't wait to find out more about it!"

"I'm glad you enjoyed it," Anita replied, shaking the hand of the last person waiting in line to speak with her.

"I'll watch the newspaper for your opening date," the woman added. "I plan to be the first person in line." She gave their clasped hands a warm squeeze before disappearing into the library.

Anita turned to Gordon. "Wow," she said. "I didn't expect people to line up to chat with me after my little talk."

"Your speech was absolutely riveting," Gordon said. "Well organized, interesting, and beautifully delivered. You, my dear," looking her straight in the eyes, "are a natural."

She flushed with pleasure. "I don't know about that."

Sunday approached them from the side. "What a complete success! People are going to leave here and tell everyone they know about this exhibit. We'll be busier than we ever imagined. Talk about the perfect way to launch our new exhibition space in the library!"

"I'm glad you're pleased," Anita said. "Old sewing machines—who knew? I've been pushing to finish the renovations to Candy Alley so I could get out of your hair. I thought you'd want to install a more interesting exhibit."

"Based on today," Sunday said, "the library will be happy to offer you an extension."

Anita placed her hand on her forehead. "I never would've imagined such a successful outcome twenty-four hours ago."

"I did," Gordon said simply.

"I'm glad Laura saved that extra dozen cookies for you," Sunday said. "There's not a single one left on the table."

"Can we help put away the chairs and fold the table?" Gordon offered.

"Absolutely not," Sunday said firmly. "Our student staff will do that. Follow me to get your coats and your box of cookies." She led them toward the break room. "What are the two of you doing to celebrate your success?"

"We've got dinner reservations at seven at The Mill," Gordon said.

"Very nice," Sunday replied and went to fetch their coats.

"It's only three o'clock," Anita said to Gordon. "I'd like to drop these cookies at the bridal shop. My crew will be eager to hear how everything went."

Sunday handed them their coats.

Anita drew her in for a hug. "Thank you so much, Sunday. I'll never forget this day."

Sunday gave her a squeeze in return. "Have a lovely Valentine's dinner," she said.

"One more thing," Anita said. "Have you heard anything more about your wedding dress?"

"Yes!" Sunday snapped her fingers. "I meant to tell you and forgot. I got an email yesterday that it'll be delivered tomorrow. It got delayed in Chicago, but it finally started moving again. Will that be soon enough for alterations?"

"Of course," Anita said. "I'll be in the shop the entire day. Bring it over to try on, if you'd like."

"I'm having it delivered here to the library," Sunday replied. "I didn't want it sitting by my front door. If it arrives before you close, I'll call to see if you have time."

"I'll make time for you," Anita said. "And tell that young man of yours the flowers he sent you are beautiful."

They hugged again, and Anita and Gordon were on their way.

∾

ANITA LOCKED the door of Archer's Bridal and turned the sign from 'Open' to 'Closed.'

"I loved seeing how excited your seamstresses were for

you," Gordon said. "Your crew feels more like a group of sisters or cousins than employees."

"We've been together so long that we feel like family," Anita agreed. She looked at her watch, then tilted her eyes up to meet his. "Do you mind if we pop over to the museum? They completed refinishing the floors yesterday, but I was so busy practicing my talk that I didn't get over there. I know we can't walk around in there yet, but I'd love to open the door and peek inside."

"Sure," Gordon said. "I'd like to see them too. We've got plenty of time before our dinner reservation—and, frankly, neither of us needs to change clothes. Unless you want to, of course," he added quickly.

She patted his arm. "I was thinking the same thing."

"It's still wickedly cold," he said. "Let's drive over."

They got into his car and drove to the other side of the square. The new lock opened without effort, and a wall of warm air enveloped them. Dusk was falling. Even in the scant light from the open door and the window, the rich warmth of the original wooden floors glowed.

Anita gasped. "They look even more beautiful than I imagined. We'll have to come back tomorrow to see them in full daylight."

Gordon pulled his keychain from his pocket and switched on the small flashlight attached to it.

"How resourceful you are," Anita said, smiling.

Gordon grinned. "Any appraiser worth his or her salt carries a flashlight." He trained the beam slowly across the gleaming floor. "They did a beautiful job." As he swept the light toward the back wall, an irregular, oblong shape reflected in the beam.

"What's that?" Anita asked, her voice rising in alarm.

Gordon circled the dark patch with the light. He glanced at her, then slipped off his shoes.

"That's water, isn't it?" Her panic flared.

Gordon walked carefully across the floor to the spot. He bent to touch it, already knowing what he would find. He turned back to her and nodded.

Anita kicked off her shoes on the sidewalk and hurried to join him.

Gordon traced the wall with the flashlight beam to a spot on the ceiling that was saturated with water.

Anita and Gordon looked at each other.

"A broken pipe," she said, gripping his arm. "A pipe in the new upstairs bathroom must've frozen in this cold snap and then thawed when they cranked up the temperature to cure the floors."

"I'm afraid so," Gordon said.

Anita groaned. "We just completed so many things." She gestured around her. "Now we'll have to rip out walls and pipes, rebuild the bathroom, redo the ceiling, and refinish the floor." Her words came fast as she pointed out the affected areas.

"Call Sam and Jeff," Gordon said. "I'll go around the back to shut off the water."

"Do you even know where it is?" she asked.

He was already outside, slipping on his shoes. "I'll find it. Don't worry."

Sam and Jeff arrived fifteen minutes later.

"Tell Joan and Judy I'm sorry to ruin your Valentine's Day plans," Anita said as they came inside.

Sam turned on his flashlight and headed to the second floor without comment. The stern expression on his face spoke volumes.

"This never should've happened," Jeff muttered. "The flooring contractor was supposed to leave the water running at a trickle before they left."

Sam trotted down the stairs to rejoin them. "This is my fault. I should've turned the water on myself. I didn't want to walk on the floors before they're fully cured."

"Don't blame yourself. The flooring contractor knew what to do. How bad is it?" Jeff asked.

"A pipe burst in the bathroom wall upstairs," Sam said. "But there isn't much damage up there. I think most of the water ran down the wall. There must've been a low spot on the first floor where you found the puddle. Either the break just happened, or ..." he pointed to the basement door, "you've got a basement full of water. I'm going to find out."

Jeff clicked on his flashlight and followed Sam. Gordon and Anita hovered outside the doorway.

Sam hadn't taken more than three steps down the stairs when he called up to them. "Yep. The basement is flooded. You could go swimming down here."

He and Jeff returned, their expressions grim.

"I'll have the basement pumped tomorrow," Sam said. "I know you planned to remove the wood planks on the basement walls in the future, but they're waterlogged. Mold will be a problem, so we'll rip them out now. We'll repair the bathroom, and some of the drywall on the first-floor ceiling will need to come down. The wet spot on the floor may need attention, too. We'll dry it now and be back at first light to get started."

"I guess it could've been worse," Anita said, trying—but failing—to sound upbeat. "What do they say? Every dark cloud has a silver lining? I suppose us not having to redo everything is mine."

"We'll come see you tomorrow after we know more," Sam said.

"Looks like you two had plans tonight," Jeff said, taking in their dressy attire. "There's nothing more you can do here. We'll dry the floor and lock up."

Anita and Gordon stepped out onto the sidewalk. She checked her watch.

"We've missed our reservation," she said. "I'm sorry, Gordon."

"Don't be," he replied. "This couldn't be helped. If you've got eggs, cheese, and a few vegetables, I'll make omelets."

Anita rested her forehead against his shoulder. "Breakfast for supper?" she asked. "My absolute favorite." She tilted her head back to look up at him. "You, Gordon Mortimer, are the most remarkable man I've ever met."

CHAPTER 34

*a*nita answered Sunday's call on the first ring.

"It came!" Sunday cried.

"Hallelujah," Anita replied. "You must be relieved. Is it a great big box?"

"Surprisingly, no," Sunday said. "They must've really jammed it in there."

"Have you opened it?"

"Not yet," Sunday said. "It just arrived. I take my lunch in twenty minutes. Can I bring it to your shop then, and we'll open it together?"

"I was going to suggest that," Anita said. "We want to make sure we don't cut the fabric when we open it. I have the perfect tool."

"I'll be over in half an hour," Sunday said. "I can't wait to see my dress."

Anita prepared the larger of their two dressing rooms for Sunday. In the corner, she placed three-inch heeled pumps in various sizes. They kept them on hand for brides who forgot to bring their own heels. She didn't know if Sunday had purchased a veil, but their shop made them, so she hung several samples on a hook just in case.

She checked her watch. Sunday would be here any minute. Anita closed her eyes and inhaled. She never got over the thrill of watching a woman don the dress she'd said yes to. A wedding gown lit up a woman like no other garment she'd ever own.

The bell over the door tinkled.

Sunday entered the shop, hugging a cardboard box to her chest.

Anita intercepted her in the showroom, casting a wary glance at the box. It was too small for the dress in the photo that Sunday had shown her. The seller must have vacuum-packed it in place. It would take hours of steaming to remove the wrinkles. If it was too squished, Sunday would need to come back after work so Anita could spend the afternoon reviving the dress.

"I'm so excited I can hardly breathe," Sunday said, handing the box to Anita.

"Let's go into the workroom to open this," Anita said, leading her into the adjacent room. Her seamstresses were on their lunch break, and they had the space to themselves.

Anita opened the box, keeping the blade of her special knife angled outward. She expected the compressed dress to spring out the moment she cut the tape. But the flaps stayed put.

Sunday hovered over Anita's shoulder.

Anita opened the flaps and withdrew a slim package wrapped in iridescent tissue, sealed with a silver sticker. She felt Sunday's sharp intake of breath.

"No," Sunday cried. "That can't be my dress. It's way too small."

Anita broke the sticker's seal and lifted a narrow column of satin from the tissue. She held it up by its thin crystal straps, which connected to a plunging V-neckline and criss-crossed over a daringly low back.

Sunday burst into tears.

Anita draped the dress across the worktable and took Sunday into her arms.

"It's the wrong dress," Sunday sobbed. "It's completely wrong."

Anita nodded. "I'm so sorry, sweetheart. This isn't the first time I've seen this happen." She glanced over Sunday's shoulder at the dress. "It *is* beautiful and would look lovely on you—"

"But it's not me," Sunday said. "I hate that dress. I'd feel so out of place in it."

"We can't have that," Anita said firmly.

Sunday stepped back, wiping her face.

Anita's head seamstress, who had heard the commotion from the break room, rushed forward with a box of tissues and handed it to Sunday.

Sunday took a tissue and blew her nose. "I'm sorry about this," she said. "I'm acting like a petulant child."

"You're doing no such thing," the seamstress said. "Anyone would react the way you did. This is awful."

"I agree completely," Anita said. "What will you do?"

"I'm going right back to my office to contact the seller."

"Do they have a phone number?" Anita asked.

Sunday shook her head. "Just email." She pressed her eyes shut and groaned. "Based on how unresponsive the seller was when the dress was lost in transit, I don't know if I'll ever get the one I ordered."

"Did you pay with a credit card?" Anita asked.

Sunday nodded.

"At least you won't get stuck paying for something you don't want," Anita said.

"But what am I going to do for a dress? I'm getting married in six weeks."

"We have a few sample gowns we can sell," Anita offered. "But we don't have anything like the photo you showed me. Do you want to try on this dress? Just to see how it looks on you?"

"That's a good idea," the seamstress said. "People come in with an idea of what they want and end up saying yes to the exact opposite."

Sunday sighed. "I guess I should."

Anita showed her to the fitting room. Sunday stepped onto the raised platform, and the seamstress helped her into the slim satin dress. Sunday studied herself from every angle.

Anita watched Sunday's face in the mirror. The dress looked stunning on her—anyone could see that. And Sunday knew it too. But there was no sparkle in her eyes. She looked like a cashier relieved her register had balanced—satisfied but not overjoyed.

"Did you see it from behind?" Anita asked, adjusting the three-way mirror. "It's not as low in the back as I first thought. We can shorten the straps to bring it up even higher. Other than that, it fits you perfectly." Anita stepped onto the platform behind Sunday and lifted the dress by the straps so she could visualize the suggested alteration.

Sunday wiped the tears from under her eyes. "It's not as bad as I thought. I still want my dress, though. I'm going to go back to my office, find a phone number for the seller, and raise hell." She looked at Anita. "If they send me the correct dress now, will you have time to do the alterations?"

Anita glanced at her head seamstress.

"We'll get your dress ready," the woman said. "Even if we have to work the entire night before your wedding."

Sunday stifled a sob. "That's very nice of you," she whispered. She glanced at herself in the mirror again. "Really, this dress is fine. I mean—I'm marrying the man of my dreams. I'm being silly. It doesn't matter what I wear."

"Honey," Anita said gently, "if what a woman wore to her wedding didn't matter, we wouldn't be in business. Of course it matters. Let's get you out of this dress. Leave it with me for now. Go back to your office and see what you can do to get your real dress."

"Okay," Sunday said in a small voice.

The seamstress helped her step out of the dress and carried it to the workroom.

"I'll let you get dressed," Anita said, pulling the curtain closed behind her.

"Do you have a picture of the dress she wants?" the seamstress whispered when Anita caught up to her.

"I've seen one," Anita said. "It's a Cinderella ball gown style."

"Lots of lace appliqué or beading?"

"Not that I remember."

"We could make that dress for her," the seamstress said. "She's a perfect size six if I've ever seen one."

Anita looked at her, and the two women exchanged a conspiratorial smile.

"We already have yards of fabric on hand that we could use," the seamstress said. "Can you get your hands on a picture of that dress?"

"I'll ask her to send it to me," Anita said, snapping her fingers. "I'll tell her I'm going to make inquiries in bridal shops around the state."

"Ooh, I like that," the seamstress said.

"I'm afraid she's going to find out pretty quickly that this online seller doesn't have her dress," Anita said. "I'll get Sunday to send me the photo before she leaves."

"And we'll spend the afternoon figuring out how to make that sweet woman her dream dress."

CHAPTER 35

The young man bounded up the basement stairs two at a time and hurried across the first floor to where Jeff was studying a set of engineering plans unrolled on top of a glass display case.

"Hey, Jeff," he said, slightly out of breath.

Jeff kept his finger in place on the plans and looked up.

"I'm sorry to disturb you," the young man continued, "but you'll want to see this."

Jeff flipped his reading glasses to the top of his head and followed without a word.

They descended into the dank, musty basement. Workers had pumped out the standing water the day before. The young man had spent the morning removing the old white-washed wooden planks from three sides of the foundation, revealing uneven, rough, irregularly shaped fieldstone walls —typical of 19th-century construction.

But the fourth wall told a different story. He'd pried away two planks, and, instead of revealing stone, the standing work lights now shone into a dark, cavernous void. The stale air that seeped from the space carried the sharp tang of rust, the acrid hint of old coal smoke, and the earthy smell of soil.

Jeff stepped off the last stair and gasped. "It's a false wall, isn't it?" he said. "There's a room behind it."

The young man nodded and handed him a flashlight.

They pressed their foreheads to the narrow rectangular opening and beamed the light inside. It illuminated a rusted metal cylinder, pocked and green with age. Wires and copper tubes curled from the top like skeletal fingers.

"That's an old still," Jeff said, a low note of wonder in his voice.

"That's what I thought," the young man said. "There's a pile of broken bottles next to it."

Jeff swept the light around. "Those bottles look like the ones we found in the crates. There's a rolltop desk and an old banker's chair. That must've been where they kept the ledgers. This was a full-scale bootlegging setup."

He set the flashlight down. "Do you have an extra pair of gloves? Let's widen the opening."

The young man pulled a pair from his back pocket, and the two set to work. Nails shrieked as they pried boards loose. Dust and dry rot filled the air, clinging to their skin and clothing like soot.

"I'll move one of the standing lights in here," the young man said, stepping through the widened gap.

Jeff followed. The air inside was cooler, heavier. He crouched and scraped the dirt floor with his fingernail. "Strange. This side doesn't feel as wet."

The young man circled his flashlight. "The watermark's lower—only about eighteen inches."

Jeff walked toward the still, his boots crunching on loose gravel. "It feels like a slight incline. Perhaps that explains why this area stayed dry."

"Do you think the false wall helped?"

"Possibly," Jeff replied. "Somebody built this to last."

The young man stumbled over a rusted metal lunchbox. It landed with a hollow clang. "Holy cow," he breathed. "I feel like I've walked into the past."

Jeff turned to him. "Would you get Sam? And bring us more flashlights."

The young man nodded and disappeared up the stairs.

Jeff crossed to the rolltop desk and shifted the wobbly chair. The tambour door was stuck. He didn't force it, suspecting it to be a valuable antique. He opened the lap drawer instead. Inside was a fountain pen, a half-full bottle of ink, a tarnished ring of skeleton keys, and a cellophane-wrapped package of dusty peppermint candies. The scent of old ink mingled with the faint sweetness of aging sugar.

Footsteps thundered down the stairs. Sam and the young man ducked through the opening.

"We knew they had to be making the stuff somewhere,"

Sam said, sweeping his flashlight. "I should've realized the size of the basement didn't match the footprint of the first floor."

"There'd be no reason to suspect it," Jeff said. "Buildings often have smaller basements."

Sam trained his light on the lunchbox. "It feels like they walked out yesterday."

"Whoever ran this was tidy," Jeff murmured.

The young man had ventured to a far corner. "This doesn't match the rest of the room," he said, kneeling beside a bucket, a pickaxe, and a trowel. A square of deteriorating carpet, the color of dried blood, sat nearby. He peeled the carpet back.

The room went silent except for their breathing. Beneath the carpet, the dirt was uneven and loose. A rounded, dark brown object jutted from the soil.

He brushed it gently. The surface was smooth. "Looks like a tree root," he offered uncertainly. "But it's huge. And there aren't any trees on this side of the street."

Jeff crouched beside him, running his hand across the exposed object. The surface was cold, unyielding.

Sam did the same. Then both men stood, locking eyes.

"You'd better call Anita," Jeff said.

Sam nodded.

"Want me to keep digging?" the young man asked, eyes wide.

"No," Jeff and Sam said in unison.

"We leave everything where it is," Jeff added firmly. "Don't touch another thing."

"What about removing the rest of the boards?"

"Make a wider opening for access," Jeff said. "But after that? Nothing. Construction stops. That stack of planks is the last thing leaving this basement—until we know exactly what we've found."

~

ANITA ANSWERED SAM'S CALL.

"You're on speaker in my car," she said. "I'm taking Gordon to the airport."

"Hey, Gordon," Sam said. "Sorry you're leaving town. There's something at the museum I'd like you both to see."

"Hi, Sam," Gordon replied. "That sounds mysterious. What's up?"

Anita and Gordon glanced at each other. She shrugged.

"You sound like you've got news," Anita said. "Are the repairs from the broken pipe going to cost more than we thought?"

"No," Sam said. "They won't exceed the estimate." He paused. "I'm calling about something we found—literally, a few minutes ago. You know we got the water out of the basement yesterday and planned to remove the damaged wooden planks from the walls today."

"Yes," Anita said. "What's happened?"

Sam hesitated long enough to make it clear he was

enjoying the suspense. "It turns out the basement we've seen is *not* the entire basement."

"What do you mean?" Anita asked, straightening in her seat.

"The wall where the crates were stacked was a false wall. There's a separate room behind it."

"No kidding!" Gordon said. "Have you been back there?"

"We sure have. And I think there's something Anita needs to see—as soon as she returns from the airport."

"I won't get back until almost seven," Anita said. "Don't you want to go home? We'll pick this up in the morning."

"You need to see it tonight," Sam said, his voice firm. "We'll wait for you."

"Are you going to give me a hint?" she asked, half laughing.

"Not a chance," Sam said. "You've got to see this. Drive safely. We'll wait—no matter how long it takes." He ended the call.

"Oh my gosh," Anita said, her voice tight with anticipation. "He sounded excited—not upset—so I don't think it's bad news."

"They must've found the still," Gordon said. "Or other pieces of the bootlegging operation. In any case, I want to be there for the great reveal." He reached for his phone. "Turn around at the next exit. I'm headed back to Westbury with you."

"But you have meetings in New York tomorrow."

"Nothing I can't reschedule," he said, already tapping on his phone. "I'm canceling my flight right now."

She stole a glance at him, then turned her eyes back to the road, a smile springing to her lips.

"No way I'm letting you do this alone," Gordon said. "To quote a certain Broadway play—I want to be in the room where it happens."

CHAPTER 36

"We just pulled into a parking spot at the curb," Gordon said into the phone. "We'll be at the front door in under a minute."

Sam disconnected the call and stepped out onto the sidewalk, holding the door.

Gordon and Anita raced up the sidewalk. Without breaking stride, they slipped through the open door.

Jeff was waiting inside and handed each of them a flashlight.

Sam stepped in behind them. "That was a quick trip," he said, raising an eyebrow at Anita. "If you were almost at the airport, you must've driven like a bat out of hell to get back here."

Gordon and Anita exchanged a glance.

"Let's just say we're thankful the highway patrol wasn't

out tonight," Gordon said. "Anita has a lead foot when she's in a hurry."

"Enough conversation," Anita said, her impatience clear. "Show us what you found."

Sam switched on his flashlight and led them down the steep basement stairs.

"Oh my gosh," Anita whispered, casting her beam over the wall with the newly cut opening. "There's a big room back there."

"Yep," Sam said. "Jeff and one of the workers found it. I'll let Jeff tell you."

"We uncovered this hidden room when we removed the wooden planks on the wall. Follow me," Jeff said, stepping through the jagged opening into the space. "This is where the bootleg operation took place."

He swept his flashlight over the rusted still, then across the massive rolltop desk. "We haven't gone through everything, but it appears the bookkeeping happened at that desk."

"That's interesting," Anita said, angling her beam toward the floor as she approached the still.

"I'd love to examine any records in that desk," Gordon added. "This is an exciting find."

"That's not all," Sam said. "They found something else." He trained his flashlight on the smooth, dark brown object protruding from the soil in the corner.

"What's that?" Anita asked, stepping toward it.

Sam motioned for Gordon to follow.

"Someone's been digging," Gordon said, gesturing to the nearby bucket, pickaxe, and trowel.

"I spent the summer after sixth grade with a setup like that," Anita said. "Judy and I were fossil hunting." The levity in her voice vanished as she dropped to her knees and ran her hand lightly over the curved surface. Her fingertips lingered, reverent.

Gordon knelt beside her and did the same. They both turned wide-eyed to Sam and Jeff.

"Is this …?" Anita let the question hang in the air.

"We can't say for sure," Sam said, "but it's almost certainly a prehistoric bone. Judging by the curve and size, my guess is it's a tusk. Both mastodon and woolly mammoth remains have been discovered in this region." He looked down at the exposed surface. "The only other possibility is a tree root—but, with no trees nearby, that's unlikely."

Anita brought one hand to her head. "This is unbelievable," she said. "First, a basement full of whiskey … then a hidden room from a Prohibition-era operation … and now the remains of a prehistoric creature?"

Gordon stood and held out both hands to help her up. "I'd say you bought the most interesting piece of real estate I've ever heard of."

"Do I have to report this to anyone?" Anita asked. "I hate to sound selfish, but … will this interfere with the museum?"

Sam shook his head. "I hope you don't mind, but we called Tim while we were waiting for you. He said bones found on private property belong to the property owner.

Have them excavated or leave them alone. It's entirely up to you."

"I'm not leaving them alone," Anita said. "This is an incredible find. What if there's an entire skeleton under there?"

"There's no way to know until excavation begins," Jeff replied. "Sometimes the skeleton is intact, but other times scavengers dragged off parts, or the ground shifted."

"Who should I contact to handle this?" Anita asked.

"Maggie," Gordon, Sam, and Jeff said at once.

"This is routine for universities," Gordon stated. "Highpointe probably has a geology department."

"The Joseph Moore Museum at Earlham College in Indiana has one of the most complete mastodon skeletons on public display," Sam said. "My parents took me to see it when I was a kid. If Highpointe can't do the dig themselves, I'm sure that museum would point you in the right direction."

"How do they do an excavation like this?" Anita asked. "Will it mess up the work you've already completed?"

"It shouldn't," Gordon assured her. "If it's done like an archaeological dig, they'll establish a grid using string and stakes to map the site. Every find will be photographed, documented, and logged by location. They'll use trowels, brushes, even dental picks. Everything's removed with care."

"No bulldozers?" Anita asked.

"Nope," Gordon smiled. "Bones are far too fragile. Once they're uncovered, they're stabilized with plaster or a preservative and then carefully removed. It won't be noisy or messy."

"I was reading online," Jeff said, "about a university dig where they unearthed an entire mastodon in a single day. That specimen was in an open field, so it was easier than a basement—but I don't think this dig will derail your plans."

"The broken pipe has already delayed us at least four weeks," Sam said. "And the elevator is on back order. Don't worry about opening your museum. It'll be a while yet."

Anita stood still, arms crossed, eyes fixed on the dirt. "I've got a new byline for the museum," she said. "It'll be Stitches in Time: Linking the Past to the Present."

"And you could refer to this as the Hidden Histories Room," Gordon offered.

"I like that," Anita said. She turned to Jeff and Sam. "Thank you for waiting for us."

"I'm glad we turned the car around and I came back with Anita."

"Do you mind if Sam and I bring Judy and Joan here in the morning?" Jeff asked. "We told them we found something interesting in the basement. As soon as we tell them what it is, they'll want to see it."

Anita chuckled. "Of course you can."

"Unless," Sam added, "you'd like to keep this a secret."

"A secret? In Westbury?" Anita laughed. "You know better than that, Sam. Everyone in town will know this news by lunchtime tomorrow."

She turned and headed for the stairs. "I'll text Maggie

tonight. If she's still up, I'm sure she'll call. As soon as I know more, I'll let the two of you know."

The four of them stepped out into the crisp winter night and said their goodbyes.

Anita and Gordon climbed back into her car. The street was quiet, the stars faint behind a veil of clouds.

"And people say New York City is exciting," Gordon scoffed. "It has nothing on Westbury."

CHAPTER 37

*A*nita hovered by the front window of her new building, watching the activity on the street in front of her. The familiar figures she was waiting for soon came into view. "I knew you'd be here first thing," she said, hurrying to meet Judy and Joan on the sidewalk. Their husbands trailed behind them.

"I wonder if Charlotte knew there was a mastodon in her basement," Joan said with a grin.

"She probably didn't know about the hidden room or the bootleg operation, either," Judy added. "Those secrets have stayed buried for decades."

"We're not positive that whatever is sticking out of the ground down there is a part of a mastodon," Anita reminded them.

"When will you know?" Joan asked.

"I spoke to Maggie last night," Anita said. "She'll contact the head of Highpointe's geology department first thing this morning. She doesn't know what's on Dr. Locke's schedule, but she's certain she'll rearrange her schedule to come out and look."

"That's Dr. Fiona Locke, isn't it?" Judy asked. "She's one of my customers—smart as a whip. I'll bet she'll know just by looking at it."

"I hope so," Anita said. "I'm on pins and needles."

"Okay, ladies," Sam said. "Enough talking—let's get down there and see this thing!"

Jeff handed out flashlights, and they followed Sam and Jeff down the steep basement stairs and into the hidden room. They approached the protruding object slowly—almost reverently.

"Would you look at that?" Judy whispered. "The exposed part is—what—two feet long? I wonder how big it'll be when it's excavated."

"Who knows," Sam said. "It may not even be in one piece."

Joan looked down at the ground beneath her feet. "I wonder if we're standing on its skull or something."

"Oh, I hope so," Judy said. "Imagine having a complete skeleton—wouldn't that be incredible? What would you do with it?" she asked, turning to Anita.

"Whatever's down there needs a new home," Anita said. "If Highpointe wants it, I'll donate it to the college. Gordon and I were talking last night—he suggested an exhibit down here that details the excavation. We'd post photos of the process and recreate the dig site. He even suggested we reproduce some of the bones."

"That sounds really interesting," Joan said.

"We'd use half of the basement for that, and the other half to display the still, the desk"—she pointed to the other side of the room—"and information about Prohibition and bootlegging. He suggested calling it the Hidden Histories Room."

"Genius," Judy said. "Love that idea."

"He's not only my biggest supporter, but a tremendous help," Anita said. "I don't know what I'd do without him."

Judy and Joan exchanged a knowing look.

"From what I see," Joan said gently, "I don't think you'll ever have to find out."

The basement was too dim for anyone to notice the color rising into Anita's cheeks.

"Well," Anita said, her voice brisk. "That's all there is to see. I need to get back to the shop. Sunday's bringing in the wedding dress she bought online for alterations."

"Don't your seamstresses mark the alterations?" Joan asked.

"As a rule," Anita said with a smile. "But we've got a surprise in store for Sunday."

She led them out of the basement and up the stairs, telling them the story of Sunday's wedding dress misadventure.

"That was clever of you to get a photo of the dress she really wants," Judy said.

"I love that your shop is going to make her the dress of her dreams," Joan added. "It would be great to see her face when you give her the news."

"That's why I'm heading back to the shop. I told her I contacted other bridal shops in the state, and no one had anything like the dress she wants in stock. She's convinced she has to make do with the one that was sent to her. I want to be there when she finds out she doesn't have to settle at all."

"You'll have to work fast to complete it in time," Joan said. "If you need another pair of hands to finish the work, let me know. I have free time—I'd be happy to help."

"I'll take you up on that," Anita said. "I know what a fine seamstress you are, Joan."

"I wish I knew how to sew," Judy said with a shrug. "But I don't, so I can't help in that way."

They were at the door when Judy suddenly turned back.

"I have an idea," she said. "Something to help advertise the museum during the excavation—no matter the results."

Anita and Joan stopped and looked at her.

"You said that vintage Singer on display at the library still works, right?"

"Yes," Anita said. "It's in perfect order. I still enjoy sewing on it, actually."

"Is it a lot slower than the machines you use at the shop?"

"It's slower, but not bad—just different."

Judy took a deep breath. "This might seem impossible given your deadline, but what if you used the Singer to sew Sunday's dress?"

"You mean bring the machine back to the shop?" Anita asked, puzzled. "Why on earth would I do that?"

"No—sew the dress right there at the library." Judy's eyes lit up. "I know seamstresses need large tables—I've seen yours at the shop. The library has lots of big tables. I think people will find it fascinating."

Joan clapped her hands. "That's a fabulous idea, Judy! Post a schedule so visitors know when you'll be there. I'll bet people will come just to see you work."

Anita raised a skeptical brow. "It sounds a little like inviting people to watch paint dry."

"That's only because you've been sewing your whole life," Judy said. "Lots of people haven't seen a sewing machine in operation, let alone a vintage one."

"The library might even livestream it," Joan offered. "You know, like that eagle cam that was so popular. They could call it 'Dress Cam.'"

"I think you've lost your minds," Anita said, laughing.

"Judy's right," Joan insisted. "Even if you can't sew the whole dress there, doing part of it would be great."

Anita looked at the earnest, hopeful faces of her two closest friends.

"I'll ask Sunday what she thinks when we tell her about the dress," she said. "If she likes the idea, I'll give it a go."

"Dress Cam, here we come!" Joan said, high-fiving Judy.

Anita's phone chimed. She glanced at the screen and smiled. "Showtime, ladies. Sunday just arrived at the shop. I'll let you know how it went the minute she leaves."

~

ANITA'S HEAD seamstress intercepted her at the front door to the shop.

"She's in the dressing room," the woman said. "She's slipping into the dress she believes she's stuck with."

"Good," Anita said. "I don't want to suggest we'll make her dream dress if she's now decided she likes this one. It really is lovely on her."

"I agree. We never try to change a bride's mind about her dress," she said, reciting the shop's mantra.

"Exactly," Anita replied. "Come with me to the fitting room. We'll know if she's fallen in love with this dress the moment we see her."

"I'll catch your eye and nod if I think she's still disappointed but making the best of it."

"Perfect," Anita said. "Okay … let's see if we're about to launch a sewing frenzy around here."

"I hope we are," the woman whispered as she followed Anita.

Anita tapped on the fitting room door. "Ready?" she called.

"Yes," Sunday replied, her voice flat.

Anita shot a knowing look at the seamstress and opened the door.

Sunday stood on the raised platform wearing satin wedding pumps and the gown. She was facing them, not the mirror.

"You look lovely, dear," Anita said, stepping into the room.

Sunday forced a smile. "Thank you," she said.

"Turn to face the mirror, please," Anita said gently.

Sunday turned around.

Anita stood behind her, and their gazes met in the reflection.

"I'd like you to take the straps up, like you suggested before. I think I'll be happier if the dress doesn't sit so low on my body," Sunday said.

Anita caught the seamstress's slight nod out of the corner of her eye.

"I've got a better idea," Anita said. "One that will make you even happier with your wedding dress."

Sunday ran her eyes up and down her reflection in the mirror. "What could that be? There isn't much to work with."

"We've been talking," Anita said, gesturing to the seamstress and the workroom behind them. "All of us here at Archer's Bridal. The dress in that picture—the one you originally wanted—is a classic design. It would look stunning on you. We've made dozens like it over the years."

Sunday tilted her head, then turned to face Anita. "What do you mean?"

"We decided," Anita said, "that, if you came in and weren't thrilled with this dress, we would offer to make you the one in the picture."

Sunday clapped her hand over her mouth, her eyes wide as she looked from Anita to the seamstress.

"We have most of the fabric we'll need on hand, and we can purchase the rest of the materials by the end of the week," the seamstress said, smiling. "And, as Anita said, we already have the patterns. We'll take measurements today, and you'd have to come in frequently for fittings."

"You guys …" Sunday's voice caught. "I can't believe you'd do this. You realize the wedding is in four and a half weeks, right?"

"We'll be working overtime, that's for sure," Anita said. "But it will give us great joy to do this for you."

"Then … yes." Sunday's voice trembled. "I'd love for you to make that dress for me."

"I'll grab my notepad," the seamstress said. "Let's get your measurements." She stepped out of the room.

Sunday cleared her throat. "Before you get started, I need to make sure I can afford this. Do you know what it will cost?"

Anita gave her a figure.

"That can't be right," Sunday said. "That's less than the one I ordered online. And your dress will be a custom-made wedding gown!"

Anita took her hand. "I'm only charging you for the materials. Archer's Bridal will donate the labor."

"You can't do that," Sunday protested. "That's way too generous."

"Because of you, my sewing machines are on exhibit at your library. That's turned out to be the best publicity I could've hoped for. I've already had dozens of inquiries." Anita took a deep breath. "You've heard about the possible archaeological dig in the basement?"

Sunday nodded. "It's the talk of campus. I assume it'll delay your grand opening. We'll leave your machines on exhibit at the library until you're ready to move them to the museum."

"You see," Anita said. "That's more than kind."

"Oh, for heaven's sake," Sunday said. "That's what librarians do. It's no big deal."

"It is to me," Anita said. "I want to make your dream dress to repay your kindness."

Sunday swept Anita into a tight hug. "This is the most special thing anyone's ever done for me. I promise I'll be here promptly for every fitting. Just say the word."

"About that," Anita said. "Judy had an idea. At first, I thought it was crazy, but the more I considered it, the more merit I see."

Sunday pulled back and raised her eyebrows.

"She thinks we should sew the dress on the Singer machine on display at the library."

Sunday shrieked. "That's a terrific idea! People will find that so interesting. It'll bring patrons into the library and generate more excitement for your museum." She gasped. "I can't wait to tell Lyla!"

"I'm glad you agree," Anita said, smiling.

"My office on the third floor is tiny, but it's private," Sunday said. "We could do fittings there if that works for you."

"I was hoping you'd say that," Anita said.

Sunday ran her hand through her hair. "We'll put this all over social media! Let's livestream parts of the sewing process, similar to the recent eagle cam."

Anita chuckled. "I didn't watch it, but I'm learning about it now. Joan and Judy had the same thought and were going on about it."

"Perhaps they have other great ideas as well," Sunday mentioned. "I'm pulling Lyla in on this as soon as I get back to the library. We'll call Judy and Joan to see what else they've come up with."

The seamstress returned, a tape measure around her neck and a notebook in hand.

"I'll let the two of you get started," Anita said. She turned to the seamstress. "We've decided to construct the dress at the library."

The woman's eyebrows shot to her hairline.

"I'll fill you in later. When do you think we'll begin sewing?" Anita asked.

"I called our vendor. Everything we need is in stock, and I plan to swing by after we finish the measurements. We'll have the pieces cut by the end of the week, so you could start sewing on Monday."

"Then Monday it will be," Anita said with a nod.

"If I know Lyla," Sunday added, "she'll get the word out before the day's over. Is there anything you need from the library?"

"A long table," Anita said.

Sunday chuckled. "You're in luck—libraries are full of those. I'll have one set up next to that sewing machine before Monday."

CHAPTER 38

"They're here!" Sam called from the second floor, where he and Jeff were supervising repairs to the bathroom. "They must've parked near Celebrations—they're walking through the square."

Anita inhaled deeply and pushed her shoulders back.

"Nervous?" Gordon asked.

She nodded. "After all the excitement … I'll be disappointed if it's only a tree root."

"You'll know in the next few minutes," Gordon said gently.

He opened the front door to Maggie, who entered with a tall, thin woman in slim black trousers tucked into hiking boots, a heavy anorak, and a field bag slung across her shoulder. Dr. Fiona Locke pushed her hood back, revealing close-cropped, dark hair peppered with silver and aquamarine eyes that sparkled with excitement. "Anita Archer," she said warmly, stepping forward. "And you must be Gordon Mortimer."

"Dr. Locke," Anita said, shaking her hand. "Maggie tells me you cut your trip short to return to Westbury. I'm sorry to put you to the trouble."

"Are you kidding?" Fiona grinned. "I couldn't get back here fast enough. A scientific conference doesn't hold a candle to the possibility of an actual dig. And, please—call me Fiona."

Anita twisted her hands together. "I just hope it's the real deal. I'll feel terrible if we wasted your time."

"Don't worry about that. You did the right thing calling us in before unearthing it yourselves. Better safe than sorry."

"We're grateful you reached out to the college," Maggie added, smiling.

"Well," Gordon said, "are you ready to take a look?"

Fiona nodded enthusiastically.

"The lighting in the basement is poor," Anita warned as she led the way to the basement stairs. "Grab a flashlight from the basket by the door." She and Gordon led Fiona and Maggie down the narrow basement steps.

"The floor is packed earth," Anita said as she looked down at Maggie's expensive pumps. "It's still muddy in spots from when the pipe burst. Are you sure you want to risk those shoes?"

"You know me better than that," Maggie said.

"I'm not leaving without seeing this for myself. I'll clean the mud off later."

They stepped into the basement, and Anita pointed to the rough opening in the plank wall. "It's through there, on the left-hand side."

Fiona hurried past her, moving carefully toward the corner. At the dig site, she dropped to her knees and set her field bag beside her. She pulled on a pair of nitrile gloves and retrieved a small brush, a soft cloth, and a magnifier from her bag.

Maggie stood behind her, leaning in to get a better look at the object protruding from the dirt.

"Would you shine a light on it as I work?" Fiona asked.

"Of course," Maggie replied, training her flashlight on the object.

Fiona traced her gloved hand along the exposed length of the object, then brushed and wiped a patch clean. She leaned in close, examining the surface through her magnifying glass.

Anita, Gordon, and Maggie watched in breathless silence.

Fiona finally rocked back on her heels and looked up at them. The smile on her face told them what they wanted to know before she spoke.

"It's real, all right," she said. "I believe this is a mastodon tusk. The shape and texture are textbook. You can see the striations and age cracks. The surface is solid. You have a beautiful specimen under here."

Anita let out the breath she hadn't realized she'd been holding. "Thank goodness," she whispered.

"Do you have any idea how old it is?" Gordon asked.

"It's probably late Pleistocene," Fiona said. "Creatures like this roamed the Midwest more than 10,000 years ago."

"Gosh," Anita said. "Imagine that."

"This tusk—and any other bones—belong to you," Fiona said. "Maggie tells me you'd like the college's help with the excavation?"

"Definitely," Anita said. "You think there could be more?"

"Very possibly," Fiona replied. "There could be a full skull —or even a complete skeleton. Based on the condition of this tusk, I'd say the preservation here has been exceptional."

"Well then," Anita said firmly, "I want all of it carefully excavated, and I'd like to donate it to Highpointe—if the college wants it."

"There's no question about that," Maggie said. "The college would be grateful for your donation."

"What's the next step?" Gordon asked.

"I'll take photos and record preliminary measurements," Fiona said. "Then I'll write an initial field report and assemble a paleontology team."

"I understand you've done this before?" Maggie asked.

Fiona nodded. "I attended Earlham College and worked at the Joseph Moore Museum as an undergrad. I've been on multiple digs with them, and I still have strong ties to their staff. We'll recruit graduate students from Highpointe and experienced volunteers from the museum to do the excavation properly."

"Can I continue remodeling for the museum upstairs?" Anita asked. "I'm opening a sewing machine museum here."

"Absolutely," Fiona said. "We shouldn't interfere with that. I went through the exhibit at the library, by the way. It's fascinating. I plan to watch Dress Cam while you're making Sunday's dress."

Anita laughed. "I can't believe you heard about that."

"It's the talk of campus," Fiona said, smiling. "If the only thing we find is the tusk, we'll finish the excavation in about a week. If we uncover additional bones, it'll take longer. We'll work in phases, and we'll stay out of your way."

"I want you to do this the right way," Anita said. "Even if it delays the museum opening. Uncovering and preserving this guy—" she looked down at the exposed tusk—"is my top priority."

CHAPTER 39

*A*nita paused to read the sign posted at the library's front entrance. The attractive poster, designed with a delicate lace background and elegant scrollwork font, declared:

Watch History in the Making: Sunday's Wedding Dress—Sewn Live!

A bold QR code beneath the title promised streaming access and details.

She glanced at Gordon. "I'm still not convinced this is going to be interesting to anyone," she said.

"Oh, ye of little faith," he replied. "I think you're going to go viral—and so does everyone else who knows about the project." He shifted the tall garment bag he carried over his shoulder.

Anita held the door for him. "Thank you for schlepping

the fabric," she said. "We didn't think through the logistics of transporting the cut pieces from the shop to the library."

"I don't mind," Gordon said. "I wouldn't miss your online debut for anything."

"I'm glad Sunday cleared a space in the storage room for my dress form and supplies. It'll be a relief not to haul the dress back and forth every day."

They walked past the circulation desk. The student working there looked up and gave Anita an enthusiastic thumbs-up. "I'll be watching on my phone," she said in a stage whisper.

Anita smiled and nodded as they passed.

Gordon laid the garment bag on the long library table positioned beside the black Singer treadle machine. Anita had oiled it, threaded it, and adjusted the bobbin's tension the day before. All was ready.

She unzipped the garment bag and carefully unwrapped the tissue-wrapped bodice pieces, spreading them flat on the table. She caressed the ivory satin gazar, smoothing out the edges of the first seam she intended to stitch.

Gordon stepped back and watched, admiration in his eyes. He knew an artist at work when he saw one.

Sunday slipped into the exhibit room from the back, taking a seat beside a laptop on a nearby stand. She would manage the livestream setup, and had the perfect vantage point to watch the first seam of her wedding dress take shape.

Lyla adjusted the camera tripod and then moved to the small microphone positioned near the machine.

"Okay, Anita," she stated. "Are you ready to go live?"

Anita swung to face Lyla. Her expression shifted from concentration to surprise as she caught sight of the crowd now staring at her. "Is everyone here to see me?" she asked, voice trembling slightly.

"They sure are," Lyla said with a smile. "You're the woman of the hour. I can't remember the last time the library was this busy on a weekday."

Anita blew out a breath and reached for the first fabric pieces. "Let me sit down before you start, okay?"

"Suggestion?" Gordon called from his spot at the edge of the crowd. "Why don't you start by describing the dress to the audience?" He looked at Lyla. "Does the camera show the worktable?"

Lyla leaned in to check. "It does."

"I'd stand at the table to begin," Gordon said. "Describe the dress, then walk to the sewing machine. Tell the audience about it and mention that your grandmother taught you to sew on it. Then start stitching."

"That's a great idea," Sunday said, nodding.

"I can do that," Anita agreed. She stood beside the table, hands resting lightly on the pattern pieces.

"And we're live in five ... four ... three ... two ... one ..." Lyla nodded.

"Welcome to Dress Cam," Anita said, looking directly into the camera. "I'm Anita Archer, owner of Archer's Bridal here in Westbury. I'll be sewing a wedding gown for Sunday Sloan, rare book librarian at Highpointe College Library—right here in an exhibit filled with vintage sewing machines I've collected over the years."

She smiled, her posture relaxing.

"First, let me tell you about the dress. It's going to be spectacular on our beautiful bride. We're making it from satin gazar. The dress will have a fitted bodice, a V-neck, and long illusion sleeves in hand-appliquéd lace. A line of covered buttons will extend the length of the back. If you watched the royal wedding of Kate Middleton and Prince William, you'll recognize the style—elegant, timeless, and romantic."

"I'm going to begin by sewing the right front bodice to the right back." She picked up a pinned piece of fabric and took her seat.

"Before I begin, let me tell you about this sewing machine." She ran her hand across the shiny black enamel with its gold-leaf nameplate. "It's a Singer 15K, manufactured in Scotland in the 1930s. My grandmother bought it in 1939, and it was used at Archer's Bridal until 1980—when she and the machine retired together."

She smiled warmly. "She taught me to sew on this machine. It's been in use for over 80 years, and, with a bit of loving care, it'll keep going for many more. It produces beautiful, even stitching—and I love working on it."

Anita turned the wheel to raise the needle, positioned the fabric, lowered the presser foot, and began pumping the

BARBARA HINSKE

treadle. The needle moved with a steady hum as the fabric glided forward. She removed each pin and set them to the side in her pin cushion, guiding the seam with practiced hands. When she finished the first seam, she cut the threads and held the completed piece toward the camera.

"There. Our first seam is done." She laid it at the far end of the table and picked up the next pieces. "Now we'll do the same for the left side of the bodice."

She continued working, narrating each step. When she finished a seam, she held it up to the camera, explaining its place in the design. And every time she glanced up, she was surprised to see the crowd hadn't thinned; instead, it had grown.

When she finished stitching the last of the day's pieces, Sunday asked, "Would you like to take some questions?"

Anita looked out at the crowd. No one raised a hand.

"We've got questions from viewers online," Sunday said, lifting the laptop. "Nancy in Ohio wants to know why you chose satin gazar instead of plain satin."

"That's a great question, Nancy," Anita replied. "Satin gazar has a beautiful shine, like traditional satin, but it has more body. It doesn't cling—it flows. Sunday's skirt will move gracefully when she walks."

"Three more online," Sunday said. "Let's answer those, then open it up to folks here at the library." For fifteen more minutes, Sunday read questions, and Anita answered them with confidence and warmth.

Lyla stepped forward when they were done. "Dress Cam

276

will be back tomorrow," she announced. She shut off the camera and microphone. The crowd dispersed.

Anita leaned back in her chair. "I can't believe we had questions from people online."

"One viewer suggested we post daily photo updates," Lyla said. "I'm creating a Dress Cam Journal for the library's website."

"You're a natural at this, Anita," Gordon said, joining them.

"We've already had over five hundred views," Sunday cried. "Hashtag Dress Cam is trending!"

"I'm astounded," Anita said.

"I think people love the entire story," Gordon said. "It's not just about stitching a wedding dress—it's about the disappointment of Sunday getting the wrong dress, the kind bridal shop owner saving the day, the short deadline, the vintage sewing machine, and the beautiful library where it all takes place. It's romantic, generous—human. You're a modern-day fairy godmother."

Anita burst out laughing. "I never dreamed this would be so successful," she said. Her smile suddenly vanished. "What if Josh sees the dress?" She turned to Sunday. "Do you believe that old wives' tale—that it's bad luck for the groom to see the dress before the wedding?"

"I sure do," Sunday said. "He promised me he won't go snooping online. Maggie said she'll watch on her phone from her office but will keep him away from the screen."

"Whew." Anita exhaled. "Let's store what we've finished

in the closet. I need to get back to the shop to prepare tomorrow's pieces."

"I'm going to ask our custodian to make more space for viewers," Lyla said. "We're already up to 800 online viewers. We'll have more in person the next time."

"See you tomorrow, fairy godmother," Sunday said to Anita after they'd stashed the completed pieces.

Anita chuckled. "Goodnight, Cinderella."

CHAPTER 40

*J*osh was the final one to climb into John's Suburban. "I can't believe you got six tickets to the playoff game," he said, scanning the group of men in the car as he maneuvered into the third-row seat and buckled in next to Frank.

"We've got Glenn to thank for that," Frank said. "He used his connections."

"It helps to have been a season ticket holder for more than fifty years," Glenn replied with a grin. "It's been at least a decade since I've been to a playoff game. I'm excited about going with a group of guy friends. Makes me feel young again."

"You're the youngest-thinking person I know," Tim said from the second row, smiling at Glenn beside him.

"Thank you for inviting me," Josh said sincerely. "I've never been to a college basketball playoff game."

"We wanted to do something special for you," John called from behind the wheel. "You're getting married in ten days. We figured this would be our version of a bachelor party."

"You didn't have to do that," Josh said. "Sunday and I both feel like bachelor and bachelorette parties—especially those whole destination weekends—have gotten out of hand. We're not doing any of that stuff."

Everyone in the car—except John, who kept his eyes on the road—turned to smile at him.

"What?" Josh asked, his brow furrowing.

"About that ..." Gordon said, glancing at him from the passenger seat. "What do you think Sunday is doing tonight?"

"She's going to Archer's Bridal for the last fitting on her gown. They finished it two days ago and moved it from the library to the shop so they could make any last-minute alterations."

The car fell silent for a beat.

"That's not the only thing she's doing tonight, is it?" Josh asked, suspicion creeping into his voice.

"I think a certain group of women may have other plans for her," Gordon said lightly.

"We promised our wives we wouldn't say anything," John added. "So you'll hear about it when you get home." He signaled and merged onto the highway. "Now," he said, his tone shifting, "we've got a 60-minute drive ahead of us. I want to hear everyone's analysis of the remaining teams and your predictions for who's taking home the national title."

～

SUNDAY STOOD on the pedestal in the dressing room, examining herself in the three-way mirror.

Anita squatted behind her, arranging the fabric of the train. She glanced at Sunday's reflection and quickly stood.

"What's wrong, honey?" she asked.

Sunday wiped a tear with one hand and flung out the other. "Tissue," she said in a choked voice.

Anita grabbed the box from the corner and handed it to her. Sunday snatched one from the top and dabbed at her cheeks, catching her tears before they fell onto the dress.

"I feel so beautiful," she whispered. "When the wrong dress arrived, I told myself I was being silly—that it didn't matter, that I'd be fine. But I've had a picture of a dress like this tucked in the back of my journal since I was in middle school." Her voice cracked. "I can't believe you made this for me."

Anita took the damp tissue from her. "You'd be a beautiful bride no matter what you wore," she said. "But I'm thrilled with how this turned out."

Sunday sniffled. "We better get me out of this dress before I start crying again and ruin it."

Anita began unbuttoning the long line of covered

buttons. "I once sewed the sleeves on a wedding dress backward," she chuckled.

Sunday stopped sniffling and turned wide eyes to Anita.

"Didn't discover it until the bride came in for her first fitting."

"Oh my gosh," Sunday said. "That must've been—"

"Awful?" Anita finished with a wry smile. "We fixed it easily, but it sure was embarrassing. I checked and double-checked the sleeves on your gown. I'm not making that mistake again."

Sunday continued to sniffle, and Anita handed her another tissue.

"There's a pocket on the right side," Anita said as she helped Sunday step out of the dress. "Every weepy bride needs a pocket."

Sunday laughed. "I'm afraid that's going to be me. A pocket for tissues will be very helpful."

"You're not stuffing a tissue in that pocket," Anita said, shaking her head. "You need an old-fashioned, lace-trimmed hanky."

"You're right," Sunday said. "I'll poke around the antique shops this weekend to find one."

Anita nodded, her eyes twinkling.

Sunday slipped back into her slacks and sweater while Anita carefully positioned the dress on its padded hanger and hung it from the elevated hook on the dressing room wall.

"I'll steam everything first thing tomorrow and put it in a garment bag. You can pick it up whenever you like," she said.

Sunday crossed the room and pulled Anita into a tight hug. "Thank you again." She took a step back. "Josh went to a playoff game with John, Gordon, and the others. I'm on my own for dinner—and I know you are too. Want to join me at Pete's?" She slipped into her puffer jacket.

A loud pop sounded from the back of the shop.

"What was that?" Sunday asked. "I thought we were the only ones here."

Anita shrugged. "We better go check before we head to dinner." She opened the fitting room door.

"It sounded like a champagne cork," Sunday whispered, following closely behind her.

They walked through the showroom and into the break room. Anita flicked on the overhead light just as a chorus of voices rang out: "Surprise!"

Sunday gasped and brought her hands to her cheeks.

A cluster of smiling women stood along the far wall. Someone had set up two tables—one with trays of finger foods, the other piled high with wrapped gifts. Bouquets of iridescent white balloons bobbed above them, and a shimmering 'Bride to Be' banner hung from the ceiling. Champagne and sparkling cider chilled in ice buckets on the counter next to rows of flutes. A circle of chairs had been set up in the center of the room.

"You didn't think we were going to let you get married without a bridal shower, did you?" Susan stepped forward.

"You're all so busy," Sunday said. "And we planned our wedding so quickly … I didn't think anyone would have time."

"You should know us better than that," Judy said, hugging her.

"Thank you all for doing this," Sunday said, her eyes shining.

"We know you're not a fan of tiaras and sashes or noisy bar nights, so we planned something a little more … you," Susan said. "Let's eat and drink first." She gestured to the food table. "The bride goes first."

Sunday grabbed a plate and filled it with one of everything.

"Everyone wrote their best piece of marital advice on a note and dropped it in that box." Susan pointed to a rectangular box covered in an ivory and mauve floral chintz. "We thought you could read those aloud before we open gifts." She guided Sunday toward a cozy armchair in the middle of the circle. For the next hour, Sunday sipped sparkling cider and nibbled cheese straws, caprese skewers, and meatballs while her friends shared stories, advice, and more than a few hilarious wedding mishaps.

"These crab puffs are heavenly," Nancy said. "Who brought them?"

Loretta raised her hand. "I'm glad you like them. They're easy."

"I'd love the recipe," Joan said.

"I'll email it to you tomorrow," Loretta replied.

"Keep eating," Susan said. "There's plenty of food, but I think we need to move on." She handed Sunday the fabric-covered box. "Now it's time for the advice."

Sunday pulled out the first slip. "This is from Gloria Vaughn. She writes, 'The most useful words in marriage—or parenting—are: 'Tell me more.'"

She looked over at Gloria. "I'll remember this."

"They matter most when you're angry or don't agree with someone," Gloria said. "My instinct was always to argue to prove my point. But we resolve things faster—and with more compassion—when we really listen."

"I'm writing that down," Susan said, grabbing a pad and pen from under her chair.

Sunday finished reading the rest of the notes, then hugged the box to her chest. "I can't wait to share these with Josh. I love that you did this."

"Now—time to open gifts," Susan said. "I'll record who gave what so you can write thank-you notes. Mom's going to hand out the gifts."

Maggie handed Sunday a small rectangular box. "This one's from Judy."

Sunday untied the narrow satin ribbon and opened the box. Inside was a delicate white linen handkerchief, embroidered with forget-me-nots and edged with blue satin.

"Oh, this is perfect," Sunday said, her eyes wide. "Anita and I were just talking about how I need a hanky for my gown's pocket."

Anita winked at Judy.

"You two planned this," Sunday accused, laughing. "It's absolutely beautiful. I can't possibly use it to wipe my tears."

"I made it for that exact reason," Judy said. "You're supposed to use it."

"And now you've got something blue, too," Loretta added. "New and blue."

Maggie handed Sunday a large box. "From Lyla."

Inside was a scrapbook filled with printed screenshots from Dress Cam, photos of the gown's progress, and online viewer comments. Sunday flipped through the pages and passed it into Nancy's outstretched hands.

"This will be as precious as our wedding photos," she said.

Lyla smiled so wide her cheeks pushed her glasses up on her nose.

Sunday unwrapped a set of luggage organizers and packing cubes from Loretta, a kitchen wisdom book from Gloria, an ivory silk robe from Anita, a blank travel journal from Nancy, and a china jewelry tray from Joan.

Susan and Maggie lifted the cloth from under the gift table to reveal the final surprise: a robin's egg blue luggage set.

Sunday scooted to the edge of her chair. "These are gorgeous!"

"TSA-approved locks, built-in phone charger, cupholder, and a hook for your bag," Susan explained.

"I remembered that your luggage was damaged on your London trip," Maggie said. "Josh mentioned you hadn't replaced it. We thought this would be useful."

"You're all set to travel now," Loretta added. "Do you have a honeymoon planned?"

"Not yet," Sunday said. "We're saving for a house. We plan to take a trip on our first anniversary. But now, with all these amazing travel gifts ... I don't know if I can wait!"

"How's the house hunt going?" Nancy asked.

"We want to stay in this area, but everything's so pricey. We need more time to save. Once we've got a larger nest egg, we'll call Tim," Sunday said, smiling at Nancy.

"He'd be happy to speak with you now—even if you're not ready," Nancy said. "He'll have ideas for you."

"I'll talk to Josh," Sunday said. "Maybe after the wedding."

"I grew up in a house across the street from the Olsson House," Judy said. "It's a wonderful neighborhood to raise a family."

"We love that street," Sunday said. "I drive down it on my way home from work at least once a week. Which house?"

Judy began describing it.

Sunday interrupted her with a squeal. "I know exactly which one that is. We stood on the sidewalk and lusted after it for the longest time on New Year's Eve. That's our dream house. I hope we can find one just like it."

Judy bit her lip and didn't say anything else.

"I'm sure you'll find the perfect home for you and Josh," Anita said.

"And now," Susan announced, getting to her feet, "there's just one thing left to do."

All eyes turned to her.

"We've got a cake from Laura's Bakery—and it won't eat itself."

Maggie cleared a space on the food table and Anita brought the cake in from the kitchen. Judy passed slices around.

Conversation quieted as everyone enjoyed the sweet treat. Sunday set her fork down and dabbed her lips with her napkin.

"Thank you for being such good friends—and for making tonight so special. I love you all. One thing is certain—Josh and I want to spend our lives in Westbury."

CHAPTER 41

The early morning mist vanished as the sun rose in the cloudless day. The old stone chapel on the Highpointe College campus—its Gothic Revival arches outlined against the azure sky—looked like something out of a fairytale.

The faint scent of flowers drifted through the sanctuary, greeting wedding guests as they entered. An enormous spray of lilacs, white tulips, and forget-me-nots graced the altar, their fragrance unmistakably that of spring.

Maggie and John strolled, hand in hand, through the massive wooden double doors into the narthex.

Gordon, who had been leaning against the stone wall near the coat rack, straightened and stepped forward to greet them.

"Where's Anita?" Maggie asked, glancing around expectantly.

"She just stepped into the bride's room," Gordon said, nodding toward a closed door on the other side of the narthex. "She wanted to see if Sunday needed help getting into her wedding gown. Lyla's with Sunday now, waiting to walk her down the aisle. Anita said she'd be right out."

Maggie nodded. "We'll see you at the reception." She and John turned to go, but Maggie looked back over her shoulder, a twinkle in her eye. "This is the most beautiful place to get married, isn't it, Gordon?"

He smiled, his eyes following her for a moment. "It really is," he said softly.

John squeezed Maggie's hand and guided her forward. "If that was a hint," he murmured, "it wasn't very subtle."

"What are you talking about?" Maggie replied, her voice full of mock surprise.

"You and Judy—and, let's be honest, all of your friends—think Gordon should marry Anita and move to Westbury."

They made their way down the aisle and slid into a pew near the front. Sunlight streamed through the stained glass above the altar, casting colors like watercolor brushstrokes across the stone floor.

Maggie leaned close to John and pressed her lips near his ear. "You have to admit, they're perfect for each other."

John turned his face toward hers, raising an eyebrow. "Let's allow them to make that decision," he said with a smile.

~

ANITA FASTENED the final button on the back of Sunday's wedding gown, her fingers steady with practice. She smoothed the back of the satin skirt, coaxing the fabric into a flawless fall.

Sunday's long blonde hair was swept into a reverse French braid, its delicate weave secured by a vintage hair comb glinting beneath her cathedral-length veil. The lace-edged tulle cascaded down her back, softening the structured lines of the gown.

Anita turned the bride toward the door and adjusted the train one last time.

Lyla stood beside Sunday, looking regal in an eggplant-colored A-line gown. Her thick silver hair framed her face in a sleek, chin-length bob.

"Thank you for showing me how to bustle the train," Lyla said. "I've never done that before. It's complicated with all those hooks and loops."

"If you need any help, you know where to find me," Anita replied with a smile.

Lyla nodded, her expression tender as she looked at Sunday.

Anita stepped toward the door and turned, her eyes sweeping over the bride.

"You look radiant, my dear. I know I'm not objective, but I think you look even more beautiful in that dress than Kate Middleton did in hers."

Sunday, who had been twisting her embroidered handkerchief in her hands, let out a small laugh.

"It's almost time," Anita said. "I need to join Gordon so we can take our seats. You'll be coming down that aisle in a few moments." She opened the door and slipped out.

Gordon, who had been waiting near the sanctuary doors, extended his elbow as Anita approached.

"I was getting worried there was some last-minute snafu," he said.

Anita shook her head as they walked together. "Everything's going as planned. And Sunday looks perfect."

On the outskirts of campus, Jeff turned into the western entrance of Highpointe College and followed the signs to the chapel.

"We're going to be late," Judy said, wringing her hands. "And I'm entirely to blame. I made the decision this morning while I was getting dressed. I should've made it weeks ago. Sunday and Josh—they're exactly the couple I want living in my old house."

"What did Tim say when you called him?" Jeff asked, eyes on the winding drive.

"He said there are lots of legal ways to handle a sale when a buyer doesn't have their financing in place. Lease with an option to purchase, seller carry-back—all kinds of things. I wrote in their card that, if they want the house, it's theirs. We'll work out the details whenever they're ready."

"I wish we could see their faces when they open it," Jeff said. "I can only imagine how thrilled they'll be."

He pulled into the chapel parking lot as quickly as he dared and slid into a vacant space. They both jumped out.

"I'm sorry I made us late," Judy said, breathless as they sprinted toward the steps.

Jeff grabbed her hand and pressed it to his chest. "They haven't started yet," he said as he pulled open the chapel doors. "We made it."

∿

"NERVOUS?" Lyla asked gently, her hand brushing Sunday's arm.

Sunday nodded, her expression open and honest. "I'm not having second thoughts or anything … but, yes. I'm nervous."

"Anyone would be," Lyla said. She handed Sunday the bouquet—a hand-tied gathering of the same flowers gracing the altar, finished with a long satin ribbon. The lilacs brought out the purple in Sunday's amethyst eyes.

A soft knock sounded on the door, and Susan stuck her head in. "Ready? It's go-time."

"You look lovely in that lavender silk dress," Lyla told her. "You're the most glamorous pregnant woman I've ever seen."

Susan beamed, gave her bump a gentle pat, and opened the door wide. "And you are the most stunning bride, Sunday." Susan picked up her own bouquet—a smaller version of the bride's—and walked to the entrance of the sanctuary.

The opening chords of the wedding march rang out from the organ. Inside, guests swiveled to face the back.

Josh and Frank stood side by side at the altar, each in a silvery gray suit and crisp white shirt. Frank's tie was lavender; Josh's a deep, regal purple. Josh's gaze never wavered from the back of the sanctuary.

Lyla extended her right arm to Sunday, who tucked her left hand into the crook of Lyla's elbow. They stepped forward and paused as the music swelled. Sunday's eyes locked on Josh's. He exhaled, visibly moved.

The guests rose to their feet.

They began their walk down the aisle. The gown floated around Sunday like wind through a field of tall grass. The hush in the chapel was broken only by the strains of the organ and an occasional catch of breath.

When they reached the altar, Lyla released Sunday and opened her arms for a loose, joyful three-way hug with both the bride and the groom. Sunday handed her bouquet to Susan, who had taken her place nearby.

Josh reached for Sunday's hand. Their eyes remained on each other, their connection filling the space between. No one else existed.

The officiant welcomed everyone and led them through the beginning of the service. Then came the moment they'd planned for:

"The bride and groom have written their own vows and will speak them now."

Josh took both of Sunday's hands. "Today I give you my

hand and my heart. I promise to respect you, trust you, and stand beside you through every season of our lives. With you, I am the best version of myself. I will cherish you and our love, honor our bond, and care for and comfort you all the days of my life."

A sniffle echoed from the pews behind them.

Sunday fished the lace-edged handkerchief from her pocket and dabbed at her eyes. Josh smiled at her, rubbing the tops of her hands with his thumbs.

She took a breath to steady herself.

"I promise to love you with patience, kindness, and unwavering faith. I will celebrate your triumphs and support you in your struggles. I vow to grow with you, and to build a life that honors the love we've been given. I will make my home in you, and thank God every day for the gift of you."

A soft chorus of sniffles followed, tissues emerging from purses and jacket pockets.

The couple exchanged rings, their hands trembling. The officiant offered a last prayer and then proclaimed, "I now pronounce you husband and wife. You may seal your union with a kiss."

Josh drew Sunday into his arms. Their kiss was sweet, certain, and sacred—the kind that bore witness to a love elevated to a lifetime commitment.

Applause rose around them as they finally parted, breathless with joy. The organist began the recessional, and Sunday and Josh turned to walk together down the aisle—their first steps into married life.

THANK YOU FOR READING

If you enjoyed *Threads of Kindness,* I'd be grateful if you wrote a review.

Just a few lines on Amazon or Goodreads would be great. Reviews are the best gift an author can receive. They encourage us when they're good, help us improve our next book when they're not, and help other readers make informed choices when purchasing books. Goodreads reviews help readers find new books. Reviews on Amazon keep the Amazon algorithms humming and are the most helpful aide in selling books! Thank you.

To post a review on Amazon:

1. Go to the product detail page for *Threads of Kindness* on Amazon.com.

2. Click "Write a customer review" in the Customer Reviews section.

3. Write your review and click Submit.

In gratitude,
Barbara Hinske

JUST FOR YOU—MAGGIE'S DIARY

Wonder what Maggie was thinking when the book ended? Exclusively for readers who finished *Threads of Kindness*, take a look at Maggie's Diary Entry for that day at https://barbarahinske.com/maggies-diary.

ACKNOWLEDGMENTS

I'm blessed with the wisdom and support of many kind and generous people. I want to thank the most supportive and delightful group of champions an author could hope for:

My remarkable husband, Brian Willis, who never fails to steer me

My life coach Mat Boggs for your wisdom and guidance;

My kind and generous legal team, Kenneth Kleinberg, Esq., and Michael McCarthy—thank you for believing in my vision;

The professional "dream team" of my editors Linden Gross, Dione Benson, and proofreader Dana Lee;

Elizabeth Mackey for a beautiful cover.

RECURRING CHARACTERS

Recurring Characters in the Rosemont Series

Rosemont and the Martins

- **Maggie Martin Allen** – current owner of Rosemont; president of Highpointe College; former forensic accountant and mayor of Westbury; widow of Paul Martin; married to John Allen; mother of Mike Martin and Susan (Martin) Scanlon; grandmother to Julia and twins Sophie and Sarah Martin

- **John Allen** – veterinarian; owner of Westbury Animal Hospital; Maggie's husband; "adopted grandfather" to Julia, Sophie, and Sarah

- **Paul Martin (deceased)** – Maggie's first husband; disgraced former college president; father of Mike and Susan; affair with Loretta Nash, father of Nicole

- **Mike Martin** – Maggie's son; lives in California with wife Amy and twin daughters Sophie and Sarah
- **Amy Martin** – Mike's wife; mother to Sophie and Sarah
- **Sophie and Sarah Martin** – twin daughters of Mike and Amy; close friends of Marissa Nash
- **Susan Martin Scanlon** – Maggie's daughter; attorney at her brother-in-law's firm; kidney donor to half-sister Nicole Nash; married to Aaron Scanlon; mother to Julia
- **Hector Martin (deceased)** – town patriarch; son of Silas, father of illegitimate son (Frank's father); donated rare book collection to Highpointe College
- **Silas Martin (deceased)** – Hector's father; amassed fortune from sawmill and real estate; built Rosemont

At Rosemont

- **Alistair** – Rosemont's longtime butler; now a loyal and witty ghost in the attic

The Scanlons

- **Aaron Scanlon** – orthopedic surgeon; married to Susan Martin; father of Julia
- **Alex Scanlon** – Aaron's brother; attorney; succeeded Maggie as mayor; partner of Marc Benson
- **Julia Scanlon** – daughter of Susan and Aaron
- **Marc Benson** – musician; Alex Scanlon's partner

The Acostas

- **Grace Acosta** – David Wheeler's girlfriend; babysitter for Scanlons
- **Tommy Acosta** – Grace's younger brother; befriended Nicole Nash and David Wheeler while hospitalized
- **Iris Acosta** – mother of Grace and Tommy; married to Kevin
- **Kevin Acosta** – professor at Highpointe College

The Nashes and Hayneses

- **Loretta Nash Haynes** – former mistress of Paul Martin; married to Frank Haynes; mother to Marissa, Nicole, Sean (with Paul); later children Bonnie and Branson with Frank
- **Marissa Nash** – Loretta's oldest; babysits for the Scanlons; friends with Sophie and Sarah Martin
- **Nicole Nash** – Loretta and Paul Martin's daughter; kidney recipient from Susan Scanlon
- **Sean Nash** – Loretta's son; apprentice to David Wheeler at Forever Friends and Westbury Animal Hospital
- **Frank Haynes** – Westbury town councilmember; business owner; founder of Forever Friends dog rescue; married to Loretta; grandson of Hector Martin; father of twins Bonnie and Branson
- **Bonnie and Branson Haynes** – twins of Frank and Loretta
- **Ingrid** – Haynes family nanny; former pediatric ICU nurse

The Wheelers

- **David Wheeler** – works with therapy dogs; helps at Forever Friends and Westbury Animal Hospital; Grace Acosta's boyfriend; son of William and Jackie Wheeler
- **Jackie Wheeler** – wife of disgraced mayor William Wheeler; mother of David
- **William Wheeler (deceased)** – disgraced former mayor; convicted of fraud and embezzlement; died in prison

Friends, Neighbors and Westbury Community
- **Anita Archer** – owner of Archer's Bridal • **Gordon Mortimer** – antiques dealer/appraiser; Anita's love interest
- **Judy Young (née Jorgenson)** – owner of Celebrations Gift Shop; town gossip and Maggie's loyal friend; wife of Jeff
- **Jeff Carson** — uncle owned the Olsson House; married to Judy
- **Sunday Sloan** – rare-book librarian at Highpointe College; Josh Newlon's love interest
- **Josh Newlon** – Maggie's assistant; son of Lyla Kershaw; in a relationship with Sunday
- **Lyla Kershaw** – Josh's birth mother; works in accounting at Highpointe College library; Sunday's close friend
- **Charlotte** – owner of Candy Alley candy shop
- **Laura and Pete Fitzpatrick** – Laura owns the bakery; Pete owns Pete's Bistro, local hotspot for town leaders; one child
- **Harriet and Larry Burman** – owners of Burman Jewelers

- **Joan and Sam Torres** – Maggie's first friends in Westbury; Joan is a police dispatcher, Sam a handyman
- **Gloria Harper Vaughn and Glenn Vaughn** – married; residents of Fairview Terraces; surrogate grandparents to David Wheeler
- **Chief Andy Thomas** – Westbury police chief
- **George and Tonya Holmes** – married with three children; Tonya is a councilmember and Maggie's friend

Highpointe College and Beyond

- **Dr. Fiona Locke** – Dean of Highpointe College Geology Department
- **Robert Harris** – rare-book librarian at Cambridge University; friend to Sunday; biological father of Josh
- **Anthony Plume** – dean of Hightpointe College English Department; rare-book thief; ally of Nigel Blythe
- **Nigel Blythe** – London rare-book dealer; poisoned Hazel Harrington; attempted to kill Sunday and Anthony
- **Hazel Harrington (deceased)** – former rare-book librarian at Highpointe College, murdered by Blythe
- **Ian Lawry** – former president of Highpointe College
- **Russell Isaac** – auto-parts heir; former acting mayor; involved in embezzlement scheme with Delgados
- **Tim Knudsen** – realtor; town councilmember; married to Nancy; grandfather to Zack
- **Forest Smith (deceased)** – attorney; died in suspicious fall off bridge
- **Bill Stetson** – attorney at Stetson & Graham

- **Yolanda and Malcolm Yates** – Malcolm, college president and late Paul Martin's colleague; Yolanda, his wife

Other Notables

- **Delgado Brothers** – embezzlers of town pension fund
- **Chuck Delgado** – former councilmember; liquor store owner
- **Ron** – CPA and investment advisor; married to William Wheeler's sister
- **Mary** – single mother; administrative assistant at Haynes Enterprises
- **Juan** – vet tech at Westbury Animal Hospital
- **Sherry and Neil Parker** – Sherry is new vet at Westbury Animal Hospital; Neil now runs Haynes Enterprises
- **Jack Rodriguez** – David's landlord in California
- **Lyndon Upton** – professor of finance, University of Chicago; Maggie's former colleague

RECURRING PETS

Rosemont Series Recurring Pets

Blossom, Buttercup, and Bubbles—Maggie and John's kittens, named after PowerPuff Girls

Cara—small female German Shepherd adopted by Josh Newlon. Black with a caramel-colored face

Cooper—Susan and Aaron Scanlon's dog, a gift from David Wheeler. A young Golden Retriever who is calm and gentle with baby Julia

Daisy—Nash children's dog, an Aussie/cattle dog mix female

Dan—Josh Newlon's dog, huge black lab, has calming effect on baby Julia

Dodger—David Wheeler's dog, mid-sized mutt with one eye. Therapy dog

Dory—Jack Rodriguez's Westie

Eve—shows up at Rosemont on Maggie's first night, stray, small female terrier mix

Magellan—Tommy Acosta's cat

Namor—David Wheeler's cat whose name is Roman spelled backward, gray with 4 white paws

Roman—John Allen's dog, gentle Golden Retriever

Rusty—Sam and Joan Torres's dog

Sally—Frank Haynes' dog, overweight border collie mix

Snowball—Nash children's dog, a terrier/schnauzer mix male

Sparky—Tim Knudsen's grandson's dog/medium-sized crossbreed with curly brown and white coat

ABOUT THE AUTHOR

USA Today Bestselling Author BARBARA HINSKE is an attorney and novelist. She's authored the Guiding Emily series, the mystery thriller collection "Who's There?", the Paws & Pastries series, three novellas in The Wishing Tree series, and the beloved *Rosemont Series*. *Guiding Emily* was made into a Hallmark Channel movie of the same name in 2023 and her novella *The Christmas Club* was made into a Hallmark Channel movie of the same name in 2019.

She is extremely grateful to her readers! She inherited the writing gene from her father who wrote mysteries when he retired and told her a story every night of her childhood. She and her husband share their own Rosemont with two adorable and spoiled dogs. The old house keeps her husband busy with repair projects and her happily decorating, entertaining, and gardening. She also spends a lot of time baking and—as a result—dieting.

ENJOY THIS EXCERPT FROM GUIDING EMILY

Prologue

Emily. The woman who would become everything to me. The person I would eat every meal with and lie down next to every night—for the rest of my days.

She was just ahead; behind that door at the far end of the long hall. I glanced over my shoulder. Mark kept pace, slightly behind me. I could feel his excitement. It matched my own.

Everyone said Emily and I would be perfect for each other. I'd overheard them talking when they thought I was asleep. I spend a lot of time with my eyes closed, but I don't sleep much. They didn't know that.

"A magical match," they'd all agreed.

I lifted my eyes to Mark, and he nodded his encouragement. I gave a brief shake of my head. Only four more doorways between Emily and me.

I picked up my pace. A cylindrical orange object on the carpet in the third doorway from the end caught my eye. *Is that a Cheeto? A Crunchy Cheeto? I love Crunchy Cheetos.*

I tore my eyes away.

This was no time to get distracted.

We sped across the remaining distance to the doorway at the end of the hall. The door that separated me from my destiny.

I froze and waited while Mark knocked.

I heard Emily's voice—the sound I would come to love above all others—say, "Come in."

What was that in her voice? Eagerness—anxiety—maybe even a touch of fear? I'd take care of all of that right away.

The door swung open and Mark stepped back. He pointed to Emily.

I'd seen her before. Emily Main was a beautiful young woman in her late twenties. Auburn hair cascaded around her shoulders and shone like a new penny. With my jet-black coloring, we'd make a striking couple.

"Go on," Mark said.

I abandoned all my training—all sense of decorum—and raced to her.

Emily reached for me and flung her arms around my neck.

I placed my nose against her throat, and she tumbled out of her chair onto her knees.

I swept my tongue over her cheek, tasting the saltiness of her tears.

"Oh … Garth." My name on her lips came out in a hoarse whisper.

I wagged my tail so hard that we both lay back on the floor.

"Good boy, Garth!"

She rubbed the ridge of my skull behind my ears in a way that would become one of my favorite things in the whole wide world.

Next to food.

Especially Crunchy Cheetos.

Mark and the other trainers were right—we were made for each other. I was the perfect guide dog for Emily Main.

Chapter 1

"Weren't you supposed to leave for the airport half an hour ago?" Michael Ward asked his boss, whose fingers were typing furiously on her keyboard. "You're still planning to get married, aren't you?"

Emily Main's head bobbed behind the computer, her eyes fixed to the screen.

"I can't believe you put off a departure to Fiji to help us launch this new program. Your wedding's in two days."

"We've been working on this for almost a year. I wasn't about to leave when we're this close. I just need to finish this last email." She hunched forward and peered at the computer screen.

"There," she said, pushing her office chair back as the email *whooshed* from her inbox. "Done."

She looked up at Michael, blinking. It was probably the first time she had looked at anything besides a computer screen in hours. "I brought my suitcase so I could go to the airport straight from the office. I don't have to stop at home."

Michael raised his eyebrows at her. "That's all you've got? A carry-on and a satchel for a week—a week that includes your wedding? My wife packs more than that for a three-day weekend."

"My wedding dress is a classic sheath and the rest is bathing suits and shorts."

"I would have thought Connor Harrington the third would have wanted an elaborate wedding—one fit for the society pages."

"Our wedding is going to be very elegant—think JFK Junior and Carolyn," Emily said, flinging her purse over her shoulder and reaching for the retractable handle of her suitcase.

Michael stepped in front of her. "I've got this," he said. "I'll walk you to the street. I'd like to congratulate Connor on snagging our office hero."

Emily hesitated.

"He is picking you up, isn't he? You're flying there together?"

"He went out over the weekend. He wanted to do some diving with his best man ... sort of a bachelor party reprise. I was traveling with my mom and maid of honor, but they flew out yesterday as planned. The company paid to change my ticket, but it would have cost almost five hundred dollars for Mom and Gina to change theirs. It wasn't worth it."

"But you don't like to fly." He peered into Emily's face. "Did you talk to Connor about that before you decided to stay an extra day? You have told him about your fear of flying, haven't you?"

Emily shrugged. "I've mentioned it, sure, but I haven't made a big deal out of it."

"So what did he say?"

"He suggested that I get a prescription for Xanax and sleep the whole way out there."

"Really? That's what he said?"

"He's a Brit, for heaven's sake. 'Stiff upper lip' and all that. He's not the sort of guy to coddle anyone—and I'm not a needy type of gal. You know that."

Michael cocked his head to one side. "Do you have to change planes?"

Emily nodded.

"You don't want to be knocked out for that."

"I'll be fine." Emily threw her shoulders back. "You don't need to worry about me."

"I know—I'm sorry. It's just that I wouldn't let my wife make the trip alone if she felt like you do about flying."

"I fly alone all the time, and nothing's ever happened to me. There's no reason this time should be any different."

Michael lifted his hands, palms facing her, and shrugged.

"Okay, but I think he could have at least offered to pay to change your mom's flight or something."

"I'll be perfectly fine." Emily walked past him into the hallway. "I promised Dhruv that I'd say goodbye before I leave."

"He's going to miss you. You're the one person here that really connects with him."

Michael watched her shoulders sag slightly.

"Hey," he said, rolling the carry-on to a halt beside her in the hall. "I'm sorry. I didn't mean to worry you. The whole team is going to step into your shoes while you're gone. We've talked about it."

"Of course you will. I shouldn't worry about him. I've got the best team in San Francisco. Scratch that. On the entire West Coast." Emily gave him a teary smile and punched him playfully on the shoulder. "I know you'll take care of everything while I'm away, Michael—including helping Dhruv stay connected with the team."

"Good!" Michael continued down the hallway. "I don't want you to give this place a second thought while you're gone. If anyone deserves a vacation—and a gorgeous beach wedding—it's you, Em. But don't get too comfortable." Michael turned and smiled at her. "We do need you to come back. We'd be lost without you here."

Emily laughed and pushed him toward the elevator. "Why don't you go push that button, you wonderful suck-up. It'll take ages to get an elevator this time of the morning. I'll stick my head into Dhruv's cubicle and be right back."

***

Emily found Dhruv, as usual, leaning into the bank of computer monitors, intently focused on the complex strings of code in front of him. She cleared her throat. When Dhruv didn't move, she tapped him lightly on the shoulder.

Dhruv sat back quickly and spun around. A smile spread across his face when he saw her.

"I wanted to say goodbye before I go."

Dhruv nodded. "Goodbye."

"I'll see you a week from Monday."

"I know. You're getting married in two days, then you have your honeymoon for a week, then you come back to work," he recited.

"That's right. You remembered."

"I remember things."

"Yes, you do. That's one reason you're so very good at programming," she said.

"I know."

"Okay ... well ... have a good week. You can go to Michael if you have ... if you need anything."

"I know."

Emily regarded the shy, socially awkward middle-aged man who was, by far, the most proficient member of her extremely talented team of programmers. "Bye."

Dhruv nodded.

Emily stepped away.

Dhruv leapt out of his chair and called after her. "Have a happy wedding."

Emily swung around and gave him a thumbs-up then turned back toward the elevators where Michael was waiting.

From *Guiding Emily*

ALSO BY BARBARA HINSKE

Available at Amazon in Print, Audio, and for Kindle

The Rosemont Series

Coming to Rosemont

Weaving the Strands

Uncovering Secrets

Drawing Close

Bringing Them Home

Shelving Doubts

Restoring What Was Lost

No Matter How Far

When Dreams There Be

Waves of Grace

Threads of Kindness

Novellas

The Night Train

The Christmas Club (adapted

for The Hallmark Channel, 2019)

Paws & Pastries

Sweets & Treats

Snowflakes, Cupcakes & Kittens

Tarts & Turnovers

Workout Wishes & Valentine Kisses

Wishes of Home

Wishful Tails

Back in the Pack

Novels in the Guiding Emily Series

Guiding Emily (adapted for The Hallmark Channel, 2023)

The Unexpected Path

Over Every Hurdle

Down the Aisle

From the Heart

Growing the Circle

Novels in the "Who's There?!" Collection

Deadly Parcel

Final Circuit

CONNECT WITH BARBARA HINSKE

Sign up for her newsletter at **BarbaraHinske.com**
Goodreads.com/BarbaraHinske
Facebook.com/BHinske
Instagram/barbarahinskeauthor
Pinterest.com/BarbaraHinske
BookBub/Barbara Hinske
Twitter(X)/Barbara Hinske
TikTok.com/BarbaraHinske
Search for **Barbara Hinske on YouTube**
bhinske@gmail.com

Printed in Dunstable, United Kingdom